I0785282

BOOK
THREE
THE WEDDING VOW

Never Romance a Rogue

REGINA SCOTT

*Once again to Kristin and Meryl, who always let me know
I am loved and appreciated; and to the Lord, for setting us in
families, even when we weren't born into them.*

CHAPTER ONE

Wey Castle, Surrey, England
Late July 1825

L ADY ABELONA DRYDEN, youngest daughter of the Duke of Wey, had never heard the word no.

Oh, it had been uttered occasionally in her presence, but her sunny disposition, winning smile, and engaging manner generally banished it fairly quickly. If those didn't work, the application of impeccable logic, a few blinks of her jade-colored eyes, and a toss of her golden curls usually did the trick. So it was peculiar that she was having such a difficult time convincing her dearest friend, Petunia Bateman, to settle on a gentleman to marry.

That it was Belle's responsibility to see Petunia—Tuny —happy, no one questioned. It often fell to Belle to right wrongs, and it was surely a very great wrong that the right fellow hadn't proposed. Tuny had been out for three Seasons to Belle's one. Her own family had sent her to live with Belle and the duke's family this Season in hopes a more suitable gentleman might present himself. Tuny was smart and kind, with a dry wit and a loyal heart. She deserved to find a match.

It wasn't as if she had no choices. Several gentlemen had shown interest this Season, but, one by one, seeing no encouragement from Belle's friend, they had succumbed to the blandishments of other ladies. Belle had held out hope for the quiet Lord Ashforde, even though Tuny insisted they were incompatible in spirit. And then Owen Canady had joined their circle. Surely, he was the one for Tuny.

Belle paused in the act of placing the last lily in the arrangement on the walnut credenza in the withdrawing room overlooking the castle courtyard. How many times had she imagined meeting the one for her? She knew exactly what would happen. Her pulse would stutter, then hammer against her chest. Fortune, her aunt's cat—who had matched every lady in the family since Belle's mother and father—would approve of him with a purr. He would be, all in all, perfection.

She sighed as she slipped the lily into place in the Chinese porcelain vase.

"That's a contented sound," her mother mused as she came to join her by the window. "Ready for this house party to begin?"

"Very," Belle assured her. "Thank you for agreeing to host it, Mother."

Her mother's face widened in a grin. Some said to this day that she did not resemble a proper duchess, having first been governess to Belle and her sisters. Rubbish. Anyone looking at that thick, dark hair wound in a coronet braid around her head, the warmth in those brown eyes, and the confident way she held her sturdy figure would know they were greeting quality.

"It was my pleasure," her mother said. "Though I was a bit surprised by your guest list. There seems to be more married or engaged couples than bachelors and ladies."

Belle wiggled her eyebrows. "Which leaves the bachelors with little to do but find the proper lady."

Her mother chuckled. "Clever girl. Which bachelor holds your interest?"

Owen Canady's face came to mind, all firm lines and planes, blue eyes whispering of untold depths. Tuny found him charming. Truth be told, most everyone Belle knew found him charming. She herself was not immune to the tousled raven hair, the neat mustache and beard, that endearing smile, and the faint lilt of an Irish accent.

"No gentleman in particular," Belle said. "This party is for Tuny."

Her mother slipped an arm about her waist as they headed toward the door. "Good for you for helping a friend. So, which bachelor is for Tuny?"

"All of them," Belle said merrily. "But I have the highest hopes for Mr. Canady."

From downstairs came the sound of carriage wheels on the courtyard outside. Belle broke away from her mother to give her hand a squeeze. "They're here!"

Her mother laughed as Belle picked up her green plaid skirts and dashed to the landing. Oh, how carefully had she selected the guests to attend a house party at her family's country estate, Wey Castle. The games, activities, and outings she had planned were designed to bring Tuny and Mr. Canady together. Frequently. Surely, under such congenial circumstances, love would blossom.

It had already blossomed for her two older sisters. Larissa and Callie were engaged to twin brothers, Prince Otto Leopold and Count Frederick Montalban of Batavaria. And it was because Belle had convinced her sisters and Tuny to agree to a vow: all four of them would be happily wed by harvest. Once she had Tuny betrothed, it would be Belle's turn. Surely, the perfect gentleman was only days away.

She clung to the polished wood railing and leaned over to gaze down at the entry hall below. Mrs. Winters, their white-haired housekeeper, was already at the door, with their footmen, Davis and Wills, flanking her in their olive livery.

"Sir Matthew, Lady Bateman, welcome back to Wey Castle," the housekeeper said as Tuny's brother and sister-in-law came through the wide double doors. Sir Matthew nodded his thanks, his broad shoulders taking up considerable space. He bent his dark head closer to his wife's russet hair and murmured something. Charlotte smiled up at him.

Tuny came through the door next, one hand clutching that of her seven-year-old niece, Rose, and the other her five-year-old niece, Daphne. Rose had the same reddish hair as her mother, while Daphne favored their father's sable hair. Both were squirming in their cape-fronted pelisses.

"That's our cue," Belle's mother said to her, and the two of them sailed down the stairs to greet their guests. From other parts of the castle, Belle's sisters Larissa and Callie, her younger brothers Thalston and Peter, and their father came to join them, until the flag-stoned entry hall was quite crowded indeed, and laughter rang up to the painted ceiling three stories above them.

"I'm so glad you came," Belle told her friend as Miss Winchester, the young governess they'd hired for the party, arrived to take charge of Rose and Daphne.

Tuny turned her attention to Belle. Her friend's dark blond hair was sleeked up under a feathered hat, and her warm brown eyes glowed with excitement. "Is he here yet?"

"*He?*" Belle teased. "There were so many presentable gentlemen on the guest list."

"Only one that I saw when Larissa and I looked," Tuny said. "Leastwise, only one who wasn't married."

She hadn't seen the name Belle had added later. "Mr. Canady has yet to arrive, but I promise you I will be watching and will bring him to you at first opportunity. I want to see you happy."

Tuny's smile burst into view. "How can I not be happy surrounded by my good friends? Don't go to any trouble for me, Belle. I've survived three Seasons. I can survive another if need be."

Not if Belle could help it. Because Tuny and her family came from trade, there were those who looked down on her, and that, in Belle's mind, was simply unacceptable. Tuny must have a husband who would love and value her, and this party was just the place to find him.

Mrs. Winters had barely sorted everyone—the children up to the schoolroom with Peter, and Sir Matthew, Charlotte, and Tuny to change from their trip out from London—when the next guests arrived.

The green and gold of the royal carriage of Batavaria gleamed as it stopped in the castle courtyard. Larissa and Callie remained in the doorway just long enough for their loves to step down before going to greet them. What a pretty picture they made—the prince and his brother both curly-haired blondes with impressive physiques, blond Larissa with her queenly air and shier, pale-haired Callie.

The prince, who was known as Leo to friends and family, held Larissa's hand and gazed down into her eyes. Belle smiled.

Count Montalban, Fritz to all who cared about him, went one further. He gathered Callie close and kissed her so soundly Belle blushed. So did her sister, but her eyes were sparkling as she led him back toward the castle. Behind him loped a massive hound, mostly black but with touches of white and gold around his face and chest. Fritz had recently adopted the *Sennenhund*, who had proven to be more polite at times in company than his master.

Three more men climbed down, flexing broad shoulders and gazing at the castle appraisingly. Because of the attempts made previously on the prince's and count's lives and reputation, some of the Imperial Guards had come with them to protect them, while their Lord Chamberlain and the other guards had remained at the palace they had been leasing outside London.

Callie introduced the blond guard as Mr. Keller, the brunette as Mr. Huber, and the fellow with the midnight black hair as Mr. Roth. They would be taking their meals with the staff but would join the rest of the party for activities where they might need to safeguard Leo and Fritz.

"And what of Mr. Canady?" Belle's mother asked as Mrs. Winters led the royal delegation to their rooms, and Belle's father and Thal departed for more interesting pursuits. "His trunk arrived from London yesterday. He's the last on the list except for Meredith, Julian, and Fortune, and they'll be joining us later for the welcome dinner."

Her Aunt Meredith, Uncle Julian, and Fortune would be staying at Rose Hill, their estate farther along the Thames. Belle's aunt had promised they would come over for some activities. Belle was just as interested in seeing the famous feline's reaction to the candidates for Tuny's hand.

"I had hoped Mr. Canady would be here by now," Belle said, craning her neck to see through the front doors to the wide gate in the wall that encircled her home. Castle Wey was built around a central courtyard, with an archway opening to the drive down to the island that was part of her father's holdings. While they had a small stable on one side of the courtyard, the main stable lay at the base of the hill, away from the house. Surely he hadn't stopped there. She had been very specific in her instructions.

"You told me Lord Ashforde might be a few days yet," her mother said.

Belle turned to put her finger to her lips. "Shh! Tuny doesn't know he's coming."

Her mother raised eloquent brows.

"She has convinced herself he isn't the man for her,

but I'm not so sure," Belle explained. "However, if Mr. Canady is half the man I suspect, he and Tuny will be betrothed before Lord Ashforde arrives, and it will serve his lordship right for waiting."

Her mother patted her shoulder before turning for the door. "Watch for him if you like, then, but don't stay out too long. It's perishing hot."

Not as warm as it had been in London, but Belle felt it too. An almost ominous heat lingered in the air, as if something was drawing closer. With the moisture off the Thames, which flowed past on either side of the island, even her clothes felt tight against her body.

If only Mr. Canady would arrive!

She had been cultivating his friendship by standing up with him at balls, chatting at soirees, receiving him when he called, and looking for him in Hyde Park ever since they had met in London a few weeks ago. He had distinguished himself by attempting to out-bid Lord Ashforde over a painting at a benefit auction Tuny and Callie had arranged to support the Society for the Prevention of Cruelty to Animals. The two men had clearly been trying to impress Tuny. Surely her friend would find one of them suitable. If Mr. Canady did not come up to scratch, Lord Ashforde might ride in to save the day. It was all very logical.

As if summoned by her thoughts, Mr. Canady rode through the gate, moving easily with his mount, carriage noble and smile pleased. As he drew up before the stable, her pulse stuttered then hammered against her chest as if desperate to reach him.

Belle blinked. Why that reaction? If he was THE ONE, he was the one for Tuny. Surely her breathless anticipation had everything to do with her plans for this party, and Tuny's future, not him.

Owen Canady considered himself a gentleman by birth, a pauper by circumstance, and a cozener by necessity. When all one had was a horse and a desire for more, one did what one must. He had been carefully cultivating a friendship with the Duke of Wey's family since first meeting their good friend, Miss Bateman, at a ball during the Season. The move had been a bold gamble, a chance to reach his goals faster than he'd previously dreamed.

And he sincerely enjoyed Miss Bateman's company. Like him, she must look to her own future, for she had neither ancient family nor impressive fortune to recommend her. His family connections were distant, his fortune nonexistent. But that had never stopped him from making his way. All he needed was the entre.

Normally, Jasper was his voucher to social circles above him. A Thoroughbred through and through, the stallion did not appear to be much, being of average build and so pale a grey as to be almost white, but he had never met another horse he couldn't outrun. So long as Owen kept to the smaller meets and moved from one part of England to the other, so no one could sing Jasper's praises, he could take part in friendly races and walk away with a tidy sum each time.

If he was careful and frugal, he'd reasoned, one day he might even be able to afford a small estate of his own. Then, he'd herald Jasper's prowess and put the old boy out to stud. But the Duke of Wey, it was said, keenly appreciated horseflesh. If Owen could convince him to sponsor a race, he might win enough to stop his vagabond life now.

And so he had captured the attentions of the Miss Bateman and the duke's daughters, never realizing that the act would shake his entire world to its foundations. Now, he must steal the duke's secrets or lose the only being who had ever cared about him.

He patted the horse as he drew up before the stable on

one side of the courtyard.

"It won't come to that," he murmured against the closest upright ear. "I won't let them take you."

Jasper tossed his head, black mane flying, as if Owen's loyalty had never been in doubt.

The stable hand pulled up short as Owen dismounted. A younger man with sandy hair and the beginnings of a beard, he eyed Jasper as if he had never seen a horse of his sort before. Likely he hadn't. White horses had fallen out of favor some years ago now. No gentleman rode one.

No gentleman had ever been blessed with a horse like Jasper either.

Owen patted the Thoroughbred again before offering the reins to the stable hand. "What is your name?"

"Walters, sir," he said, bobbing his head respectfully.

"Walters," Owen said, "this is Jasper. He's rather particular about his care. He prefers to graze rather than be fed hay, so be sure to take him out at least three times a day onto pasture, and look to see that there's no ragwort about. Treat him with a carrot, not apples. They make him flatulent. Allow no one to ride him except me. He won't tolerate it, and I would hate for anyone to be thrown or trampled on his account."

The stable hand's head kept bobbing throughout Owen's instructions, but his eyes were widening.

"Did you get all that?" Owen asked. "I can repeat it or put it in writing."

He knuckled his forehead. "I'll remember, sir. I promise."

Owen took a step back, hand on Jasper's withers. "See that you keep that promise. I'll be out to check on him regularly."

Once more the lad's head was bobbing.

Owen leaned closer to the horse. "Be a good fellow for Mr. Walters, Jasper. I'm sure he'll do his best."

Jasper snorted as if he questioned that.

Holding the reins gingerly, the young stable hand led

the horse away.

Owen nearly called the fellow back. Jasper was all he had in the world, his only true friend, his only opportunity to make something of himself. Letting the horse out of his sight for long was never easy. He often took lodging within sight of the stable in the country or the mews in the city for that very reason.

Yet surely the duke's stable was as fine as everything else His Grace had owned in London, which had been very fine indeed. No one would harm Jasper. Not if Owen did as he had sworn and discovered a secret that would satisfy his blackmailer. Or found a way to turn the tables on the fellow.

"Mr. Canady."

He turned at the sweet voice and put on his best smile. The lady standing at the edge of the stable yard was the only good part of this bargain. Golden curls offset a pleasing face above a figure with plenty of curves, and all wrapped up in a charming personality guaranteed to draw a man closer.

"Lady Belle." He swept her a bow. "Thank you for inviting me."

"You are very welcome," she said. "Everyone else has already arrived. Mother will be happy to welcome you too. And so will Miss Bateman."

She was careful to stress the last name. That had been a given since he'd become acquainted with the duke's family. It was perfectly acceptable for him to pursue the lovely Miss Bateman, but the duke's daughters were beyond his reach.

"I am honored," he said. He thought about offering her his arm, but his coat was a bit the worse for wear after the ride from London. Jasper took a perverse delight in stamping in every mud puddle, like a child let out of the schoolroom on a rainy day. After the hot weather they'd been having this summer, there had been relatively few puddles, but Owen's coat was dusty, nonetheless.

She had no such concerns. She latched onto his arm and steered him across the courtyard toward the double doors of the house. Castle, they called it. Stone walls encircled the courtyard, with windows looking down like narrowed eyes, suspicious of his every movement.

He could only hope the occupants were less observant.

"I hope you had a pleasant ride," she said.

"Not nearly as pleasant as my welcome at the end," he assured her.

She beamed. That was something about Lady Belle. When she smiled, her entire face lit. It was impossible not to smile along with her.

He shook off the feeling. He wasn't here to bask in the warmth of her smile. He had a mission, and growing attached to her or any other lady would jeopardize it. Jasper had been the one bright spot in his life since the day he'd first ridden the horse seven years ago. No one in his mother's aristocratic family had ever cared a whit for him. In fact, he'd never met a lord who didn't look out for his own self-interest first. The duke would be no different. Owen would play the game and trade His Grace's secrets for Jasper's safety, then be gone on the wind.

Doing his best not to leave a trace on Belle's heart, Miss Bateman's, or his own.

CHAPTER TWO

BELLE WAS DOWNSTAIRS for dinner before anyone else. Generally, she might have waited, timing her entrance to make a statement. Her silk gown was perfect for such a moment, with life-sized pomegranates embroidered all along the hem of the pearly white skirts, a crimson and gold striped bodice, and a turban to match, complete with ostrich plume.

But she hadn't staged this house party to make a statement. Everything was conspired to give Tuny and Mr. Canady an opportunity to further their acquaintance.

She wandered around the withdrawing room closest to the formal dining room, where everyone was to meet before dinner. When she'd been a girl, the space had been done in shades of pink with dainty gilded furnishings and a great deal of velvet. Her father had tended to avoid the room. Now, though the heavenly hosts still disported themselves about the painted ceiling, the rest of the room was more inviting, with wallpaper of cranes descending on a wooded lake, curved-back sofas and chairs upholstered in blues and greens, and a thick carpet patterned in green leaves.

Belle rearranged a pillow here, tugged a chair a little closer there. Most likely one of the older couples would take possession of the sofa, but if she could maneuver Tuny and Mr. Canady into the chairs closest to the fire, they might have a moment for a private word.

Her mother and father arrived just as she'd positioned everything to her liking. By the quirk of her mother's brow, she was the only one to notice. Larissa and Callie came next with Leo and Fritz. She would have liked Mr. Canady to appear before Tuny, so she might have a word to encourage him. Had he lost his way? Having grown up in the castle, she could navigate the dozens of rooms on the three stories of winding corridors easily enough, but she could understand why he might be struggling.

"Would you see that Miss Bateman and her family and Mr. Canady know how to reach us?" she murmured to their footman, Davis, who immediately leaped off the wall to do her bidding.

Slowly, the withdrawing room filled with family and friends, including her uncle and aunt, Lord and Lady Belfort. Belle kept defending the two seats she'd selected for Tuny and Mr. Canady, but eventually, even she had to yield. Soon, every one of the armchairs was taken, and the white marble hearth was all but eclipsed by the quartet of gentlemen—her father, Sir Matthew, Leo, and Fritz—standing in front of it in their evening black.

Waiting just inside the doorway, Belle caught herself tapping her foot and forced it to still. Really, was it too much to ask that a suitor and his lady take some part in the courtship? However did Fortune manage to match anyone up?

She glanced to where her aunt was sitting on the sofa nearest the hearth, the lady's husband leaning a hip against the side. Though Belle and her sisters shared no bloodlines with the pair, they had always considered Lord and Lady Belfort family. She smiled at the thought that that made the grey-coated cat on Aunt Meredith's lap her cousin.

As if she knew Belle was watching her, Fortune raised her head, revealing the white fur that circled her neck and ran down her front like a cravat. She blinked copper-colored eyes before turning to gaze at the doorway. It couldn't be Dolph approaching. The dog made a decided thud as he trundled across the floor. Besides, her mother had wisely consigned Dolph to the rear garden and the kitchen staff until they could arrange a first meeting between him and Fortune.

So, was it Owen who had caught the cat's attention?

Belle drew herself up, heart starting to beat faster, but Tuny walked in instead. She was wearing her golden yellow gown with the puffy sleeves, and Belle was pleased to see that the color made her sleek hair ripple with gold. She stopped to join Belle.

"Still not here?" she murmured, putting her back to the swooping cranes, as if intent on holding the wall in place.

"He arrived," Belle said. "I sent a footman for him, but I don't know what can be keeping him."

Indeed, everyone else was evident—her parents; her sisters and their fiancés; Tuny's brother and sister-in-law; and Aunt Meredith and Uncle Julian. The ladies were in fine silk, most of the gentlemen in tailored wool. She glanced at the porcelain clock on the mantle. Less than a quarter hour until Mrs. Winters would see dinner served. What was he doing?

Davis hurried back into the room and took up his place on the other side of the door from Belle and Tuny. His face was red and his tall body stiff. A moment later, Owen Canady walked in.

Like the other men, he wore a black tailcoat and trousers, with a white satin-striped waistcoat and pristine cravat. The contrast of color was even more dramatic on him, with his raven hair, mustache, and beard. And his sharp blue eyes glittered as he surveyed the room.

Belle nudged Tuny's slipper with her toe. "Go on. Tell him you're glad he could join us."

Tuny raised a brow. "That's your mother's job as hostess.

I'm certainly not going to usurp the place of a duchess."

"Then I will," Belle announced, breaking away from her.

Her mother was already heading in that direction. Belle waited for her, and her mother shot her an amused smile. Then she focused on Mr. Canady, offering him her gloved hand.

"Mr. Canady, a pleasure. We're delighted you could join us."

He took her mother's hand and bowed over it. "I was delighted to be invited, Duchess. Your home is nothing short of stunning, just like the ladies who grace its corridors."

Oh, well said. Belle dimpled at him.

Her mother retrieved her hand with a shake of her head. "And I thought I'd find the butter sauce on the fish tonight. I can see I'll need to keep an eye on you, Mr. Canady."

"Allow me to introduce him around, Mother," Belle said, stepping forward.

Her mother nodded, smile still amused, and Mr. Canady offered Belle his arm. She turned to lead him toward her friend, only to find that Tuny had joined her sister-in-law, with her brother now hovering next to them. By the way she was running a gloved hand up her arm, she was none too comfortable at the moment. Belle's heart went out to her. Perhaps she could make this a little easier.

"You know my sisters and their gentlemen," she told Mr. Canady as she drew him across the carpet toward the Batemans. "And my parents. You met Aunt Meredith, Lady Belfort, when we were at the benefit dinner in town. And of course, you know my dear friend, Miss Bateman. Let me introduce you to her family."

Tuny raised her head, as if expecting to have to give an oration, but Belle introduced Mr. Canady to her brother and sister-in-law instead. Sir Matthew looked him over, dark eyes narrowed. A former pugilist and bodyguard, he had been elevated to his position by saving the king's life when George had been Prince Regent. With a shock of dark hair and rugged features, he still looked as if he could go a round or two in the ring if he wanted. Belle wasn't sure what Tuny had told him about Mr. Canady or how he'd react, but he seized Mr. Canady's hand and pumped it, hard.

Tuny's smile appeared when her would-be suitor didn't so much as flinch.

"I've heard a great deal about you, sir," Charlotte, Lady Bateman, said when Mr. Canady had bowed over her hand as well. The light from the fire made flames flicker in her auburn hair and gleam in the silvery grey of her silk gown. "You're from Surrey too, I understand."

"I have friends in Surrey," he corrected her with a disarming smile. "I was raised farther north. But I understand you spent a great deal of your time in scientific studies in London."

Had Tuny told him? Belle glanced to her friend, but Tuny's brow was puckering as if she were surprised by the statement as well. Still, many in London might still recall that, before her marriage, Charlotte had worked beside her brilliant brother to advance the science of ballooning.

The pink in her cheeks said she was pleased to be reminded. "I've made my share of contributions."

"I am blessed by my family," Tuny put in at last, with a look all around. "Brother a baronet, sister-in-law a natural philosopher, one sister a marchioness and the other a barrister's wife, and all the nicest people you would ever want to meet."

"I can certainly see the attraction," Mr. Canady said, and he and Tuny shared a smile.

Something wiggled inside Belle, as if she'd swallowed a bug that was trying to escape. What was wrong with her? This was exactly what she'd hoped would happen—the two of them getting along, enjoying each other's company, finding commonalities. She knew her turn was coming.

Why couldn't she be happier for Tuny now?

Owen spent a little more time with the Batemans. He thought Belle might introduce him to her uncle, Lord Belfort, who must be the dapper gentleman with the red-gold hair standing near Lady Belfort, but Belle moved to distance herself, going to speak to her mother. The cat in Lady Belfort's lap regarded him fixedly, as if he were a mouse that would escape if she didn't watch his every movement. He put his back to her, excused himself from the Batemans, and went to join the duke and his future sons-in-law.

His Grace was as angular as his wife was curved. Funny how the jade green eyes that looked so warm on his lovely daughter could look so cool on him. He, Prince Otto Leopold, and Count Montalban were in conversation. Owen had been introduced to the Batavarian twins, but he still found it interesting that they were so alike, both with curly blond hair and bright blue eyes, both tall and muscular. He would not have wanted to tussle with either. He would have to be very, very careful how he approached them and the duke.

He still wasn't sure why his nemesis was so determined there were secrets to be had or what the villain intended to do with them. The fellow hadn't been forthcoming when he'd pressured Owen into this role. In truth, Owen wasn't certain how the man knew anything about him. But Owen had answered a knock at the door of the rooms he had been renting in London to find a tall, slender, dark-haired stranger with a long mustache. His smile had been apologetic.

"Forgive the intrusion, Signor Canady," he'd said in a voice spiced with a Mediterranean accent. "But I fear I own your horse."

That had gotten Owen's attention, as the fellow had likely known it would.

"And I fear you're mistaken," Owen had told him, though a kernel of fear had lodged in his chest. "My uncle left me my horse in his will."

"Ah, no," the fellow said, slipping into the room unbidden, as if he owned it as well. "Your great-uncle left everything to your cousin, and your cousin allowed you to ride away with the horse. But your cousin has now sold him legally to me."

Of course he had. His cousin Alfred was a weasel through and through. He'd seen no profit in Jasper and had been only too happy to allow Owen to take the unruly horse. One less burden on the estate. A show of gold, and Alfred would have conveniently forgotten the arrangement.

Still, proof of his cousin's perfidy would not be unwelcome.

"And the bill of sale?" Owen asked.

His visitor pulled the paper from his coat. "As you can see, perfectly legal."

The kernel of fear blossomed into panic.

"What do you want?" Owen demanded.

The miscreant spread his hands. "A small thing. Something so easy for you to do. You are used to saying the right words, smiling at the right time. I see this. Then there is the Duke of Wey. He is a difficult man to approach. He trusts few. But you have been invited to his home. Bring me his darkest secret, and I will provide you with a bill of sale that proves the horse yours. Fail, and I will have no choice but to bring in the authorities and dispose of so temperamental an animal."

Owen had babbled a promise with fear he did not have to manufacture. While the fellow finally introduced himself and issued further instructions on when and where to meet, Owen's mind had sorted through options.

Contest the sale? Alfred would have been only too happy to argue against him, and he could well lose what funds he'd put by on solicitors and court fees.

Run and hide? It might work temporarily, but Jasper would be easy to identify, and their hard-won funds would eventually run out. In the end, he'd had two choices: learn the duke's secrets or use His Grace to uncover his nemesis' secrets.

The smile his enemy had praised was difficult to maintain now. With that upright bearing and serene gaze, the duke seemed as polished as they came. What nefarious plans could possibly lay percolating beneath?

"Your Grace," Owen said with a bow when the duke acknowledged him with a look. "I wanted to thank you for inviting me to your home."

His lips quirked, but he did not smile. "I understand you will be a very welcome addition to the guest list, Mr. Canady."

Someone had pleaded his case, then. Miss Bateman? Belle? "I will do my best to be entertaining, Your Grace, as a good guest should. Your home here is lovely. Surely you must prefer it to the bustle of London."

"Indeed I do," the duke replied with a hint of a sigh that said he could not visit often enough for him. Owen had heard the gossip in town. They called him the Hermit Duke because he preferred the company of his family to the pleasures of Society.

Owen made a show of glancing around at the elegant furnishings. "There is a comfort to knowing yourself at home. I would enjoy learning more about your castle's history, if you can find the time."

Something flashed behind his green eyes. "I will see what can be done."

Good. He had the duke interested. Best to make sure others didn't notice that Owen had singled him out.

"And I would enjoy learning more about Batavaria as well," Owen put in smoothly to the prince and his brother.

Count Montalban eyed him, but Prince Otto Leopold smiled.

"I am always delighted to speak of my homeland, Mr. Canady," he said, voice holding a complex combination of accents. His former country lay among the mountains near France, Germany, and Switzerland, and he was said to have spent time in Italy as well.

"Indeed," Count Montalban said, voice slightly deeper than the prince's but no less accented. "You might find him prosing on at great length, with little provocation. Be warned, Canady."

Prince Otto Leopold chuckled. "I will try to restrain myself."

"You needn't worry on that score," Owen assured him. "I've kept up on your progress with King George from the papers." The Congress of Vienna had reapportioned Europe, with the result that the once-kingdom of Batavaria had been subsumed by the country of Württemberg. The prince, his brother, and their father, King Frederick, were attempting to enlist King George's aid in seeing their lands restored.

Count Montalban snorted. "Do not believe what you read in the papers."

Owen had also read a few stories about the count, who had been until recently the Captain of the Imperial Guard. The *London Times* had not been kind. If even half the articles were true, how could the duke agree to allow the fellow to marry into his family? Was that the secret his tormentor wanted him to unearth?

"I prefer to hear the story directly from those involved," Owen told the count.

Unfortunately, the housekeeper chose that moment to announce that dinner was served, and all the couples began pairing up to walk together into the adjacent dining room. The duke and duchess obviously did not stand on ceremony. In more traditional households, His Grace would have led the highest-ranking lady guest in to dinner, but he escorted his duchess instead at the front of the column, followed by Lady Larissa and her prince, Lady Calantha and her count, Lord and Lady Belfort, and Sir Matthew and Lady Bateman.

Belle was regarding Owen, green eyes wide. Though he ought to offer to escort her, as the daughter of a duke, she tipped her head, sending golden curls cascading to her shoulder, and aimed her gaze at Miss Bateman.

Might as well be obliging. He'd learned that as a lad. He extended his arm. "Miss Bateman, would you favor me?"

She smiled. "Of course, Mr. Canady."

He started to turn to Belle to offer her his other arm, but she waved her gloved hands at him as if shooing him ahead of her. Owen raised a brow but set off as she indicated.

Miss Bateman drew him up short, fingers clutching his arm. The grey-coated cat that had been sitting on Lady Belfort's lap was standing in front of them, her eyes, like two copper pennies, still drilling into him. Behind him, he heard Belle suck in a breath.

"Fortune?" Miss Bateman asked.

The cat turned and stalked off after her mistress.

Miss Bateman's gaze darted to Belle's. "It wasn't the cut direct."

Belle bit her lower lip a moment before answering. "No, not exactly." She managed a smile. "I'm sure she'll be happier on next meeting."

Miss Bateman nodded, and they continued into the dining room. He could not shake the feeling that something momentous had just happened, and he had been found wanting.

It wouldn't be the first time. In fact, he'd accustomed himself to being criticized for his least fault and had congratulated himself on developing a sufficiently thick skin that he no longer cared.

So why did one look from Belle make him care a very great deal?

CHAPTER THREE

FORTUNE HADN'T LIKED him.

Well, she hadn't disliked him, not precisely. Callie had told Belle the story of how the cat had hissed and bolted when confronting a certain Lord Wellmanton, who had turned out to be a thoroughly disagreeable fellow colluding with the leaders of Württemberg to prevent Fritz, Leo, and their father from retaking their kingdom. Fortune had certainly treated Owen better than that.

But the cat's ability to know someone's character was legendary in Belle's family. Fortune had allowed Belle's father to pet her on first sight, or so the story went. Belle had seen how the cat had reacted to meeting Leo and Fritz. What was Belle to make of Fortune's tepid reaction now?

She knew her parents would not force their guests to sit according to precedence, nor did they seem to mind that, without Lord Ashforde, they were odd numbers at table. A few comments, a pointed look, and a sweet smile soon saw Owen seated with Tuny on his right and Belle on his left. Tuny's brother was just beyond her, and Larissa was on Belle's other side. With her mother at the foot and father at the head, it made for a congenial group.

Just as Belle had planned.

Her father asked the blessing, and the footmen moved forward to serve their guests. Belle was less interested in the flounder in butter sauce, sweet potato rissoles, and peas with mushrooms that were placed on her plate for the first course than what was happening between Tuny and her potential suitor. Leaving Larissa to converse with Leo, which her sister would likely much rather do anyway, Belle tilted her head just enough to focus her hearing in her friend's direction. The ostrich plume in her turban tickled her ear.

"How do you find Wey Castle, Mr. Canady?" Tuny asked, cutting into her fish.

A safe if unoriginal opening gambit. Belle might have asked about any adventures on his journey out from London. And she would have to remind Tuny to find a way to use his first name.

"A delightful place, rich in history," Owen responded, digging into his rissoles. "I take it you've visited often."

"Lady Larissa, Lady Calantha, and Lady Abelona have been my dearest friends since I was a girl," she confessed. "Whenever I visited my sister, the Marchioness of Kendall, at Villa Romanesque, their country seat, I spent as much time with them as I could."

Good. Reminding others of your standing was never a bad thing in a Society that prided itself on privilege. Belle had to clamp her jaw shut to keep from adding how much she enjoyed Tuny's company. Time enough later to extoll her friend's virtues, if that were even necessary.

"Then you must know them very well," Owen said, silver fork toying with his peas. "Their father seems the doting sort."

He couldn't know the half of it. Her father had kept his distance from them when they were small, as if he couldn't imagine what one did with daughters. Her stepmother—her mother—had taught them to be a family. Now her father was nearly as determined as Belle to see all his daughters happy.

"His Grace is very kind to include me," Tuny said,

dropping her gaze.

No, no. Now was no time for humility! Tuny should be asking him about his family, his friends. She needed to draw him out. Learn everything about him.

Belle forked up some peas and shoved them into her mouth to keep from saying the words aloud.

Just then, Sir Matthew asked Tuny a question, and she turned her attention to her brother.

"You're rather quiet tonight," Owen said to Belle.

She swallowed the peas so quickly she nearly choked. "Just enjoying the company. You and Tuny seem to be getting along well."

His dark brows went up. "Tuny?"

"Short for Petunia," Belle explained. "It's an affectionate name shared among those she loves. I'm sure she'd allow you to use it, if you asked."

That was pushing it a bit. Tuny was trying to decide whether she could love Owen. But putting the idea in his head could only help.

"I'll bear that in mind," he promised. "Your father is not what I expected."

Belle glanced down the table to where her father was smiling at something Leo had said. When her father smiled, she knew all was right with the world.

"What did you expect?" she asked, returning her gaze to Owen.

"Someone more distant, less approachable," he said, nodding his thanks to the footman, who had refilled his glass.

"You've heard some of the rumors in town," Belle said, wrinkling her nose. "Some people can't appreciate his preference for family. But I certainly do. And so does Tuny. Her family is very important to her. You should ask her about her sisters."

He inclined his head. "Two, if I recall. Just as you have two. And she's the youngest, like you."

Belle beamed. "Very good, Mr. Canady. You *have* been attentive."

He chuckled. "You make it sound as if I just won top marks in school."

"In knowing more about a lady, definitely," she assured him. She glanced around him, but Tuny was still busy talking with her brother. Now Belle's mother was chiming in from the end of the table. How did her friend expect to win a fellow's affections if she ignored him?

"And what more should I know about you, Lady Belle?" Owen asked.

Belle turned her attention back to him. His gaze hadn't wavered. Indeed, the warmth of it raised an answering heat in her cheeks.

"There's not a great deal to tell," she said. "I'm a duke's daughter and the youngest, as you noted. I'm fond of riding and dancing, but you already knew that from our time together in town."

He leaned closer. "And what secrets lie behind those lovely green eyes?"

Her mother really needed to speak to the staff. It was entirely too warm in here. Belle glanced to the hearth, only to find it empty. It must be the summer. It had been unseasonably hot. Everyone remarked on it.

"I have no secrets I am prepared to share with a gentleman," she informed him.

His dark eyes lit. "Ah, but you do have secrets."

Belle leaned closer, until their foreheads nearly touched, and lowered her voice. "You should ask Petunia."

He chuckled, straightening.

"So, Your Grace," Fritz ventured, voice carrying down the table, "what have you planned for us this fortnight?"

That was all it took for everyone to focus their attention on her father.

"I'm sure my duchess will be happy to tell us," he said, lifting a glass in toast to her mother.

All gazes now swung her way. Belle would never get Tuny and Owen back into conversation now!

"Tomorrow, we'll start with a tour of the area," her mother said, smiling at them all. "There will be mounts available for those who wish to ride and carriages for those who prefer a more leisurely pace. Later in the week, we'll have archery, games, and other contests, as well as an opportunity to show your theatrical skills with a set of *tableaus vivant*."

That had been one of Belle's better ideas, if she said so herself. Working together to bring a scene to life had so much potential for building admiration, affection. Her sisters must have thought so too, for they were grinning at their fiancés.

"Everything will culminate in a ball here at the castle late next week," her mother continued. "The Earl of Carrolton and his family will be joining us, as will the Marchioness of Kendall and her family and a number of acquaintances from around the area."

Leo raised his glass. "To new friends."

"To new friends," the others chorused, lifting their glasses in response.

After they'd all taken a sip and lowered their glasses, Belle looked pointedly around Owen at Tuny, but she was already talking with her brother again.

She cornered her friend as the group rose from the table, the men as well as the women. Her father had never been one to tarry behind when he might be with her mother.

"You must press your advantage," Belle hissed as she and Tuny followed the older couples down the corridor, Owen walking with Sir Matthew not far behind and Belle's sisters with their betrotheds just ahead.

"It's early days," Tuny whispered back. "Plenty of time."

Belle held back a sigh with difficulty.

They had not even reached the withdrawing room

before Tuny's brother raised his voice. "I'm for an early bed. Long trip out from London."

His wife smiled at him. "Long trip with two excited girls in the carriage." She turned to Belle's mother. "You don't mind, do you, Jane?"

"Not at all," Belle's mother assured them as the others paused. "I expect Alaric and I will be right behind you, as soon as we see Meredith and Julian off."

But if all the older couples were unavailable, who would play chaperone? Belle opened her mouth to suggest that her mother stay with her and her sisters when Tuny patted her arm.

"I'm tired as well. See you in the morning, Belle."

And she followed her brother and sister-in-law up the stairs, without even a word to Owen!

"Thank you for a lovely evening, Your Graces," Owen said before heading in the same direction.

Belle let her sigh out. Might as well make for her room too. There was always tomorrow.

She hugged her aunt and uncle, then crouched before Fortune to run a hand over her silky fur.

"He's a fine fellow," Belle whispered. "I know you'll see it when you look closer."

Fortune's ear twitched as Belle straightened, but the cat set her gaze on the door as if just as eager to be gone.

Aunt Meredith wasn't quite so ready. She turned to Fritz. "With fewer people about, now might be a good time to introduce Dolph to Fortune."

Fritz inclined his head. "Excellent thought. I'll fetch him." He strode down the corridor.

Leo offered Larissa his arm. "Perhaps we'd best leave them to it."

Larissa laughed. "Trust a prince to know when to beat a strategic retreat. Leo and I will be playing chess in the library, Mother."

Her mother nodded with a smile. "Shut the door, if

you please. I wouldn't want anyone bolting in there."

Larissa and Leo hurried to comply.

Callie put herself next to Belle. "And we can block the withdrawing room."

Belle widened her eyes. "Are we expecting a battle?"

"Possibly," Uncle Julian drawled.

All gazes turned as the door at the end of the corridor opened, and Fritz came out with Dolph. He'd put a leash on the big *Sennenhund*, and Dolph trotted along beside him happily, head high, chest puffed, and plumed tail waving.

Fortune's ears went back.

Immediately, Aunt Meredith scooped her up, but that only brought her on a level with the hound's sniffing nose.

Fritz tightened his hold on the leash to keep Dolph from bounding forward. The hound obediently sank onto his haunches, but the rapid movement of his tail across the floor told of his excitement.

"Fortune," Fritz said with all the solemnity of a courtier greeting a grand duchess, "allow me to introduce Augustus Adolphus. Dolph, this is Fortune, a very fine lady. You will treat her with the respect due her station."

Anyone outside their family would probably have burst out laughing at the statement. Belle's family nodded in agreement, and Dolph lowered his head toward the carpet in deference.

Fortune's ears came forward, and she blinked her great copper-colored eyes as if granting dispensation.

"Do we dare?" Uncle Julian asked.

Aunt Meredith dipped her skirts to lower Fortune to the floor. The cat stalked up to Dolph and bumped her nose against his. Dolph reared back with a snort, eyes widening. As if satisfied she had made her point, Fortune turned and sashayed back to Aunt Meredith.

"Well," Belle's mother said, smile forming. "That's done,

then. It seems there will be no bloodshed involved."

"Thank goodness," Belle's father muttered. "Still, we would be wise to be watchful when they meet again."

Just as Belle would be watchful when Tuny and Owen next met.

She was downstairs early the next morning, dressed in her white muslin walking dress with the gathers along the long sleeves, the bodice, and two feet of the skirts. She'd hoped to arrange everything to Tuny's advantage, but she found Owen there ahead of her. Today, he wore a bottle-green riding coat and fawn trousers, every inch the gentleman. She could only hope Tuny would appear shortly to admire the vision as well.

"I thought I might go riding this morning before activities start," he told Belle as she settled herself beside him at the table.

She looked to Wills, who was serving that morning. The older footman stood taller, the light picking out the grey in his brown hair.

"Will you see if Miss Bateman can be ready to ride?" she asked him.

He started away from the wall, but Owen held up a hand. "No need. I generally ride alone. A gentleman can benefit from a moment of quiet before the day starts."

She liked riding first thing as well, particularly in London. The mist rising from the grass and the birds flitting from tree to tree made Hyde Park a delightful place for an early morning ride. Still, she couldn't forego the opportunity for her friend.

"I'm sure you've noticed that Tuny knows when to be silent and when to speak," she said. "I'll just…"

She started to rise, and he put a hand on hers.

"It's all right, Lady Belle," he said. "I don't mind going alone. And I'm sure Miss Bateman would prefer to eat breakfast first."

Belle sank back onto her chair. "Oh. Well, if you're

certain."

He withdrew his hand, leaving hers surprisingly cold. "I'm certain. A turn about your fair island, perhaps a canter into town, is all I need. I'll be back before the others are down."

Belle nodded. "Very well." She brightened as another thought hit. "Or perhaps I can send Tuny to meet you along the way."

He cast her a glance. "You are being very kind to think of your friend, but I don't need help courting."

Heat flushed up her. "I'm not nearly so selfless, I assure you."

"Ah, but it seems that you are." He set aside his napkin and rose. "Thank you for your concern. I can take it from here."

Belle nodded again, but she couldn't help thinking that he was being far more optimistic than the circumstances warranted.

She was a wonder. Owen clucked to Jasper, who set off down the hill from the duke's castle at a canter. He was used to the matchmaking schemes on the *ton*, even though they had seldom been directed at him. Mothers looking for a strategic alliance for their daughters sought position and wealth; fathers looked for connections and advantage. He had none of those qualifiers. But watching others maneuver had always been interesting.

Belle clearly wanted him to court Petunia Bateman. He could see the lady's attraction. She wasn't mercurial, but one could never tell when a particular situation would be met with skepticism born of harder living or delight at the wonders of the world. It was a heady combination. But falling for Petunia Bateman didn't align with his plans.

And falling for Belle would be far, far worse.

"Can you see a duke wanting us in the family?" he asked Jasper as the horse trotted down the lane toward the graceful stone bridge that arched over a side branch of the Thames. Wey Castle rested on the highest point of an island, and the bridge was the only way to connect to the village. Owen had noted that on the way in.

Jasper snorted and picked up the pace, as if trying to distance himself from the very idea.

Owen chuckled. "Smart fellow. Still, you can't help but admire the lady's optimism and her determination to help those she loves. A shame we've never had anyone with that kind of influence in our lives. We might not have to race for our supper."

Jasper tossed his head. But he slowed his steps as they neared the village on the other side of the Thames.

Weyton was little more than a cluster of whitewashed cottages, all neat and tidy, plus shops for a blacksmith, cooper, dry goods merchant, and baker. A few larger cottages for the more prosperous families lay on the outskirts. The inn along the river likely drew a crowd most nights.

He'd lived in a few such villages as a lad, first with his mother in Ireland after his father and brother's deaths, then with his mother's relatives in England after her death. He'd been only six at her passing, too young to understand why her family hadn't wanted to take her in when she'd been widowed. She had made a choice to marry an Irishman, and one who had seen fit to join with the firebrand Wolfe Tone when he'd rebelled against the English. Bringing her back into their homes would have meant disapproval, gossip. Bringing in her orphaned son was a duty, a way to be praised for their charity, their generosity.

Even if love had never been part of the bargain.

He shoved aside the memories that threatened and rode to the end of the town and along a little byway as if he fully intended going further. When he was certain he had not been followed, he circled back to the house he had been told to find. The cream-colored two-story cottage was ringed by tall hedges, and the drive up to the green-lacquered front door had seen fresh gravel of late. He caught no sign of workers, but he wasn't sure he wanted to leave Jasper alone, particularly knowing who waited for him inside.

"If someone tries to untie you," he murmured to the stallion as he loosely looped the reins over the porch railing, "you run as far and as fast as you can. I'll find you." With a pat on Jasper's withers, he climbed the stairs to the door.

He didn't bother to knock. He had been instructed to appear this morning; his host would be expecting him. Pushing open the panel, he stepped into a small entryway that opened onto a sitting room. If he hadn't been forced to visit by his blackmailer, he might have found the cottage charming with its walls partly paneled in wood and fine furnishings scattered about.

The man standing by the empty stone hearth turned at the sound of Owen's bootheels against the polished wood floor. His black hair was pomaded back from a sharp-featured face, and his thin mustache drooped on either side of his mouth.

"Do you have my answer?" he asked in his accented voice.

"Not yet," Owen admitted, moving to join him. The position was as much to keep an eye on Jasper through the gauzy curtains as to watch the man who held his future in an uncertain grip. "The duke and his family are reticent."

"And you are persuasive," his nemesis said. "I have confidence you will learn his secret."

"That's just it," Owen said, widening his stance. "I begin to believe the duke has no secrets. What exactly did you hope I would find?"

The question was a gamble, but anything he could learn about his enemy might stand him in good stead.

The fellow eyed Owen a moment, head cocked and dark gaze thoughtful. "I will tell you, then. Perhaps it will speed your work. I must know what the duke has planned to support the Batavarians." The last word simmered with loathing, as if the fellow had picked up an apple only to find a worm crawling out from inside it.

As if the man in front of him wasn't the worm himself.

"And why should the duke's support be any secret?" Owen pressed. "His oldest daughter is marrying the crown prince, and his middle daughter is marrying the prince's brother, Count Montalban."

He curled a lip, making his mustache hitch. "He has made clear his support. What is unclear is how he plans to express that support. We must know how to counter his arguments, poison his plots. With another man, we would learn what he cares most for in the world and threaten it. That is how you find yourself in this position." His smile to Owen was knowing.

"But the duke cares only for his family," Owen reasoned. "And you dare not threaten them without risking his wrath."

Alonzo Mercutio, informant to the King of Württemberg, nodded. "Exactly so. A shame you are not in such a position, Signor Canady, but I very much fear the only way you will keep your beloved horse is to bring me the information I seek, and soon. I do not have the luxury of patience."

CHAPTER FOUR

MEREDITH MAYES, LADY Belfort, sat at her dressing table in her lavender satin dressing gown, pulling a brush through her dark hair. A few strands of silver, well earned, were beginning to appear, along with lines around her eyes. The lavender shade so many had remarked upon was still evident. She fluttered her lashes at her husband, who had bent to stroke a red-gold hair of his own into place.

"Are we planning to join the house party today?" he asked as he straightened.

Meredith set down the brush and swiveled to meet his gaze. He was as handsome as the day he'd first proposed to her, under the kissing bough at her mother's annual Christmas Eve party. She rose and adjusted the cravat at his throat. "No, though I begin to regret I said we'd wait."

Julian's brows rose. "Something happening I don't know about?"

She ran her hands along his shoulders, relishing the strength beneath her fingers. "I will own to a curiosity about Mr. Canady. We met a time or two in London, but I find I know nothing about him, save that Belle seems determined that he and Tuny should suit."

Julian smiled. "Noticed that jockeying at dinner, did you? What does Fortune say of him?"

As if she had heard her name, a mew came from the other side of the bedchamber door. It sounded the least bit perturbed.

Meredith went to open the door for her pet, who scampered in and went to take possession of the bed. Her look to Meredith was knowing.

"I'm not sure Fortune and Mr. Canady have met," Meredith admitted to her husband as he moved to join her by the door. "But I can't help the feeling that he's hiding something. Perhaps we should have a conversation. I would not want Petunia or Belle to lose her heart to a rogue."

Julian pressed a kiss against her cheek. "Always thinking of your ladies and our girls. I'll send word to my office, see if we can look into his background."

She grabbed his lapels before he could pull away entirely. "Perfect. Now, perhaps we could find other things to converse about."

Julian wrapped his arms about her. "Conversation can wait."

Belle found a dozen excuses to linger near the front of the castle with Tuny, watching for Owen. She insisted that they bring a carrot to Unicorn, her horse for some years. The powerful white mare had been meant to work the castle's home farm on the island, but Belle had fallen in love with her the moment her mother had spit on her gloves and turned the horse's forelock into a horn. Unicorns were on the family crest, after all.

"And she still can fly like the wind," Belle told Tuny as she watched Unicorn chew on her treat.

"With you on her in Cossack trousers," Tuny said, glancing down at her serviceable blue day dress. "You'll never catch me riding astride."

"Father only allows me to do it on the island," Belle

admitted, moving on to the next stall. Her father's latest acquisition, a fine dapple-grey mare with a silky black mane and tail, ambled closer, as if hoping there might be a carrot for her too.

"Probably not with Mr. Canady in company," Tuny said.

Belle grinned at her. "I'll bring Father around."

She would have been happy to bring Owen around as well, but she had reacquainted her friend with each of the other horses in the small stable nearest the castle without the least sign of him.

"Good day for a ride," she speculated, coming out into the sunlight to gaze up at the blue sky. "I don't see a single cloud."

"Next you'll have us counting the windows in the wall of the castle," Tuny predicted with an amused smile. "Or perhaps estimating how many stones cover the yard."

Belle shook her head. "That won't be necessary. He should return shortly. He was only going to the village and back."

Tuny nodded toward the gate. "And here he comes now."

They both turned to look at the man passing out of the shadows. Belle wasn't the only one to sigh in appreciation. She shared a grin with her friend before the pair hurried to meet him as he was dismounting.

"What a fine animal," Belle said. She raised a hand, and Owen stepped fluidly between her and the horse so that her fingers landed on the chest of his coat. She pulled back, face warming.

"This is Jasper," he said, offering the reins to Walters, their stable hand, who had come running. "He's a bit particular about those with whom he associates, and he's just had a long ride, so it might be best if I introduce you another time." He nodded, and the lad began leading the horse away.

"Particular, eh?" Tuny said, aiming a look at Belle. "Like Fortune."

"Fortune?" he asked, facing them once more.

"Lady Belfort's cat," Tuny explained. "You met her last night. She's famous for knowing a person's character."

His look remained pleasant, but he seemed to have grown an inch or two. "And she wasn't excited about mine. Imagine that."

Belle linked arms with him, finding the bands of muscle unyielding. "A passing fancy, I assure you. She will come to see your sterling qualities, just as we have."

"No doubt," he drawled. He seemed to make an effort to recover himself, for his smile edged into view. "And what delights do your parents have planned for us today? A tour of the island, if memory serves."

"Some on horseback and some in carriages," Belle said, nodding to Tuny to fall in on Owen's other side as they started back for the great doors of the castle. "I fear dear Tuny isn't as comfortable in the saddle as you are. Perhaps you could tutor her."

He turned to Tuny. Belle couldn't see his face, but she could hear the warmth in his voice. "I'd be happy to offer my assistance, Miss Bateman."

Any lady would jump at such a chance. Helping Tuny into the sidesaddle meant Owen might allow his strong hands to round her waist. Eyes and hands might meet, often. And surely he would need to ride closely beside her to encourage her. Perfection!

"Thank you, Mr. Canady," Tuny said. "But I'm satisfied with what skills I possess. After all, I don't really need a horse in London. I can walk most anywhere I please, and I can use my brother's carriage if the journey is longer than my legs allow."

Belle slumped. She and Tuny needed to have a conversation about how to better encourage a gentleman.

They came inside to find that everyone was indeed

gathering for an amble about the island.

"The open carriage would suit me just fine," Charlotte was saying to Belle's mother as they entered the withdrawing room. "I'm sure the girls would enjoy it too."

"Then Peter and I will join you," her mother said with a nod to Belle as she moved closer to the sofa.

"Me too," Tuny said, following her.

That would never do. There wasn't room for Owen as well. Even riding beside them, he would find it difficult to converse with Tuny if her attention strayed to her nieces.

"Perhaps we should take a second carriage," Belle suggested. "Mr. Canady could drive me and Tuny."

"One carriage should be sufficient," her father said. "We have horses available for anyone else who wishes to ride."

"Of course, Father," Belle said. "I was only thinking of our guests. Some are not as comfortable on horseback as we are."

He glanced at Owen. "We can likely find a horse to accommodate a less practiced rider."

"Excellent suggestion," Owen said with an easy smile. "I regret that my horse doesn't deal well with strangers. I'll keep Jasper. One less horse for you to provide, Your Grace."

Her father inclined his head. "Then it seems we are settled. Meet at the stable in a half hour?"

Everyone was agreeable, and most hurried off to change. Leaving Owen to his own devices for the moment, Belle hurried to catch up with Tuny on the first floor corridor.

"Why don't you want to ride with Mr. Canady?" she asked.

Tuny shrugged, blue skirts flapping with her stride. "I thought I should show off my best traits, not my worst."

"Which is why I asked him to tutor you," Belle

explained. "Working together builds camaraderie."

"You sound like a matchmaking mama," Tuny accused her with a grin. "Don't worry, Belle. If Mr. Canady is the one for me, I'll know it, and so will he." Her grin slipped. "Unlike some others we could name."

She must be thinking of Lord Ashforde. Tuny had confessed to having conceived a passion for the fellow in her first Season. She seemed certain he could not return her affections.

"All I ask is that you put yourself forward a little," Belle encouraged her as they neared the room Tuny had been given, just down the corridor from her own. "He cannot become better acquainted if you do not allow him closer."

Tuny nodded, and they separated to change into suitable clothing. But Belle vowed not to let Owen finish his ride before he knew just how fine a lady Petunia Bateman was.

Mercutio's threats were still ringing in Owen's ears. He had to find a way to determine how the duke planned to use his considerable influence on the Batavarians' behalf. Failing that, he had to find some fatal flaw in Mercutio's plans that would give Owen an edge over the fellow's masters in Württemberg. But Belle's father remained elusive.

Owen had hoped to ride beside him as they left the castle, but the duke divided his attention between leading the cavalcade and helping Sir Matthew. Like his sister, the baronet did not appear comfortable in the saddle, listing first one way then the other and hands fisting on the reins as if he meant to drag his mount across the island by sheer force. In contrast, His Grace had an easy seat, moving with the horse as if born to the saddle. So did his eldest son, Lord Thalston, who rode on his other side. He might have been an ally in racing Jasper, if Mercutio hadn't made him Owen's target. But then, what aristocrat had ever offered Owen help?

He had no opportunity to converse with the Batavarians either. Prince Otto Leopold was riding next to Lady Larissa, with Count Montalban beside Lady Calantha, and two of the three Imperial Guardsmen rode right behind. They were followed by the carriage with the duchess, Lady Bateman and her young daughters, Miss Bateman, and the duke's youngest son, Peter.

That left Owen with Belle at the rear.

"I'm very sorry about this," she said as they followed the group down from the castle. "I'm sure Jasper could go much faster and farther, given the opportunity."

That she'd remembered the name of his horse warmed him. Her horse, though older, moved with its own grace. The mare would have been a good contender to pit against Jasper, but he fought down the urge to suggest it. This time, he was after bigger game.

"He has been known to speed over hill and dale," he allowed. "But I am content in present company."

She beamed at him. "As am I. Unless, of course, we could have Tuny beside us. Would you prefer to ride next to the carriage?"

The only person in the carriage who might have been able to tell him anything of import was the duchess, and she had her hands full with Peter and the two Bateman girls.

"No, thank you," he said. "Miss Bateman and I will have ample opportunity to chat in a more congenial setting."

"I have always found the island to be quite congenial," she said, glancing around.

Owen followed her gaze. Except for an occasional copse of woodland, fertile fields rolled across gentle rises giving views to the sweep of the Thames beyond.

Cottages and barns dotted the landscape, their owners out working among the greenery in the warmth of the summer day. Easy to imagine having an estate in such a setting, sitting in his withdrawing room, gazing out across the river. Taking Jasper for a run down the lanes.

"It is lovely," he said. "Small wonder your father enjoys his time here."

"He says he feels the most alive on the island," Belle said, giving her horse a pat. "I love it too, but I will admit that I found the Season thrilling."

It had been her first. It had also been the first time he'd spent the spring and summer in London. Generally, as soon as the roads were hard enough for racing, he'd be moving about the country, in search of competition willing to pay for the privilege. He'd thought ingratiating himself to the right families might open bigger doors.

Not cost him his future.

"There is a certain excitement to the Season," he allowed as they followed the cavalcade past a larger set of stables, likely with room to hold carriages. "Everyone jostling to see and be seen, wondering who will catch whom first."

"Celebrating being caught," she added with a smile that set her jade-colored eyes to gleaming in the sunlight.

"Commiserating about not being caught," he reminded her.

She laughed. It was deeper than the giggle he'd expected, warmer, brighter, as if he'd come out into the summer sunshine after weeks of rain.

"I have a feeling it won't be long until Tuny is caught," she said with a nod to the carriage in front of them.

Back to her friend. He shouldn't be surprised. She was that determined. "No doubt," he offered.

"She is very clever, you know," Belle said, as if warming to her theme. "And good with children. See how she helps manage her nieces? She'll make a wonderful mother."

He would not rise to that bait. He'd find himself betrothed before dinner. He merely nodded as they passed the turn to the village. Jasper gave the faintest of tugs in that direction, as if expecting they were going back to see Mercutio. Owen kept him moving forward.

"She's not afraid to economize, either," Belle said. "Why, I've known her to remake dresses and retrim hats, so she always looks fashionable even with a smaller budget."

Perhaps she thought he'd find that attractive. Did he appear so lacking in funds? Like her friend, he'd done all he could to appear an equal with the aristocracy from which his mother had come. The duke's housekeeper, Mrs. Winters, had seemed surprised he had not brought a valet with him. He'd fended off her suggestion that the duke loan him one with the truth.

He was used to doing for himself.

Indeed, he knew how to turn a cuff, repair the lining of a coat, and replace a collar. He'd shined his own shoes more times than he could count and traded favors with the cobbler to keep his boots and shoes functioning. It was troubling to think he'd missed something. Or perhaps Belle was simply used to so much more.

The carriage bounced over a rut just then, sending a cloud of dust into the air. She waved a hand to keep it from her face. Owen waved a hand to keep it from Jasper's eyes.

"You are very fond of him, aren't you?" she asked as if she had just noticed.

"I am," Owen admitted readily. "I was orphaned as a lad and raised by various relations until my great-uncle took me in. He seemed to think he'd made a good bargain. In bringing me to live with him, he had footman, valet, and groom all in one, without having to pay for more than the food I ate and the clothes I quickly outgrew. I was seventeen when he purchased Jasper, also at a bargain price. But Jasper had more spirit than I did. He wouldn't allow the stable master to break him, and he wouldn't allow my uncle to ride him. He wouldn't pull a carriage, much less a plow. The only one he'd consent to have on his back was me."

He ran a hand along the pale grey neck, and Jasper twisted his head to eye him, mouth twitching on the bit as if he were laughing at Owen.

"Your uncle must have had some confidence in you to give you the horse," she ventured.

Owen chuckled. "Uncle Wentworth had wanted to see the horse put down, but he hated losing money more than he loved his pride, so he agreed that I might take care of the horse, in addition to my other duties. When he passed away, he left Jasper to a distant cousin of mine, who was willing to allow me to keep him."

His parsimonious uncle had left him nothing directly, but she didn't need to know that. Nor did she need to know that his cousin had now sold Jasper into Mercutio's hands. Unless Owen did as he asked, the Italian could bring Owen to court, take Jasper away from him. That he would never allow to happen.

No, he couldn't tell Belle that part of the story. In fact, he wasn't sure why he'd told her what he had. What was it about those big green eyes that made a fellow spill his secrets?

He would have to be more careful, or this house party could be his undoing in more ways than one.

CHAPTER FIVE

THEY FINISHED THEIR tour of the island at her father's lock. Belle always smiled to see the mechanism he had worked so hard to install on the channel between the island and the village. Though they had been repaired and improved many times over the thirteen years they had stood, the massive wooden gates and bronze capstan and chain had helped protect the island and village from floods time and again.

"An impressive feat," Owen said as the carriage headed back toward the castle, the riders following. "It seems your father is a man of vision."

"That he is," Belle agreed. The carriage had picked up speed, as if the occupants were eager to return to the castle. So was Belle. The sooner they dismounted, the sooner she could bring Tuny and Owen back together again. She urged Unicorn a little faster.

Jasper lengthened his stride to keep up, the movement effortless.

"And what vision is he pursuing now?" Owen asked. "Funding a scientific expedition, perhaps? Supporting the re-establishment of Batavaria?"

Belle laughed. "Not the former, to my knowledge, but certainly the latter. King Frederick and his sons have been cruelly used for political purposes."

He nodded as if wholeheartedly agreeing. "Yet how can one fight from a distance?"

"Oh, I don't think physical fighting will be necessary," Belle assured him. "Father is working with Uncle Julian, Leo, and Fritz to see things settled. I have no doubt they'll bring the matter to a satisfactory conclusion."

"I commend you for your faith in your father," he said as the castle mount appeared ahead. "The matter seems daunting to me. King William of Württemberg is surely not amendable to ceding lands his family has held for more than ten years now. How can your father hope to persuade him?"

"You haven't seen my father at his finest," Belle told him. "When he sets out to accomplish something, nothing will dissuade him."

"Rather like his youngest daughter, I see," he said with a smile.

"Exactly like his youngest daughter," Belle agreed, grinning. "Still, it's not my father whose good opinion you should be seeking. Perhaps when we return to the castle, you should have a talk with Sir Matthew."

He cocked his head to one side to eye the broad back of the man beyond the carriage. "Sir Matthew? Is he involved in the Batavarian restoration as well?"

"No," Belle said with a shake of her head. "But he'll be the one you'll want to approach when you decide to offer for Tuny. He is the head of the family, you know."

"Ah, yes," he said, relaxing back in the saddle, but she couldn't help noticing he made no promises.

"He isn't as fearsome as he might look," she said. "He was a pugilist of some renown years ago. They called him the Beast of Birmingham. He was elevated when he saved King George's life. Sir Matthew and Charlotte are devoted to each other and their daughters. And I know he has Tuny's best interests at heart. He'll listen."

He nodded, but his gaze seemed to have gone off into the distance. Belle looked in that direction as well.

Near the lane that led to the bridge to the village, a man

sat on a chestnut horse. He appeared to be watching the cavalcade's progress, but a broad-brimmed hat shadowed his face, so she couldn't be sure. She didn't recognize him, and she was certain she hadn't seen the horse before. She'd have remembered such an elegant creature.

"Do you know him?" Owen murmured.

Belle shook her head. "I don't think so, and that's rather odd. I know everyone on the island and many of the people in the village."

"We seem to be lagging behind," he said, facing forward again. "Shall we?"

Belle nodded, and they urged their horses into a canter to close the distance between them and the other members of their party.

Owen was everything she could have asked for the remainder of the day. He partnered Tuny for a game of whist, praising her for her inspired play. The two were so attuned that they won hand after hand. Surely Tuny appreciated that! He also spent dinner in conversation with her friend, with only a polite sentence here and there to Belle. She should be in alt, but, for some reason, the veal in mushroom sauce was less delicious than usual.

Where were the longing looks, the stolen moments with heads close together, holding hands, looking deeply into each other's eyes? Where were the blushes, the kisses! The latter might require some privacy, true, but she never saw either Tuny or Owen slip away from the rest of the guests.

Until she discovered him disappearing down the stairs Wednesday morning.

It was only by chance that she caught a glimpse of raven hair under a tall-crowned riding hat over the top of the stair railing. She'd just come out of her room in her tailored black riding habit, hoping for a ride before breakfast. She lifted her skirts and hurried to tap on Tuny's door.

Her friend opened it, blinking sleep from her brown eyes. "Belle? What time is it?"

"Morning," Belle assured her. "Mr. Canady is going for a ride. I thought you might want to wish him off, if nothing else."

She glanced down at her blue flannel nightgown. "I'll never change in time."

"I'll hold him up as long as I can," Belle promised. "Hurry!"

Tuny snapped shut the door.

Belle dashed for the stable, raising the footman's brows as she passed through the entry hall.

"Mr. Canady?" she asked Mr. Walters, who was standing just inside the main doors of the stable, broom in hand.

"You just missed him, your ladyship," he said apologetically. "He went riding with the prince and count."

It would have been rude to call him back for no better reason than that Tuny wished to see him off, but Belle ventured to the gate just to see how far they'd gone. Easy to spot the three gentlemen, their Imperial Guard attendants, and Dolph near the turn that led to the bridge.

Nearly as easy to catch sight of the chestnut horse and its rider watching them from the cover of the nearest group of trees. Why did he find her father's guests so fascinating? Or was it Leo and Fritz who had drawn him to the island?

Owen congratulated himself on winning a place at Prince Otto Leopold's side as he ambled along the lane leading east along the side branch of the Thames. The sun on His Highness' curly hair made it appear he wore a halo instead of a riding hat. A shame Owen could not believe he'd earned a heavenly sign of approval. He hadn't met anyone among the aristocracy who had.

"Fine day for a ride," His Highness ventured, blue gaze moving leisurely from the reeds along the water's edge to the grass of the fields inland.

His brother made a sound that appeared to be agreement, his gaze following the track of the massive hound that paced them, head down and sniff audible . The more muscular of the two brothers, Count Montalban sat with less ease on the saddle of a fine dapple grey. Perhaps he'd had less call to ride in Batavaria. Certainly the two Imperial Guards following them looked stiff in the saddle, but it might be hard to relax with all that braid crossing their chests.

"Thank you for allowing me to join you," Owen said to the prince. "I'd hoped for a ride this morning, but I'm still learning my way about the island."

"As are we," Prince Otto Leopold assured him. "This is our first visit to His Grace's home here."

There was his opening. "But I thought the duke was a staunch supporter of your cause. Surely you've needed to retreat here to plot strategy before."

"I prefer not to retreat," Count Montalban informed him. "Even to plot strategy."

"The duke has been all graciousness in allowing us to take up his time," the prince said, "here and in London."

"Then you know your next move," Owen said, as if the matter was no more than a passing fancy.

The count narrowed his eyes at his brother as if in warning.

"We do," the prince said. "Rest assured, all is in hand, Mr. Canady. But I thank you for your interest."

Just as quickly as the door had opened, it closed. He could not demand answers without raising questions he could not afford to address.

But perhaps he could ask a few questions from a

different direction.

"By the by, I believe I met an old friend of yours," Owen said as they reached the end of the island and turned for the north. The waters of the Thames tumbled past, and the hound planted his feet along the shore before the count called him to heel.

"Oh?" the prince prompted.

"I believe you know him from your travels in Italy. Alonzo Mercutio?"

The prince's horse shied. The count urged the dapple grey to cut off Jasper. Jasper tossed his head and stomped his feet in challenge, even as the hound bounded around the group, lifting his head and bellowing a bark.

Owen managed Jasper. It took a moment for the others to bring their horses back under control. But it was clear the count wasn't nearly as calm.

"When did you meet him?" he demanded, eyes flashing. "Where?"

Owen stroked Jasper's neck and kept his voice measured. "Earlier this summer, in London."

"Have you seen him recently?" the prince asked. His voice was cooler, but it reminded Owen of the calm before the storm. He must go carefully if he wished to avoid a lightning strike.

"It was a chance encounter," he extemporized. "He seemed to know I was an acquaintance of the duke. He asked me a few questions about what you were up to. That's what gave me the impression you knew him well. I take it I was mistaken."

"We know of him," the prince allowed.

"But Alonzo Mercutio is friend to no one," his brother added. "Least of all the House of Archambault."

"Our family is not on good terms with some of the Württemberg noble houses," Prince Otto Leopold allowed, but the dangerous tone had left his polite voice as he guided his horse forward once more. "Signor

Mercutio serves as their spy. Fortunately, he was sent home in disgrace, and we have every hope we will not meet again."

Owen wouldn't have been surprised if Mercutio didn't share that hope. He managed to keep up a conversation about commonplaces as they continued along the shore, but he couldn't forget the prince's words.

Mercutio was in England illegally. A word to His Highness or the duke might see him imprisoned. But what of the bill of sale for Jasper? Could Owen find it and destroy it? That wouldn't make the horse any more his. Alfred would know the horse had value since Mercutio had paid him. If Owen approached him to purchase Jasper outright, his cousin could well ask a price beyond what Owen could pay.

Until he had that bill of sale in his hands, he would never feel secure that Jasper was safe. He needed more information if he was to best the Italian. He would have to continue playing the game, for now.

Belle made a point of telling Mr. Quayle, their Master of Horse, about the strange rider. A tall fellow with sandy hair, Mr. Quayle had succeeded his father in the position a few years ago. Like his father, little rattled him, so she wasn't surprised when he gave her a nod and promised to look into the matter. She did not doubt he would do just that.

She returned to the castle to find Tuny coming down the stairs. The white satin ribbon at the dress's high waist was crooked, testimony to the speed at which she'd donned the green gown.

"Missed him," Belle reported.

Tuny shrugged. "There's always breakfast."

But though they made the beef steak and eggs last as long as possible, Owen never appeared. In fact, Belle didn't find an opportunity to bring the couple together until they all ventured down to a field near the main stables for an archery tournament.

Her father had had erected a long earthen mound across the field, about a hundred yards from where he stopped. Affixed along the mound were targets, a set of concentric circles painted on linen. She recognized the colors—gold in the center, surrounded by red, then blue, black, and white at the edge. Quivers of arrows and bows of various lengths sat waiting on a worktable nearby.

Her mother and Sir Matthew had stayed at the castle with his daughters and Belle's brothers, but Charlotte, Larissa and Leo, Callie and Fritz, Mr. Huber and Mr. Keller of the Imperial Guard, Tuny, Belle, and Owen all stood up before her father as he explained the rules.

"The next quarter hour for practice," he advised, pacing off the summer grass in front of them. "Then we will take turns shooting. We'll start at sixty yards, then eighty, and finally one hundred. A hit within the gold earns you nine points, with seven for red, five for blue, three for black, and one for white. Highest score of the three flights wins a prize." He held up a gold medallion on a silk ribbon.

Mr. Huber and Mr. Keller exchanged glances, then joined most of the others in heading for the plank table to select a bow and quiver.

Belle sidled closer to Owen as they followed. "I don't recall Tuny ever shooting with us before. I'm sure she'd appreciate your tutelage."

Owen glanced around Fritz in front of him. Tuny had already chosen a bow and was standing to one side, pulling back on the string and mimicking the actions of Mr. Huber beside her.

"I have a feeling the Imperial Guards will be the ones

to beat," Owen said, straightening. "You might ask them to instruct Miss Bateman."

Oh, why must everyone be so stubborn! "She doesn't know the Imperial Guards half as well as she knows you," Belle told him. "Besides, Mr. Huber and Mr. Keller must divide their time between practicing and keeping an eye on Leo and Fritz."

He glanced around. "Do you expect an attack here?"

"No," Belle admitted. "Please, just help Tuny so she doesn't feel left out."

He went to speak to her friend.

Belle took her turn at the table, selecting one of the shorter bows and drawing it to test the strength. Out of the corner of her eyes, she spotted an arrow heading for the target, where it struck and quivered, nearly in the center.

"Well done, Miss Bateman," Owen said, offering a blushing Petunia a bow.

Well!

Belle moved to take up her own stance, nocked an arrow, and let it fly. It landed in the grass about a foot short of the target. Disappointing!

A moment later, and strong arms came around her. "Perhaps you'd allow me to tutor you too," Owen murmured in her ear.

She couldn't breathe, couldn't think. She must have managed a nod, for his hands cupped hers, steadying the bow.

"The key, I find," he said, voice caressing her ear, "is to point in the direction you want it to go and keep the pressure consistent."

His hands guided her fingers against the string as he helped her pull it back. She closed her eyes a moment, reveling in the feeling of being held next to his lean body. She almost cried out in loss when he released her.

"It helps to open your eyes, Belle," her father said.

She snapped them open to find her father regarding her with an upraised brow from a few feet away. Face heating, she scrambled for an arrow from the quiver and nocked it to the bow. This time, it flew completely over the mound.

She bit her lip a moment before turning to Owen. "Perhaps a little more instruction would be advisable, Mr. Canady."

CHAPTER SIX

THE MINX. OWEN was fairly sure Lady Belle Dryden could shoot an arrow as easily as she rode a horse or danced a waltz, both of which she did with grace and style. She'd encouraged him to teach her friend. He wasn't entirely sure why *she* wanted his instruction now.

But he wasn't about to refuse.

He pulled an arrow from her quiver and offered it to her, then took up his position just behind. Her curvy body fit against his as if the two had been designed for each other. She trembled just the slightest as he wrapped one arm around her to hold the bow and the other to hold the arrow.

"Pull it toward you," he murmured, bending his knees a little so his head was on a level with hers. "Relax your arm. That's right. Do you see your target?"

She twisted enough to glance back at him. "Oh, yes."

Why was he having trouble concentrating? He knew what he was doing. He may not have been raised in a castle, but he'd learned all the gentlemanly pursuits—archery, fencing, riding, shooting. Uncle Wentworth would never have wanted to admit he'd failed in his duty to bring Owen up properly. And Owen had never had difficulty besting his competitors.

"Ready?" he made himself ask.

She faced front, silky curls brushing his cheek. He swallowed.

"Loose!"

She let go of the string, and the arrow flew to embed itself within the blue circle of the closest target.

"Much better," the duke said when Belle made no move to leave Owen's arms. "I suggest you prepare your own bow, Mr. Canady."

Owen didn't think it was his imagination that the warm tone the duke had used with his daughter had cooled considerably when applied to him instead. He released Belle and stepped back. She cast him a grateful look, cheeks pink, as he moved away.

The duke held up his hands. "Halt! Practice is over. Retrieve your arrows and take up your positions for the flights."

Owen hadn't had a moment to shoot his own bow, so he waited while the others ventured to their targets and pulled the feathered barbs from the linen. As he'd suspected, the Batavarians—guards and masters—had managed to hit the inner rings. Lady Bateman had hit the outermost. Miss Bateman's body hid her target from his view as she retrieved the arrows and returned to her spot next to his.

As if she'd noticed him watching, she arched a brow his direction. "Care to make a wager, Mr. Canady?"

Something inside him rose to the challenge, as it always did. "What did you have in mind?"

She pulled an arrow from the quiver on her back. "You win, and I'll give you the first dance at the ball Her Grace is planning for next week. I win, and you ride to the village for plums. I understand Mrs. Turnstable at the market has them in at the moment. I'm rather partial to them."

Owen grinned at her. "You're on."

With a nod, she nocked the arrow.

Along the row, everyone else was doing the same. The duke strode up and down, then finally took himself off the course to one side.

"Ready!" he called, and bows tilted up. "Loose!"

Arrows sped through the air to thud against the ground and various parts of the target. Owen peered closer as His Grace moved out as well.

"Seven points to Miss Bateman, Mr. Huber, and Lady Bateman," he declared. "Five points to Leo and Fritz. Three points to all others, except Belle." He eyed his daughter. "You are aiming at the target, aren't you?"

She dropped her gaze. "Yes, Father."

Owen took a step closer, even though it put him out of line for his target. "You can do it, Belle," he murmured. "I have faith in you."

Her head came up, green eyes shining. It was all he could do to force his gaze at his own target.

"Ready?" the duke called.

Owen hastily nocked an arrow and drew it back.

"Loose!"

He let go of the string, and the arrow whizzed past his cheek to land in the outermost circle. So did Belle's. She beamed at him. A man could ride to the ends of the earth for such a smile.

"Another seven points to Miss Bateman," the duke said, sounding impressed. "Five points to Mr. Keller and Mr. Huber. Three points to everyone else except Belle and Mr. Canady, who each get one. Ready your bows for the final flight at this distance."

The results were similar. The duke then ordered everyone back another twenty yards, and they shot again. Owen was keeping score in his head. Petunia was behind Keller by only two points, with Owen trailing.

As they moved back to one hundred yards for the final round, Belle closed the distance between them.

"I can see your strategy," she murmured. "But I would advise that if you let her win, she will not thank you for it."

"You are too kind," he told her. "But I assure you, I'm not letting her do anything."

Her brows went up.

They took up their positions, and even the Batavarian guards were eyeing Petunia as if wondering how they might best her.

"Ready," the duke called.

Everyone's bows went up. Owen couldn't help noticing that the two guards, the prince, and his brother had all aimed slightly higher than before, as if they had calculated the arc of the flight. He adjusted his aim as well.

"Loose!" the duke commanded.

Arrows flew. The Batavarian contingent's arrows joined Owen's in the red circle.

Petunia's fell short.

She narrowed her eyes at the target, then slowly pulled out her next arrow.

"Three for Lady Bateman and Belle," the duke informed them. "Seven for the others, except for Miss Bateman. You'll get the feel of it, my dear."

She nodded to him and nocked an arrow.

The second flight, Owen scored a five and the Batavarians managed sevens. So did Petunia.

It looked as if he'd be riding for plums shortly.

Owen pulled out an arrow and offered it over to Belle. "For luck."

"For luck," she agreed, offering him one of hers in exchange.

They nocked together.

"Ready!" her father called.

Owen's bow aligned with Belle's.

"Loose!"

They flew in tandem, Owen's outpacing hers by only a few moments as the other arrows thudded into the targets.

The duke nodded as he paced down the line, pulling

to a stop in front of Petunia's. "A perfect nine for Miss Bateman. Well done!"

The others applauded, and she grinned at her arrow sticking out of the gold circle.

"Five points for Mr. Huber, Lady Bateman, Belle, and Mr. Canady. Three points to all others. The winner, Miss Bateman!"

The others surrounded Petunia to congratulate her. Belle moved up beside Owen.

"Nicely done," she said, face turned up to his in admiration.

He nodded, throat suddenly tight. He ought to acknowledge her friend's win, but he couldn't seem to turn from Belle's bright smile. Those rosy lips were only inches below his own. A kiss was out of the question.

So why did everything in him demand he offer her one?

He forced his gaze up. Beyond the mounds, just visible among a copse of trees, a man sat astride a chestnut horse. Owen narrowed his eyes.

She must have seen his look, for she turned to glance in the same direction, then started. "Him again? I warned Mr. Quayle, our Master of Horse, about him, but he must not have had time to catch the fellow. Perhaps we should point him out to Mr. Huber and Mr. Keller."

He was not about to let the Imperial Guards near the rider, not when he was growing more certain of the stranger's identity.

"Don't let it concern you," Owen said. "He's probably just curious about the fine ladies and gentlemen visiting the castle. But I'll see if I can close the distance when I go for Miss Bateman's plums."

Belle and Tuny walked back to the castle together with most of the others. Belle's father had stayed behind to have a word with Mr. Quayle. Belle could only hope the Master of Horse would speak to her father about the stranger. Owen might dismiss the fellow, but she didn't like the way he kept turning up, for all the world as if he were spying on them. Leo and Fritz had had enough intrigue in their lives, and no one wanted more.

Perhaps Owen would learn something. He had borrowed a horse from the main stables and excused himself to head for the village.

"Riding for plums," Belle said with a shake of her head as Larissa and Leo moved past them, deep in conversation. "A decent gambit."

"Better than some," Tuny allowed, swishing her summer green skirts away from a clump of dirt on the path. She cast Belle a glance out of the corners of her eyes. "Since when have you needed tutoring in anything?"

Belle raised her chin. "I haven't shot an arrow in ages. And I didn't know you'd ever shot."

"I haven't," Tuny admitted. "But it was more fun than I expected."

"You have a gift," Belle told her.

Tuny grinned. "At least it got me a gold medal and plums."

Belle laughed. "You earned them. And I believe you're earning Mr. Canady's regard."

"Perhaps," Tuny said, smile fading. "I am trying, Belle, but sometimes I feel like a gown in a clothespress—squeezed and waiting for a moment to breathe. I know Matthew and Charlotte just want me to be happy, and I never held out for a prince, like Larissa, but I keep thinking I ought to feel more than friendship for the fellow I intend to wed."

How could she argue with that?

Mr. Keller moved up on Tuny's other side just then,

giving her and Belle a respectful nod of his blond head. "You are very good with a bow, Miss Bateman."

"Just lucky," Tuny demurred.

"A natural skill," he argued. "And one I admire. Batavarian women are often encouraged to learn how to protect their families."

Tuny rubbed her chin with one finger. "Not enough men in Batavaria, then?"

He colored, but the other guardsman joined them as well.

"Not at all," Mr. Huber assured Tuny, steps as steady as his temperament. "The winters can be harsh, and the summers fleeting. Everyone in Batavaria—men, women, and youth—must work together to thrive."

"I like that," Tuny said. "The same could be said of a marriage, in any country. Good times are joys, but you want someone at your side who can help in times of trouble."

"I came in second," Mr. Keller seemed to feel compelled to point out.

"Behind a woman who had never shot before," his comrade reminded him with a good-natured grin.

His look darkened. "But ahead of you."

"Gentlemen," Tuny interrupted, "shouldn't you be watching your prince and Count Montalban?"

They eyed each other a moment longer before offering her a bow and striding off to join the men they were bound to protect.

"It seems you've made more than one conquest," Belle told her.

"Who knew a bow could be so useful?" Tuny asked, smile returning. "Perhaps I should carry one in London. Just think of the number of suitors who might show interest."

That set Belle to laughing again.

The news of Tuny's success appeared to have reached

the castle a little faster than Belle and her friend, for her mother took them aside as they were coming into the entry hall, and Charlotte moved to join them.

"What's this I hear about Mr. Canady riding for plums?" Belle's mother asked, linking arms with Tuny.

Tuny winked. "Can you think of a better use for a suitor?"

"A suitor, eh?" Charlotte said, giving Belle's mother a look. She turned her misty grey eyes on her sister-in-law. "Is there something Matthew and I should know, Tuny?"

"If there is, I'll be sure to tell you," Tuny promised. She pulled away from Belle's mother and shook out her arms. "Archery is enough to tire a body. I think I'll have a rest before dinner." She trotted for the stairs.

"Something *I* should know?" Belle's mother challenged her.

"Only that things seem to be coming along well," Belle assured her.

Charlotte had been watching Tuny climb. Now she looked to Belle. "I don't know a great deal about Mr. Canady."

The last thing Tuny needed was for her family to grow protective. "He is a fine fellow," Belle told her. "Raised by his great-uncle here in England, and from a good family. I gather he's an orphan with a fortune of his own."

Charlotte stuck out her lower lip. "Good to know."

"Better to know all," Belle's mother said, and the two women nodded as if in understanding.

Not her mother too! "What do you two have planned until dinner?" Belle asked brightly. "I'd be happy to keep you company."

Her mother patted her hand. "No need, love. You'll want to change. We'll be right behind you."

She could only hope that was true, and that Owen would slip back in while they were upstairs, so that Belle had a chance to warn him.

Still, she couldn't help thinking about what Tuny had said as she changed for the evening. Her friend truly could choose whichever suitor she fancied, from Imperial Guards to gentlemen. The daughter of a duke faced other expectations. Larissa had always claimed she'd marry a prince, and she was betrothed to one. Callie hadn't stated a preference, but she was betrothed to a count with ties to the royal family of Batavaria.

Their mother and father had never told Belle she must search for a gentleman of noble title to wed, but she heard the whispers at balls and events. Lady Abelona, the Belle of the ball. It seemed the *ton* expected her to make a brilliant match: a marquess, perhaps, or the heir to a dukedom. Someone with similar power, prestige, and position to her illustrious father.

A shame there were so few fellows to match that description. And none of the ones she had met had touched her heart.

Of course, all was not lost. She had until harvest to fulfill her vow to Larissa, Callie, and Tuny to find a husband. She'd made a strategic error in not inviting more eligible gentlemen to this house party, but her father said the prime minister intended to call everyone back to London and Parliament sooner than usual. A lot could happen before harvest.

What she needed was someone like Owen: Honest and true, charming and clever.

Always ready to lend a hand.

Encouraging and so very handsome.

She sucked in a breath, causing Anna, the maid she shared with her sisters, to glance around her, as if concerned she'd pulled the corset strings too tight.

"I'm fine," she told the dark-haired maid, who went back to her work getting Belle into her blue satin evening gown.

And she would be fine. First, she would make sure

Tuny was betrothed, then she would look for her perfect match. All she had to do was stick to the plan, and all would be well.

Owen rode through the village and out the other side, heedless to who saw him. Locating the cottage again, he slid from the saddle and tossed the horse's reins over the porch railing before climbing the stairs and striding into the house.

"Who else do you have working for you?" he demanded, coming to a stop in the little sitting room.

Mercutio, who had been seated on the sofa, long legs out in front of him, gathered in his extremities and stood. "That is not for you to know. Why are you here? Do you bring urgent word?"

"No," Owen spat out. "Only that someone is watching me."

"Of course," Mercutio said, spreading his hands. "Did you expect otherwise? You should be more careful in your movements. You might have been followed."

"His Grace and the Batavarians think me a fine fellow," Owen told him, hands fisting at his sides. "You're apparently the only one who doesn't trust me."

Mercutio held up his long-fingered hands, but his words were far from placating. "But I am the only one who truly knows why you are at Castle Wey. If they knew, they would not trust you either."

There was that. Owen drew in a breath. "Who do you have watching me?"

Mercutio lowered his hands. "An underling. No one to concern you. He will not act until you prove you are incapable."

The fetid air of the cottage felt cooler. "What do you

mean?"

"Only that I must see the job done, no matter which tool is used to do it." Mercutio seated himself back on the sofa. "You are my first choice, but if you are discovered or lose heart, I must have another ready to take your place."

He made it sound so logical, but all Owen could see was potential danger to the duke and his family and friends.

To Belle.

To Jasper.

"I'm doing all I can," Owen told him. "I'll get you the information, but you must give me time."

"Ah, but that is the one thing I cannot give you," Mercutio lamented. "Only today I received word that the Batavarian king is making progress. He thought himself so clever, this father of the prince and count, to travel to Württemberg and confront King William. Who would have thought William would listen?" He tsked. "The Batavarian king cannot be allowed the right to restore his throne. Too many people will lose money."

"Is that what this is about, money?" Owen pressed, hoping against hope that the Italian would give him something he could use to free himself.

Mercutio's mustache tilted up on one corner. "It is always about money. Or power. This is a little of both. If King Frederick and his sons have their lands returned to them, they will stop practices that make certain people in England and Württemberg very rich. Those people want assurances that the king and his sons will not succeed. And they will not succeed if we ensure the Duke of Wey does not succeed. That is all you need to know."

It wasn't nearly enough. Owen tried for a commiserating look. "Your task is difficult, but I begin to fear I can be of little help to you. And the more I know, the more I might prove a liability. Give me a bill of sale for Jasper, and I will walk away, saying nothing to anyone."

"You can walk away," Mercutio offered. "I will keep

the horse. Someone might find a use for him—pulling wagons of coal for the mines, perhaps? A mount for an eager cavalry officer to ride into battle?"

Either situation could well cost Jasper his life. Owen made himself shrug as if the matter did not concern him overly much, even though his stomach churned. "I'll do my best to honor our agreement. But surely you see the danger as well. I doubt the duke, prince, or count would be pleased to discover you or your man in the area. Perhaps you should walk away. It isn't as if you care about the fortunes of some far-off forgotten kingdom."

Mercutio's lean face turned hard. "I am paid to care. And so are you. Do what was asked of you, and no one will be hurt. Fail?" He spread his hands again. "I cannot be responsible for the results. Now, go. Your pretty duke's daughter will be expecting you."

He had little choice. Owen pivoted and went for his mount.

Frustration sat like a second rider in the saddle with him. Every moment around the duke and his family, and he wondered at his own choices. Was it really worth ruining their lives, destroying their dreams, to save a horse?

But it wasn't any horse. It was Jasper. In a way, Owen was merely trading their dreams for his own.

It still didn't sound just.

CHAPTER SEVEN

OWEN WAS IN no kind of mood to play the charmer as he procured Petunia's plums and returned to the castle. At least it now was only an hour until dinner, so he ought to be able to hide in his room until then and regain some semblance of civility. Perhaps this evening he could find a moment in His Grace's library to look for clues as to his plans regarding Batavaria.

But he hadn't even set his foot on the stair when Mrs. Winters bustled down the corridor. White-haired, well-padded, she nodded to him.

"Mr. Canady. The duchess is expecting you in the withdrawing room, if you please."

It pleased him not at all, but he couldn't very well insult his hostess. He set down the two baskets of plums he'd purchased, put on a smile, and turned for the room she'd indicated.

Not just the Duchess of Wey but Lady Bateman was waiting for him inside. Her Grace wore a simple blue gown with a few tucks around the modest neck, but anyone looking closely would have noticed the sheen of the fine material. Lady Bateman, in a grass-green frock with puffy sleeves, offered him a smile as he bowed before them.

"Your Grace," he said, straightening. "I understand you wished a moment?"

Belle's mother patted the empty spot on the sofa beside

her. "Not just a moment, Mr. Canady. Several moments. It's come to our attention that you have been spending time with our girls."

It took him a moment to realize she meant Belle and Petunia. Keeping his smile in place, he settled himself beside her. "Lady Abelona and Miss Bateman have been kindness itself to offer their friendship."

"And is it friendship you hope to offer in return, Mr. Canady?" Lady Bateman put in, russet brows up in question.

"What more could a gentleman offer?" he asked.

"An estate in Surrey," the duchess suggested.

"Or a townhouse in London," Lady Bateman hurried to qualify.

The duchess nodded. "Just so. Income to support either…"

"And perhaps a carriage," her friend added.

"Character worth emulating," Belle's mother said as if building up a head of steam, like the engines being used in so many industries. "Friends who admire you."

"A charming presence in public," Lady Bateman said. "Though I will grant you that one."

The duchess grinned. "And the ability to ride well. I'll grant you that one too."

Even Uncle Wentworth had not been so exacting in his expectations. Owen's cravat seemed unaccountably tight.

"Tell me, Mr. Canady," Lady Bateman said, edging forward on her seat as if she feared he was about to bolt like a foal startled by a rabbit. "Do you support the church?"

"Support the church?" Owen repeated, stalling for time. What sort of support did she have in mind?

The duchess apparently knew. "Giving of yourself," she clarified. "Participating in events, tithing from your income, providing gifts to the less fortunate."

"Being of service to others," Lady Bateman agreed.

They demanded perfection. "I hadn't considered the matter in that way," Owen told them.

The duchess patted his hand. "Time enough in a life well lived, with your wife at your side, Belle or Petunia." She regarded him, brows up as if encouraging him to share his hopes.

"You honor me," Owen said, picking his words with more than his usual care. "Both Lady Abelona and Miss Bateman are fine ladies, and a fellow would be humbled to find himself betrothed to either."

The duchess cocked her head. "So, which one do you intend to become betrothed to?"

If he said a name, he might find himself engaged by dinner. If he said nothing, the duchess could well order him from her home.

"I cannot find it in myself to choose at the moment," he said. "Neither has given me sufficient encouragement to assure me a suit would be well received."

"Ah." She straightened and glanced to Lady Bateman. "Well, we can fix that, surely."

"Indeed," Lady Bateman purred. "But I still would like more information about you, Mr. Canady. What is your aim in life?"

"To live as a gentleman should," Owen answered easily. That was as close to the truth as he could come.

The duchess wasn't content. "And that means?" she asked.

"A home, a place in the community," Owen extemporized. "Respect for my contributions and position."

"A family?" Lady Bateman asked.

He had never dared to dream of such. He could not remember a happy family with his father and older brother, both of whom had been killed in the rebellion. His mother had done what she could, but their lives hadn't been particularly happy either. And only the law required him to consider Uncle Wentworth family instead of master.

"I can see family is important to you both," he told them. "As it is to Lady Abelona and your sister-in-law, Lady Bateman."

"Family is important to everyone," the duchess said, "whether they know it or not. I'll be keeping an eye on you, Mr. Canady. I see great potential, but I think you may need to prove yourself, if only to yourself, before you're ready to wed my Belle or Petunia."

Belle was pleased that Owen presented Tuny with a basket of plums, a red satin ribbon tied around the handle, as they were waiting to go into dinner that evening.

"A gentleman who pays his debts, I see," her brother commented with a nod of approval.

"Particularly when the debt is owed to such a lovely and talented lady," Owen acknowledged with a bow to Tuny.

"Best I get these to the cook," Tuny said, cheeks turning red, before hurrying to take them to Davis, who was on duty along the wall.

"Nicely done," Belle murmured to Owen as he watched Tuny.

"I left another for you with your maid," he murmured back.

Now she was sure her cheeks were turning color as well.

He was the perfect gentleman at dinner, dividing his time between Belle and Tuny on either side, and he took part in the games that evening in the withdrawing room. Her mother had taught them various entertainments over the years, so they had a set of family favorites. The

Bateman girls, Peter, and Thal were invited to join them, and much merriment and laughter was to be had.

They all headed upstairs together, and Belle could only smile at the tender looks flashing between Larissa and Leo and Callie and Fritz as they bid their betrotheds goodnight. Owen bowed over Tuny's hand, and her friend blushed, but he didn't even attempt to kiss her knuckles. And Tuny entered her room without a backward glance.

Oh!

How was she to ever find her own true love if she couldn't see Tuny settled first? Perhaps it was her frustration that made sleep hard to find. The clock chimed midnight before she rose and lit a candle. What she needed was a good story, preferably with a happy ending, to see herself to sleep. She pulled on her quilted satin wrapper and padded down the stairs to the library.

The cavernous space with its bookshelves along the walls and at right angles was like a maze, but she knew where the adventure novels were found. Thal had mentioned Mother had recently acquired a bound edition of *The Talisman* by the author of the Waverly novels, just the sort of thing for tonight. She lifted her candle with one hand and her nightgown with the other and ventured deeper among the treasure trove of knowledge.

She had just located the book, the leather cover warming in her grip, when she heard a noise. She straightened, frowning. Were those furtive footsteps across the wood floor? The sound of a drawer opening? The only drawers were in her father's desk, and surely he would have lit a lamp by now.

Who was in the library with her?

She blew out her candle and waited as the darkness wrapped around her. With the shutters closed on the windows, not even moonlight trickled in. Still, her father must have had a fire lit in the hearth at some point, for she made out its red glow as she peered around the bookcase.

Silhouetted in the light, a man was standing beside her father's desk. She could make out no features or even clothing. Belle crept closer.

Owen hugged the wall as he slipped down the stairs. Very likely the duke kept his home in better repair than Uncle Wentworth had, but he was taking no chances a squeaking tread might awake a servant. The last thing he needed was someone offering to help him find his way.

At least the duke left a wall sconce lit here and there so his guests could find their way if needed. He started down the corridor for the doors a footman had pointed out earlier to him. The library must have been huge, for he could not make out neither walls nor ceiling as he entered. By the light of a dying fire, he spied something large hunkering some ten feet distant. The desk, perhaps?

He tiptoed across the floor. He had just reached the piece of furniture, which was indeed a desk, when a lamp sprang to life.

Owen froze, lie ready on his lips.

"Did you see him?" Belle asked, shaking out the sliver of kindling she must have lit from the coals.

"Him?" Owen asked, willing his galloping heart to slow.

"The fellow who was in here before you," she explained. "I came downstairs for a book, but I heard someone else enter after me."

"A footman checking all was settled for the night?" Owen suggested. Anything to keep her from wondering why he'd suddenly appeared.

"A footman who opens desk drawers? And any of our staff would have brought a lamp along." She shook her head, and the light caught on her tousled curls. Belatedly he realized she was dressed for bed, a quilted robe hugging her curves. He made himself focus on her face.

Immediately, she turned for the door. "We must find him."

If she had surprised an intruder instead of a staff person too busy to light a lamp and too frightened to admit as much, Owen could think of only one person it might have been. Mercutio's man, the one who rode the chestnut horse. Surely he would react badly if Belle discovered him.

In three steps, he put himself ahead of her. "Might I suggest we call for your head footman? You do not appear to be dressed for the occasion."

She tugged on her sash, tightening the satin around her. "I'm perfectly dressed to protect my home."

But not herself. She had been nothing but kind to him. He could not see her harmed.

"And what a home," he reminded her. "Miles of twisting corridors, dozens of rooms. It might be difficult to search them all by yourself."

She slumped. "You're right." She glanced back at the desk. "Still, a thief? Surely none would be so bold as to enter the castle, and I would think there would be easier things to make off with than the contents of Father's desk."

Unless the thief had been after those contents. Owen's questions to Mercutio earlier must have made the Italian doubt him sufficiently to employ his other so-called tool.

"Perhaps we should check the desk," Owen said. "See if anything is missing." He started back that way, and she followed.

"I have no idea what Father was storing, so I wouldn't know if anything was missing," she warned as Owen surveyed the teak desk. The top was surprisingly clean, enough so that he could make out an inlay of ivory in the shape of a unicorn, one leg extended and head down, as if it were bowing. Only one of the drawers had a keyhole, and there were no scratches around it to indicate the intruder had tried to force it.

Owen turned to her. The lamplight shadowed her eyes, gilded her cheekbones. He might have stolen a kiss as easily as the intruder had attempted to steal her father's secrets. She didn't appear to notice as she puckered her face as if in thought.

It had never been harder to pretend to be a gentleman.

"You should tell your father," Owen said, stepping back from her. "Tell the count as well. The Imperial Guards may be able to keep closer watch."

And if that stopped him from pursuing his goals, it might be all to the good.

Wait, what was he thinking? He had to follow through on his task. He had to protect Jasper.

"Good idea," she said, oblivious to the thoughts churning madly in his mind. "I'll go now." Once more, she turned, only to look back at him. "Why did you come down to the library?"

Owen opened his mouth, and her smile flared to life, stunning in its beauty. She seized his arm and gazed up into his face. "Please tell me you came down to meet Tuny!"

"Alas, no," he said, his own smile feeling tight. "Like you, I was searching for a book."

"Oh." She puffed out a sigh as she released him. "Well, I can tell you where to find what you're after."

Doubtful. "Thank you," Owen said. "But I doubt any book would see me off to sleep now."

CHAPTER EIGHT

BELLE'S FATHER WAS not pleased at her news when she woke him, even though she was careful not to mention Owen's presence. Oh, most people wouldn't notice the change in her father's unflappable demeanor, but she saw the nostrils flare and the lips tighten.

"Thank you for telling me, Belle," he said. "I will see to the matter. Stay in your room until your maid comes for you in the morning."

To be a prisoner in her own home, even for her safety, appalled and rankled. But Belle nodded and returned to her bedchamber. She was only surprised how quickly she fell asleep and how well she slept. It was rather pleasant to be able to place one's problems in the hands of a duke.

Thursday, they were all to go on a picnic out along the Thames with Aunt Meredith and Uncle Julian. Belle went first to suggest to Constance, the older maid Tuny and Charlotte shared, that she put out her mistress' blue-skirted gown with the plaid accessories. Tuny would look very fetching in her bonnet trimmed in plaid ribbon, a plaid scarf about her neck, and a plaid sash under her bosom.

Owen was out riding when Belle came down to breakfast, and her mother, father, Leo, and Fritz were missing at the table.

"Plotting strategy," Larissa remarked when Belle asked. Callie, who was seated between her and their older sister, beckoned them closer as the Batemans chatted at the other end of the table. With her pale looks and quiet nature, people tended to overlook her sister, and they said the most outrageous things in her hearing as a result. Belle had no doubt Callie had already heard about the intruder.

"Mrs. Winters told Davis and Wills to keep closer watch," her sister reported. "Someone was in the castle last night."

Larissa frowned, but Belle nodded. "I came down to the library for a book and nearly caught him."

"I'm certainly glad you didn't," Larissa scolded.

Belle wrinkled her nose at her. "Go on, Callie."

"Father wanted to dismiss all the temporary staff hired for the house party," her sister said. "But Mrs. Winters convinced him they were all good sorts, and some sorely needed the extra income. One came all the way from Walton-on-Thames for the work. It wouldn't be fair to dismiss them all when only one might be at fault."

"Well, whoever it was," Belle said, "he'll know we're on to him now. I doubt he'll be so bold as to try again."

"And if he does, Father and Leo will make sure there is nothing for him to find," Larissa added.

They turned their attentions to their guests then, until it was time to prepare for the picnic. Belle did her best to put the matter from her mind. She'd had a goal for this house party, and chasing intruders was not part of the plan!

Her aunt and uncle arrived to join them. They had brought Fortune as far as the castle but left her in Mrs. Winters' care for now to keep her safe. Unfortunately, that meant Belle had no opportunity to coax a different response to Owen from the cat.

Instead, she tried to maneuver Tuny and Owen into traveling to the site together, but she somehow found herself with Owen in the gig her mother generally used, while Tuny climbed into the landau with her family.

"This will not do," Belle told him as he directed the horse along the lane that led toward the river. The royal carriage led the cavalcade, followed by their gig, then the landau, her aunt and uncle's carriage, and the wagon carrying the necessary supplies. With a blue sky dotted with puffy clouds and the river rolling smoothly, she could not have asked for a better day, only a more cooperative couple.

Owen glanced around at the gig. "Hood not deep enough to protect you from the sun?" he guessed.

Belle adjusted her broad-brimmed hat so that one of the ostrich plumes curled down toward her ear. "The hood is perfectly fine. But there's only room for two people."

"Ah," he said. "I do believe there's a saying about the sky being our chaperone."

"It's the roof being our chaperone, and only if both parties have been invited to the same event," she replied, nose in the air.

"I would not have taken you for a stickler when it comes to the rules," he said with a look her way.

Belle shifted on the padded leather seat, her apple-red skirts brushing his boots. Hadn't Tuny noticed how handsome he looked in his cinnamon-colored coat and tan trousers? The shadows from his tall-crowned hat made his dark eyes most mysterious.

"Rules have a purpose," she told him. "But when that purpose runs contrary to good sense, I do think we should amend if not abandon them."

"A woman after my own heart," he assured her, clucking to the horse to pick up her paces as the distance widened between them and the royal carriage. "Why, if I hadn't come across you last night in the library, I believe you would have stormed off after the interloper all on your own after all."

"I would," Belle allowed. "Sometimes one must take a stand for what's right, regardless of the personal cost."

He cast her a glance. "You truly believe that."

"Of course! Read any good novel, and you will find the hero or heroine doing the same."

"Easy to do in stories," he said, gaze returning to the road. "Harder in life."

"Necessary in life as well," she insisted. "Look at Father. I'm sure he would rather have been entertaining his guests this morning, but he was closeted with Leo and Fritz, trying to determine what to do about this intruder last night."

The horses slowed, as if he had tightened his grip on the reins. "Did they catch the miscreant, then?"

"Not to my knowledge," Belle admitted. "But you can be sure my father has the matter well in hand. Now, you will not distract me from my purpose, sir. You called me a woman after your own heart. The woman after your heart is Petunia Bateman. And she should be the one seated beside you."

He was silent a moment, then he heaved a weary sigh. "Forgive me for continuing to disappoint you, Lady Belle. I fear I haven't the dash to accompany your dear friend."

Belle regarded him. "Balderdash."

He blinked. "I beg your pardon?"

"You just attempted to beg my pardon, but we both know it's a humbug. I am convinced that you are perfectly capable of pursuing a lady, should you set your mind to it."

He sent her a grin that set her pulses to fluttering. "In that case, perhaps you won't feel the need to keep inserting yourself into the process."

Well! Belle aimed her gaze at the river, which was growing closer with each thud of the horse's hooves. "I'm sure I wouldn't need to *insert* myself if you and Tuny would simply get on with it."

"Shall I importune her from under her window?" he asked. "Perhaps throw her over my shoulder and ride for Gretna?"

Despite her pique, Belle felt a laugh bubbling up. "Sir Matthew might have a thing or two to say about the latter."

"Only if he could catch Jasper."

She gave it up and laughed. "Very well. I concede the point. You and Tuny can handle things on your own. All I ask is that you handle them in a more expeditious manner."

She glanced at him to find he had raised a brow. "Is there a reason Miss Bateman requires a husband in a hurry?"

Belle flamed. "No! I'm sure I never implied… Tuny is a lady… How could you be so unfeeling!"

"Peace!" he said, raising the hand that was not on the reins. "We are agreed that Petunia Bateman is a diamond of the first water, and the man whose suit she accepts will be fortunate indeed."

"Yes, yes he will," Belle said, chin up. "I'm glad you realize that."

"So, why are you so intent on seeing your friend betrothed?" he asked.

Oh, how to find the right words so he would not think Tuny lacking?

"Tuny has been on the *ton* three Seasons," she started. "I'm sure it's at least partly because she enjoys it, despite her protests to the contrary. I have only had one, but I can see people don't appreciate her as they should. The four of us—Larissa, Callie, Tuny, and I—vowed we would see each other wed by harvest. I will not rest until I know Tuny can fulfill that vow."

"Admirable," he asked. "And what of Belle?"

She clasped her hands in her lap. "Once Tuny is settled,

I'll be free to find my own prince."

"No more Batavarian princes wandering around, to my knowledge," he allowed.

She couldn't tell whether he was teasing or somehow concerned for her future.

"He doesn't have to be Batavarian," she told him. "He doesn't have to be a prince, as far as I'm concerned. I'll know him when I see him."

"So, this paragon has yet to appear," he mused. "Do you expect him to come floating past on the river?"

"Moses did," Belle reminded him with a grin. "And he ended up leading all of God's people."

"So he did," he said with a smile.

They pulled onto the grass beside the royal carriage in perfect charity with each other.

Belle glanced around for Tuny, but the landau and her aunt and uncle's carriage had fallen behind the wagon and had yet to reach the picnic area. Her sisters and the Batavarian contingent were already on the ground, and Fritz was watching Dolph lope about the grass, nose down and plumed tail up.

While Owen went to talk with Leo, Belle went to speak to their footman, Wills, who was overseeing the unpacking of the picnic supplies along with the help of the temporary staff. She had to agree with Mrs. Winters that none looked particularly nefarious. They all worked with heads down and hands busy.

She focused on Wills. "Miss Bateman and I will be sitting together near the shore," she explained to the older man. "Please give us one of the smaller blankets. Mr. Canady tells me he prefers to stand."

"I'll see to the arrangements, your ladyship," Wills promised her, bowing his greying head.

Humming to herself, Belle moved away from the wagon.

As soon as the other carriages arrived and the passengers

alighted, she went to link arms with her friend.

"I have a nice blanket near the water," she assured her, tugging Tuny in that direction.

"I promised Daphne and Rose I'd sit with them," Tuny protested.

"Daphne and Rose can spare you a moment," Belle said. She sat on the blanket, and Tuny sank down beside her, arranging her skirts.

Soon the others were finding places—Larissa and Callie, their betrotheds, Dolph, and the Imperial Guardsmen around one blanket; Sir Matthew, Charlotte, the girls, and Aunt Meredith and Uncle Julian around another. Her mother, father, and the boys had a blanket to themselves.

Belle put a hand to her lips. "Oh, dear! It seems we've left out Mr. Canady!"

Tuny craned her neck to where Owen was surveying the group as if trying to determine where he was supposed to sit to eat. She waved a hand. "Mr. Canady! Over here!"

Belle hid her grin as he approached.

Tuny rose. "You can have my spot. I promised to eat with my nieces."

Belle opened her mouth to protest, but Owen smoothly took Tuny's place across from her while her traitorous friend moved off to join her family.

"That didn't go as you planned," Owen said, watching Tuny.

"No," Belle said, eyes narrowed. "Not a bit."

She would not let the matter go. Vow or no vow, Owen had never met anyone so determined to achieve her goals. England should be very, very glad Lady Belle Dryden was a woman. Had she been a man, she might have toppled the entire kingdom!

Then again, who said a woman couldn't topple empires? He could imagine men fighting and dying at a word from her lips, just as men had died for Helen of Troy centuries ago.

The servants began bringing food then, laying down platters on each blanket, and Owen performed the expected role and served himself and Belle. Belle bit into the buttery roll as if she might sever it in half. He could almost hear the furious thoughts churning through her mind.

"What will you do if she won't have me?" he asked.

She blinked, her focus coming back to him. "Of course she'll have you. You are the most presentable gentleman who has ever courted her."

Such praise was designed to set a fellow to preening. A shame he couldn't believe it. "Surely there have been others. Lord Ashforde appeared ready to lay down his life for her at the dinner for the Society for the Prevention of Cruelty to Animals last month."

She nodded at the mention of the charity her older sister and Miss Bateman sponsored. "She has taken him in dislike. You are the chief contender." She set down her roll to wag a finger at him. "But do not think you are the only contender, sir. You said it yourself: Tuny is a diamond of the first water. Someone else will snatch her up if you don't."

No doubt. But Owen could not bring himself to offer. Even when he managed to clear himself of this mess and Jasper was safe, he had little to bring to a marriage. A lady had every right to expect her husband to provide for her. Winning stakes in every county in England hardly qualified. And he didn't like thinking what would happen if he hadn't finished raising the funds to maintain a small estate before Jasper was too old to keep winning.

"I have been admonished," he said, dropping his gaze humbly to the rolls, cheese, fruit, Scotch eggs, and potted tongue in front of them. "Please believe me when I say that I take your words very seriously indeed."

She humphed as if she wasn't too sure of the matter, but she didn't press her case further.

They sat companionably, watching the blue-grey waters tumble past, listening to the sounds of them brushing up against the rocks and plucking at the reeds that grew in patches along the shore. The other guests called questions and comments to each other, laughing, chatting. Dolph moved from blanket to blanket, soliciting donations. The company was as warm as the sun on Owen's shoulders.

He could only hope he was the only one to notice the movement of another figure among the trees beyond the wagon. Dolph didn't raise his head or bark, but it was possible the fellow was upwind of him. Certainly none of the servants gave a cry of concern, but perhaps they were too busy ensuring everyone had what they desired. He could not like the fact that Mercutio's man would be so bold as to watch them this closely, especially after his foray into the castle last night. At least his continued presence all but guaranteed he hadn't found what Mercutio wanted.

But sooner or later, he was bound to give himself away, and he might give Owen away in the process. It would be best for all concerned if the fellow left. The question was how to convince Mercutio's man of that fact.

Owen rose as the others began to walk along the shore. "I think I'll stretch my legs."

Belle climbed to her feet as well. "I'll join you."

Another time that might be pleasant indeed. Now he had no doubt she would steer him closer to Petunia when he only wanted to reach the wood. He glanced around, hoping for inspiration. Lord Peter was chasing Daphne and Rose across the grass in a game of catch-me-who-can while twelve-year-old Lord Thalston attempted to look above such things. Count Montalban had secured

Dolph, who humphed and sank onto the grass as if resigned to his fate.

Before he could decide how to make his escape, Lady Belfort and her husband wandered closer. Plumed hat on her dark hair, the lady wore a lavender walking dress with ribbons along the hem and sleeves. He had met her enough times in London to know the color would match her unusual eyes.

"How are you enjoying our corner of the Empire, Mr. Canady?" she asked.

"It is as lovely as its ladies," he assured her, hiding any sign of impatience from long practice.

Lord Belfort smiled. "Well said, sir."

"Indeed," his wife agreed. "I fear I don't recall what area you call home."

"The Yorkshire Dales, your ladyship," Owen replied. "North of Harrogate."

"Beautiful country," Lord Belfort said. "Windswept and wild."

"And is your family concerned you have been so long from it?" Lady Belfort asked.

She was good. The War Office could make use of such interrogation skills. "My immediate family is gone, alas. I was raised by an elderly great-uncle who has also passed. I fear I have only myself for company these days, when not in such charming company, of course." He smiled at Belle, who dimpled back.

"A shame," Lady Belfort said. "I know what it is like to have no family left. But at least you have a home. What sort of house did your great-uncle leave you?"

Peter came pelting past just then. Perfect! Owen reached out and caught him close. "Easy, there, my lad! Wouldn't want you to tumble into the Thames."

Peter scowled up at him as if much put out to have been kept from his pursuits. "I wouldn't fall in the water. I'm not a baby."

"Of course not," his sister said soothingly. "But you were running very close to the shore and very fast, Peter. Thank Mr. Canady for having a care for you."

Owen released him, and Peter sketched him a bow. "Thank you, sir. Excuse me."

Unrepentant, he dashed off again.

"Perhaps I should follow," Owen said, watching him. "Just to be safe."

He made his escape before any of them could call him back. He was only glad Belle did not insist that he ask Miss Bateman to join him.

Peter chased the Bateman girls past the wagon, but they were heading into company again, so Owen had no need to play nursemaid, if he had ever had one to begin with. Unfortunately, he was still short of the woods, and there were still too many looking his direction, from Belle to her aunt and uncle to Sir Matthew and Lady Bateman.

So, he stopped to thank the staff for their service instead of continuing on. His praise earned him smiles from the footmen and groom who had accompanied them. He then strolled closer to the trees as if admiring the qualities of nature.

"Fine property His Grace has," Sir Matthew ventured, joining him. He shoved his hands into the pockets of his trousers, which only succeeded in broadening his already broad shoulders in the tweed coat.

"Very fine," Owen agreed, once again curbing his impatience.

Sir Matthew rocked from the toes of his sturdy boots to the heels. "I understand you have designs on my sister."

Owen immediately raised his hands. "I have no such designs, sir, I promise you."

A dark scowl settled on his features, and his already gruff voice came out even rougher. "Leading her on then, are you?"

Owen took a step back, but he doubted he was far

enough out of reach of those long arms. "Never! I hold your sister in the highest esteem. I would ride off tomorrow rather than concern her, or you, in any way."

Sir Matthew nodded slowly. "I'll remember that." He stalked back to his family. Petunia sent Owen an encouraging smile.

He waited only until they all looked away, and his pulse was close to normal, before darting under the branches of the trees.

The rustle of leaves told him he wasn't alone. He narrowed in on the sound, moving from tree to tree. Some of the oaks were ancient—thick trunked and heavy limbed. The cool shadows touched on grasses that bent under his boot. But there, the chestnut horse, tied to a branch and contentedly munching whatever was in the feed sack around her mouth. Owen looked right, left, front, and back and caught no sign of the owner.

He focused on the horse again. As he'd surmised from a distance, the mare was of good quality, well balanced, with long, sturdy legs. She'd run far and fast at the least encouragement. The saddle too was of good leather. Someone with money or hired by someone with money, then. Would Mercutio or his employer be willing to equip a servant so well?

Another crack behind him had him whirling, fists up and at the ready.

Belle lifted both hands, eyes wide. "It's me. Did you catch him?"

CHAPTER NINE

OWEN'S LIPS FLATTENED, and Belle thought he might say something she would not want to hear. But then he forced his mouth into a smile, took her arm, and drew her deeper into the little copse of oaks, where their mysterious visitor had hidden his horse.

"I haven't spotted him," he murmured, head turning from side to side, as if he thought to spy the fellow sneaking up on them. His dark beard half-covered his cheek, but she could imagine a gold loop on that earlobe, as if he were a pirate or highwayman of old.

"What do you plan, then?" Belle whispered back as the leaves above them chattered in the breeze. "Should we wait for him, or should we call the servants?"

His hand tightened on hers. "Not the servants. Seeing them would only scare him away. It's not our watcher we need to know but his master. Hst!"

He hunkered lower, and Belle followed suit. His arm slipped around her waist as if to steady her. His cheek was so close she might have pressed her lips against his skin.

Oh, could this summer get any hotter!

She forced her gaze out into the woods. A man walked toward them, shoulders squared and head high, as if he had every right to be hiding here. His hair was mostly hidden by the broad-brimmed hat, but, so close, she could see whisps curling below the brim that showed a color nearly matching that of his horse. His coat was a brown that blended well with the forest, and black Cossack trousers like the ones she wore riding were tucked into well-worn boots. There was something familiar about him, but Belle couldn't place the association.

A spyglass glinted in one gloved hand. The villain! He must have been watching their every move. But why?

As if he had no concerns, he slid the cylinder into a saddlebag, sent the feed sack after it, untied his horse, and swung himself up into the saddle.

Belle bumped her shoulder against Owen's. Still he didn't move, gaze intent on their quarry. She was about to rise and demand answers herself when the man clucked to his horse and burst out of the copse in the opposite direction to the picnic.

Belle straightened to her full height with Owen, which only left her gaze on the level with the top button on his cinnamon-colored coat. "You let him get away!"

He dusted a few leaves off his trousers. "Do you know him any better now that you've seen him at close range?"

"I'm not sure," she admitted. "You?"

He shook his head. Pushing through the branches, he stopped where the horse had stood. His gaze roamed the area as he braced his hands on his hips.

"What can he want of us?" Belle asked, gathering up her skirts to follow. "If he was the one in the castle last night, he must suspect we're on to him. If he's a footpad, he must know Father will never allow any of us to be attacked. The sight of the Imperial Guards alone should have scared him off."

He turned. "I'm going to follow him. I'll rejoin you when I can."

Belle made a face. "You can't follow him on foot. We should tell Father. He'll know what to do."

Once more he glanced in the direction the stranger had ridden. The grasses rippled in the breeze, but the rider was already out of sight.

"Very well," he said, and he took her arm to escort her back to the others.

Belle went straight to her father, who had Thal along the shore and appeared to be explaining the Thames' tidal nature to her brother, who was attempting to look interested.

"Forgive the interruption," she told them both, "but we discovered someone hiding in the woods. We think he was watching us."

Thal stiffened, eyes widening, but her father's green gaze glittered as it swung to Owen at her side.

"You went into the trees alone?" he demanded.

"To be fair," Owen said smoothly, "I ventured into the woods, leaving Lady Belle with the others. She was sufficiently concerned for my safety that she followed."

Her father's look landed on her, and Belle struggled not to squirm.

"Of course she did," he drawled.

Thal mumbled an excuse and wisely slunk away.

"It's all right, Father," Belle assured him. "I knew Mr. Canady would protect me. Suffice it to say that he located the stranger. I told Mr. Quayle about him; I'd seen him before. The fellow rode off. What should we do?"

Her father's look veered into the distance, as if he could spot the fellow even now. "Leave this to me. And if you should see this man again, send word to me before going off after him. I would not want anything to happen to you, Abelona."

When her father used her full name, she knew she was in trouble. "Yes, Father," she said meekly.

"Your Grace," Owen said with a bow.

Belle took his arm, and they both moved away, steps perhaps a little faster than propriety suggested. She wasn't even sure who was leading whom.

"Forgive me," she said. "I didn't mean to put you in his black books."

He glanced back toward her father, who had gone to speak with Leo and Fritz. "Is he the type to take such a thing personally?"

"No," Belle allowed, "but he is a bit protective of me and my sisters. I suppose with Larissa and Callie betrothed, all that protection will focus on me."

He sighed as if he found it as vexing as she did.

The others were about finished with the picnic, and the groom was checking the horses. Owen excused himself to go do the same for the horse that pulled the gig.

Belle hurried up to Tuny. The breeze had left her friend's cheeks pink, and the scarf at her neck was hanging crookedly, likely because of her activities with her nieces.

"Quick!" Belle said, tugging the scarf back into place. "Go talk to Mr. Canady so you can ride back with him."

Tuny glanced at Daphne and Rose, who were arguing over a particularly colorful rock they'd found, then nodded. She gave Belle's arm a squeeze before strolling up to Owen. Belle tilted her head, but she couldn't hear what was said. Still, the next thing she knew, Owen was assisting Tuny up into the gig.

"That was kind of you," Belle's mother said, joining her.

Belle smiled. "Only fair. He is the one eligible bachelor at the party."

"I still think it an oversight," her mother said. "But I expect Lord Ashforde might even out the odds a bit."

Belle cast the gig a quick look, but Tuny didn't seem to have noticed the conversation. "Let's continue to keep that quiet, please. Otherwise, Tuny might bolt."

Her mother's dark brows went up. "That opposed to the fellow, is she? What's he done?"

"Not enough," Charlotte said, stepping to Belle's other side while her husband herded their daughters toward the landau. "She doesn't like talking about it, but I gather she was rather enamored of Lord Ashforde on her first

Season. He did not return the sentiment."

Her mother clacked her tongue. "Silly fellow."

"Perhaps not so much silly as cool," Charlotte said as the three of them headed for the carriage. "He strikes me as one of those young lords who believes he must effect a scholarly demeanor to be taken seriously. He ascended to his title early, if memory serves. I haven't heard about him pursuing any lady."

"Callie said the same," Belle offered, and the other two women nodded in understanding. They all knew that Callie had the unique gift of hearing everything and remembering.

The ride back to the castle seemed longer than the way out to Belle. She always enjoyed spending time with Tuny's nieces, but the sweet giggles were a poor substitute for Owen's teasing banter. She could only hope Tuny was learning the same lesson.

"Shall we regroup in the Green Salon for tea and cakes?" her mother offered as they came into the entry hall.

Leo and Fritz exchanged glances. Sometimes she forgot how alike they were, until they communicated with a look.

"That sounds delightful," Leo, ever the diplomat, said with a winning smile. "A shame I promised Thal I'd join him for billiards when I returned."

Thal, who had been about to pass them on the stairs, stopped and grinned, then schooled his face. "Yes, billiards. A manly sport. Surely you see that, Mother."

Their mother's lips twitched. "Oh, of course. Off you go then to your manly sports and your manly conversations. But don't be surprised if the ladies spend their time talking about *you*."

Leo laughed, and the men headed upstairs. With a smile to Tuny, Owen joined them.

Belle linked arms with her friend as they turned for the

salon, her mother having deemed no one so unfit they must go change first. Charlotte was upstairs settling her daughters back into the schoolroom.

"Well?" Belle asked her friend.

Tuny cocked her head. "Well? Well what?"

"You know very well what," Belle informed her. "How did things go with Mr. Canady? Are you calling each other by your first names yet?"

"Perhaps not yet," Tuny said as they came into the Green Salon. Belle couldn't remember the original color scheme, but her mother had been so enamored of the Green Salon at Villa Romanesque, the country home of Tuny's sister, that she'd had this room redecorated in a similar design. Now the hearth was faced with serpentine marble, and lion-footed sofas and chairs in emerald satin-striped upholstery sat about the space, inviting conversation.

"Why not?" Belle complained as they crossed the carpet, patterned in emerald and cream. "At least tell me you dazzled him with your scintillating conversation."

Tuny laughed as she dropped onto one of the chairs. "I didn't know I had scintillating conversation, and I promise you neither does Mr. Canady."

Belle ought to be disappointed, but the pink rising in her friend's cheeks told her more had happened on the ride than Tuny wanted to admit. That could only be good.

Aunt Meredith, who had gone to the kitchen to fetch Fortune, returned, stroking her pet's grey fur. Fortune's tail was lashing, as if she was much put out about being left behind, and she would not meet Meredith's gaze. It was likely a good thing that Dolph had been returned to the rear garden for now.

"Someone isn't pleased by the arrangements," Aunt Meredith said.

Belle's mother nodded to the floor. "Put her down.

She's welcome to roam. We can fetch someone to find her when you're ready to leave."

Aunt Meredith whispered something in her pet's ear, which twitched. Then she set the cat down, and Fortune streaked out of the room for the stairs.

Was she as eager to spend time with Owen as Belle was?

No, no, as Tuny should be?

Owen had come out onto the landing on the second story of the castle when the grey-coated cat flew past him. She skidded to a stop in the doorway to the room Prince Otto Leopold and Lord Thalston had already entered and glanced back at Owen as if taking his measure. Then she put her nose in the air and disappeared into the room.

Owen shook his head.

"Take heart," Count Montalban said, coming up beside him and clapping him on the shoulder. "She snubbed me at first too. She'll come around."

Owen smiled gamely, but a part of him feared the cat saw as much as they all thought she did. Fortune knew he was lacking, and she would not approve him to join the family.

Not that he had any hopes in that direction. Miss Bateman had been charming and sweet on the ride back to the castle. Any man would be delighted if she chose him. But Owen wasn't looking for a bride. And when he thought of the lady he might someday marry, she suddenly wore golden curls and had a smile that could not be denied.

The duke, Lord Belfort, and Sir Matthew had decamped for the library, leaving the four younger men to their sport. Prince Otto Leopold took one of the long, walnut cues and handed the other to Lord Thalston. Count Montalban went to sit on the high, padded bench that ran along the opposite wall. Owen joined him. Except for the duke and his duchess, here were the two people most likely to be privy to His Grace's plans. It was their kingdom at stake, after all. He merely had to find a way to bring the conversation naturally around to Batavarian restoration.

"Would you care to go first, Thal?" the prince asked.

The twelve-year-old straightened his shoulders as if much honored, then strutted to the green-baize-covered table and bent over the polished wood rim. Owen would not have expected him to have played often. He had certainly never been allowed into his great-uncle's billiard room until he'd reached his majority. But the lad struck the balls easily, sending them bouncing against the sides. One went directly into a pocket.

Prince Otto Leopold nodded, lower lip out as if he were impressed.

"You have a challenger," his brother predicted, leaning back on the seat and crossing one booted foot over the other.

Lord Thalston colored. "Father allows me to play with him on occasion. But Mother can beat him."

Prince Otto Leopold missed his shot and straightened as the count barked a laugh.

"The duchess plays billiards?" the prince asked the youth as Lord Thalston aligned himself for his turn. "Does your sister play?"

"Either of your oldest sisters?" Count Montalban put in.

"Any of your sisters?" Owen amended.

The count shot him a grin.

Lord Thalston nodded, giving another of the balls the perfect tap to send it into a pocket. "Larissa's fairly good. She knows how to calculate the angles. Callie doesn't like it. She says it's too loud. Belle will give you a good game and smile while she beats you."

Owen found himself chuckling at the image. "You're very fond of your sisters."

Belle's brother made a face, reminding Owen again of her. They both shared their father's green eyes, but the color was somehow warmer on Belle, more vibrant.

"I am fond of them," he said, as if admitting a great fault. "But they tend to fuss, as if I needed watching. I am grown, you know."

Prince Otto Leopold eyed the excellent shot Belle's brother had just made. "Apparently so. Will you keep score, Canady?"

"Happy to." Owen went to the brass wire that stretched from one side of the room to the other. He took the long pole from its place against the wall and moved the wooden markers that calculated the points. Thal's marker was easily twice as far along as the prince's.

"I take it billiards are less frequently played in Batavaria," Owen tried, taking any opening.

Count Montalban snorted. "They're played often enough. Some cannot find time for them."

"Exactly," his brother said, making his shot.

Owen moved the marker a little closer to Lord Thalston's. "I imagine it's hard to find time for leisurely pursuits when you're trying to win your kingdom back."

The count eyed him as Lord Thalston took his turn.

"And what would you know of winning back kingdoms?" Count Montalban all but growled.

"Fritz," the prince warned. "Mr. Canady surely means us no harm. You will excuse my brother, sir. He forgets he's no longer the head of the Imperial Guard."

Count Montalban leaned back once more, but Owen felt the tension in him.

"No apology necessary," he assured the two brothers. "I commend you for your efforts. I only wish I knew how to be of service. Is there a place in your plans for a man like me?"

The two brothers exchanged glances.

"Not at the moment," the prince said. "We await another audience with your king. He may grant our petition then."

"If his advisors can be swayed," the count reminded him darkly.

Prince Otto Leopold nodded, leaning on his cue. "King George has learned men, from both of your political parties, who offer suggestions on important decisions. We have heard they are fairly evenly divided on whether His Majesty ought to help us."

"Lord Ashforde is one of them," Lord Thalston volunteered, making another hit that set the prince to groaning. "Perhaps you could sway him to your side."

"A shame he isn't here," Owen commiserated, moving the marker to account for the lad's score.

"Oh, Callie says he'll arrive shortly," Lord Thalston replied, stepping back to give the prince room. "By the ball next week at the latest."

Interesting. Was this part of the duke's plan to help the Batavarians? Or more machinations from Belle? She had mentioned Petunia Bateman's antipathy for the fellow. Perhaps it didn't run as deep as she supposed. Or perhaps she hoped to give Owen competition to encourage him to offer.

Either way, the arrival of Lord Ashforde could make things interesting. He might even prove distraction enough for Owen to finish his task and free himself of Mercutio's threats once and for all.

What he couldn't understand was the unrelenting urge to unburden himself to the prince and count, and, most of all, Belle.

CHAPTER TEN

BELLE WENT TO bed fairly pleased with the results of the day, except of course for the stranger who had been watching them, but she woke to the sound of moaning. In London, she shared a room with Callie, but here at the castle she had her own room. So where was that noise coming from? She lay, blinking up at what should have been the canopy of her poster bed. It was so dark she couldn't make out the cheery, pink-striped bed hangings.

A light flared across the room, and she saw Anna bending to light a lamp.

"Is it morning?" Belle asked, stifling a yawn.

"Well into morning, your ladyship," her maid assured her. The thin piece of wood she'd used sputtered and went out before the wick caught. Anna huffed.

Belle sat up in the bed. "Why is it so dark, then?"

"A terrible storm," the maid said. Once more the flame danced into life, and she hurriedly bent to press it against the wick. "Can't you hear it?"

Belle cocked her head, listening. There it came again, low and painful, followed by pops and cracks and a faint whistling from somewhere nearby.

She shoved back the covers and set her feet on the carpeted floor. "Is everyone else awake?"

"Your sisters and most of the guests," Anna confirmed. "Sorry I didn't wake you sooner, your ladyship. Too many to help, and the lamps won't stay lit!"

As if to prove as much, a draft of air raced across the room from the hearth, setting the lamp to shuddering.

Belle shivered. "Perhaps I should get dressed."

Anna hurried to help.

A short time later, Belle was gowned in her Pomona green walking dress with the pink satin lining and muslin underskirt. She hurried down the corridor for the stairs. The servants had kept many of the drapes drawn against the storm, but, here and there, the fabric moved as if stroked by unseen hands.

She found her mother and sisters in the breakfast room. All wore wool gowns and tense faces. They knew too well what wind could do to the island and its inhabitants: outbuildings toppled, crops flattened, boats broken from their moorings, and even roofs torn off.

"Everything all right, Belle?" her mother asked as Belle took her seat beside Callie at the table.

She nodded. "You?"

"Everything packed away, and everyone prepared to entertain," her mother assured her.

"We're going to take turns in the schoolroom, keeping the boys and the Bateman girls from fretting," Larissa explained. "Leo and I will manage this morning. Callie and Fritz will cover the afternoon. I was hoping you and Petunia could spell us."

"Of course," Belle said. A footman approached with a plate of coddled eggs, but she shook her head. "Chocolate and toast, please, Davis. And plenty of marmalade."

"Meredith and Julian surely won't venture over today," her mother continued when the footman had hurried for the door to the stairs down to the kitchen. "But we ought to have something to keep the others busy. Let's start the *tableaus vivant* early. We can choose scenes out of a hat and form teams."

Callie pushed back her chair. "Brilliant. I'll write out

possible scenes. If you send everyone to me this morning in the library, Mother, I'll make sure they have their pick."

A particularly nasty gust must have hit just then, for the window groaned.

"The sooner, the better," her mother predicted with a look toward the closed draperies. "I'll see about having trunks brought down for costuming. Callie, make sure at least one family member is on each team so we can direct the others to scenery pieces."

"Of course."

The plans made, everyone dispersed. Belle hurriedly finished her breakfast, then joined her sister in the library. It was Callie's favorite room, and one of Belle's favorites. As children, they'd played hunter and hunted among the maze of shelves many a time.

"Who's picked so far?" Belle asked her sister, who was seated at their father's desk, foolscap partially covering the ivory inlay of their family crest.

Callie glanced down at the list she'd made. "Tuny, Mr. Canady, Larissa, and Leo." The castle shuddered. So did Callie.

Belle couldn't stand it another moment. She strode to the window behind the desk, pushed back a drape, and cracked a shutter. The sight made her suck in her breath.

The narrow window looked east, toward the bridge over the Thames. Trees stretched limbs across the water, as if trying to flee. Leaves and debris flew through the air. The dry dust of the road rose to obscure the main stables.

"How bad is it?" Callie asked, coming up behind her.

"Bad," Belle said. "And I fear it will grow worse."

Callie put a hand on her shoulder. "We'll get through. We always do. Father says parts of the castle have stood since 1360."

"A few of the cottages might be nearly as old," Belle said, letting the drape fall. "Which I don't think is a good thing in this instance."

"Come on," Callie said, turning for the desk. "I'll let you have your pick of scenes."

They returned to her list, and Belle glanced down the names, trying to ignore the sounds of the storm outside. She frowned. "Tuny and Mr. Canady are not in the same scene. Can we change that?"

"I suppose," Callie allowed. "Shall I put them both in your scene?"

Belle grinned at her as she straightened. "Perfect!"

"What else are sisters for but to further romance?" Callie asked, and she bent to rearrange the names. "Mr. Canady was already part of your group. I'll ask you to explain to Tuny why she's on a different team than the one she expected."

"Count on it," Belle promised. She glanced down at the list again. "The Judgment of Paris?"

"Father suggested it," Callie admitted. "Too much?"

"A mortal choosing which of three goddesses are the most beautiful and setting off the Trojan War?" Belle asked. "Hmm, I suppose I can work with that. Very well. You may tell the others on my team that our first practice will be tonight after dinner."

Callie glanced toward the window. "Assuming we have dinner."

Belle refused to think on it. She left to find Tuny, only to locate her in the schoolroom with Larissa, Leo, Mr. Huber, and Miss Winchester, the governess who was supervising the children during the house party. Fritz must have sent up the Dolph, for the big *Sennenhund* lay by the fire, wise eyes watchful.

"Thank you for being willing to help, Lady Abelona," the governess said with a quick dip of a curtsey that bowed her practical grey skirts. With her honey-colored hair and soft smile, she exuded a warmth likely to put any child in an instant good humor. "We were about to have a geography lesson. Prince Otto Leopold was going to tell us about his country."

"Then I'm just in time, for I love learning about other countries," Belle said. She slipped in behind Tuny, who was sitting on the rug next to her nieces. Peter had aligned himself closer to the Imperial Guardsman, casting him covert glances out of the corners of his green eyes. Thal was sitting on a hard-backed chair near Leo and Larissa.

"Now, then," Miss Winchester said, perching on her own chair at the front of the group. "Who can tell me where Batavaria lies?"

Peter's hand shot up, but Daphne spoke first.

"Why does Batavaria lie? Mother says it's not nice to tell false stories."

Miss Winchester's cheeks turned pink. "What I meant was who knows where the country is on the Continent."

Peter waved his hand over his head.

"Yes, Lord Peter?" the governess asked.

"It's a mountainous country between France, Germany, and Switzerland," he said, arm falling.

"Very good," she said approvingly. "Your Highness, perhaps you could tell us more?"

All the children and most of the adults swiveled to look at Leo, who favored them with a gallant smile. "I'd be delighted. Batavaria is a rugged country, bordered by mountains that reach to the sky and rivers that run cold and fast."

"Who are they running away from?" Daphne asked.

"She reminds me of you," Belle whispered to Tuny. "You took things literally when we first met."

"I've grown a bit wiser since then," Tuny whispered back.

"Some," Belle allowed, and her friend pressed her fingers to her lips to hide a laugh as Leo attempted to explain why rivers ran.

"You were on another team for *tableaus vivant*," Belle

whispered. "I asked Callie to put you on my team instead."

Tuny nodded her thanks before lowering her hand and listening dutifully to the rest of the lesson.

"Mr. Huber is also from Batavaria," Leo said as he was barraged by more questions. His look to the guardsman bordered on panic.

Brown-haired and sun-bronzed, Mr. Huber sat taller in his black uniform. "I would be happy to talk about my country, to those who will listen."

The children quieted, Rose and Daphne settling back in their seats. Peter's look was worshipful.

He lowered his voice and leaned closer to them, as if imparting a secret. "We have mountains, yes, and rivers, but Batavaria is more than that. It is the cool wind on your face as you climb, the taste of creamy cheese from cows raised on mountain pastures, the sound of church bells calling everyone to worship."

"We have wind," Rose told him solemnly.

"You can hear it outside," Daphne agreed.

"I hear your wind outside," he promised them. He patted the chest of his uniform. "But I hear the wind of Batavaria here, in my heart."

"Beautifully said, Mr. Huber," Miss Winchester murmured, and now Peter wasn't the only one to look worshipful.

He inclined his head to her.

They spent the next little while telling stories and then playing some games with the children. Thal remained aloof, as if trying to make it clear to everyone he was too old for such pastimes, but the others entered in with a will. When Fritz and Callie came to take over, Tuny expressed her desire to stay.

Belle excused herself. She wanted to see what sorts of clothing might be had for their costumes. Her family had staged the tableaus every so often as she'd been growing up. Generally a group attempted to dress and arrange the scene, for the benefit of the others. No speaking was allowed. The players simply had to stand, in character, as the others marveled. But her brothers in particular were very good at saying things that made it terribly hard for her to remember her role, and Daphne would likely be equally difficult to ignore. Belle wanted her tableau to be so good everyone stood in awe.

But as she started down the corridor, she felt the shudder of the house again, harder here near the top floor. It had been easy enough to put away the thought of the storm when she'd been with the children. Now, it seemed to be lying in wait for her, ready to snatch away her very breath.

A gust must have found its way down a chimney, for the lamps on the corridor stuttered and went out, plunging the space into twilight.

Owen stepped out onto the landing just as she rounded the corner, and she all but ran to him. She threw herself into his arms and hung on tight.

"Oh, Owen, I'm so glad to see you! This storm is terrible."

One moment, Owen had been trying to decide his next move, and the next he was holding Belle in his arms. The silk of her golden curls brushed his lips before she pressed her face into his waistcoat.

"There now," he said, surprised he could even find his voice. "It's all right. You're safe."

And he would make sure she remained safe.

The ferocity of the thought amazed him. He had fought for Jasper, fought for himself. But, in that moment, he would gladly have defeated a dragon if it meant protecting Belle.

"Thank you," she said, drawing back with a tremulous smile that tugged at his heart. "It's this wind." She rubbed both hands up and down her arms and visibly swallowed.

Owen had heard the sounds too. More, he'd felt the tension in everyone in the house. The duke had invited him and Sir Matthew for turns at the billiard table, and Owen hadn't been about to pass up the offer to spend some time with Belle's father. Alas, even in the relaxed setting of the billiards room, His Grace had been reticent to speak. And he too kept glancing toward the closed shutters on the windows.

Owen had been almost glad for the storm. It might mean that no one could safely leave the house, but it also meant that no one could enter. Mercutio would have a hard time sending his spy out in this weather.

"It's quite the gale," he said, leaning a hip against the landing's handrail. "But I have a feeling your father's castle has withstood worse."

"So Callie reminded me," she said, tucking a curl back behind one ear. "Still, it isn't easy sitting here listening to the wind howl and wondering what damage it must be doing elsewhere on the island and in the village."

"Or the stable," Owen said. The thought of Jasper in danger suddenly made his coat feel several sizes too small.

She must have noticed the change in him, for she raised her chin. "If you're concerned about the stable, I know a way in from the castle." Before he could thank her, she seized his hand. "Let's go see."

He didn't resist as she led him down the stairs.

He had already noticed the duke's country seat had far too many corridors turning in far too many directions to find his way easily, but Belle rounded this corner and that until they came up against a thick oak door. Even it seemed to pulse with the wind like a beating heart. She pulled up short and glanced at him, as if unsure whether she wanted to go any farther.

Owen eased his fingers out of hers. "It's all right, Belle. I can take it from here."

He started forward, and she grabbed his arm. "No, I'm coming with you."

He doubted there could be too much danger in the duke's private stable, or someone would have come running to alert the castle at large. So he nodded and pulled wide the door with his free hand.

It opened into a tack room, saddles and bridles hanging in easy reach and wood floor scrubbed clean. The crate directly in front of them proved that few ever used this route. Beyond lay another door, this one open. Through it, Owen could see grooms moving from stall to stall as horses whinnied and shuffled about.

"They're more scared than we are," Belle said, compassion in her voice.

Owen shoved the crate aside, and she followed him out into the stable.

The grooms had closed the big doors to the courtyard and the shutters on the windows, but the wind still managed to punch through, rustling straw and setting lanterns and leather bits to swinging. Owen went straight to Jasper's stall.

The pale grey had backed himself into the corner, head up and breath coming hard. White showed around his eyes. Owen slipped into the stall and approached, hands held easily in front of him.

"I'm here, old fellow," he said. "I won't let anything happen to you."

He reached up and stroked the long nose. Jasper pressed himself against Owen's palm and gave him a snort.

"Unicorn has been the best of the bunch, your ladyship," he heard one of the grooms saying to Belle. "But it's all we can do to keep them calm."

"Let me help," Belle said.

Owen turned to warn her against that. Though she

may have known many of the horses her whole life, surely some were more newly purchased and some, like Jasper, were strangers to her. But she didn't approach any individual horse. Instead, she went to stand in the center of the stable and took a stance.

"Sleep my dears and peace attend thee, all through the night," she sang in a sweet soprano.

"Guardian angels God will send thee, all through the night.

Soft the drowsy hours are creeping,

Hill and dale in slumber sleeping.

I my loved ones' watch am keeping, all through the night."

The clear tones of the old lullaby dipped into every corner of the stable, masking the sounds of the storm. The horses stilled, ears twitching as if to catch every note.

"Angels watching ever around thee, all through the night.

Midnight slumber close surround thee, all through the night.

Soft the drowsy hours are creeping,

Hill and dale in slumber sleeping.

I my loved ones' watch am keeping, all through the night."

Now the grooms had stilled their movements, watching her. Owen felt the pull as well. She was light, she was peace. She was every good thing they all dreamed of attaining one day. She was inspiration in a small, curvy package.

How could he ever do as he'd promised and betray her father?

Yet what would become of Jasper if he didn't?

CHAPTER ELEVEN

BELLE SANG ALL six verses of the lullaby, more than once. Her mother had first sung it over her and her sisters when Belle was a girl, but she hadn't learned the true melody until she'd heard it being sung by the Marchioness of Kendall over her little girl, Sophia. It had taken an Italian singing master to gently point out to Belle and her sisters that the Duchess of Wey was tone deaf.

By the time her throat started to tire, Mr. Walters came to her rescue.

"The storm's waning, your ladyship," he said. "We can take it from here. And thank you for your kindness."

Belle smiled at him and nodded. Drawing a breath, she looked to Owen. The awe on his face pulled her up short. She had seen admiration any number of times from a gentleman—when she rode well, when she danced well, even when she sang well at a musicale. This was more. This was deeper. She wanted to strut right out into the wind and dare it to harm those she loved.

Well, maybe not that.

"Is Jasper all right?" she asked instead, going to join him and his horse. The pale grey stallion eyed her, mouth working, as if he too thought to thank her for her singing.

Owen ran a hand down the horse's withers. "He is now. I think he liked your singing, as did everyone else in the stable."

Jasper bobbed his head as if agreeing. Belle laughed. She started to raise her hand, then paused. Owen hadn't wanted her to touch his horse earlier.

"May I?" she asked.

He glanced between Jasper and her, then took her hand. "Allow me."

He pressed her hand gently against the warm flesh of the horse, then moved it slowly from shoulder to flank. Jasper sighed as if he enjoyed her touch, but he quickly shuffled away from her to reposition himself in the box.

Where he could keep a wary eye on her.

Owen released her, and Belle let her hand fall.

"It's a beginning," Owen said.

He sounded far more satisfied than she felt.

"Did he have a harsh trainer?" she asked as Owen turned for the door to the tack room and the castle. She fell into step beside him.

"An incompetent trainer, more like," he said, stride lengthening until she had to scurry to keep up. He must have realized he was outpacing her, for he slowed his steps.

"I think I mentioned that my great-uncle was careful in how he spent his money," he explained as they reached the door to the castle. He held it open for her.

"Looking for bargains," Belle remembered as she crossed in front of him.

The last moan of the wind shut off as he closed the door behind them. "To the point of being a pinchpenny," he confessed. "Apparently, Jasper had stymied the efforts of horsemen at two other estates before my uncle decided he would be the making of the stallion. Unfortunately, our stablemaster had no better luck. I was the only one Jasper ever tolerated, and I'm still not sure why."

Belle patted his arm. "Jasper knows quality when he sees it."

He chuckled. "Jasper knows his like, I suspect. Stubborn,

determined. But I best say no more, or you will want to warn away Miss Bateman."

She had entirely forgotten about Petunia!

"Not at all!" Belle protested. "I'm sure she'd find the story as delightful as I do. There is something to be said for a man who is so devoted to his horse."

He raised a dark brow.

"There is!" she insisted. "But I will say no more on the matter at the moment either. I understand you are on my team for *tableaus vivant.*"

He did not blink at the change in subject as they rounded a corner and headed toward the main entry hall. "I did not realize it was your team, but if you are leading the tableau for the Judgment of Paris, then I'm your man."

She beamed at him. "You will make a marvelous Paris."

He groaned. "Oh, I was so hoping to be Zeus."

"I will not be going so far back in the story," Belle informed him primly, tugging on his arm just the slightest to direct him toward the library, where she knew her mother had installed the trunks of costumes. "Besides, as far as I know, you are the only gentleman on our team. You must play Paris. Charlotte, Tuny, and I will play the three goddesses."

"Hera, Athena, and Aphrodite, respectively," he mused.

She would not tell him she intended Tuny to play the goddess of love, not until she had to. She had a feeling Tuny would be no more amused. But Aphrodite was who Paris had chosen as the most beautiful. Therefore, Tuny must be the one Owen chose.

Even if a tiny part of her wanted him to choose her instead.

Owen followed Belle to the library and dutifully exclaimed over the various costumes she pulled from trunks that lay open on the floor. He would have liked far better to disappear among the many books, just the two of them, and talk of more substantive things. But talking might lead to confessing.

She wrinkled her nose at a particular set of leggings, and he couldn't stop his smile. Yes, he had a feeling spending time with Belle was a danger. How did she so easily slip past his defenses? Why did a few moments in her company set him to dreaming of a different future than the one he'd so carefully planned?

He had to think of a way out of this predicament, something that kept Jasper safe and did not harm her family. At the moment, his best option might be to keep the duke and the Batavarians at a distance. That way, Owen couldn't be tempted to do something he was already regretting agreeing to do.

"There you are, Mr. Canady," the duke said, striding into the library. "You mentioned you wanted to know more about the history of the House of Dryden."

Of course he had. Owen painted on a smile. "Certainly, Your Grace. But I wouldn't want to monopolize your time. I realize you have many other guests at present."

"All happily occupied," the duke informed him. "Belle, would you find the volume?"

"Volumes?" she asked with a teasing smile before turning to Owen. "Father has been updating the family history. Three volumes now, from the time of the Romans until today."

Well, that certainly would keep Owen from asking difficult questions. "How interesting. I'd love to know more."

Belle disappeared among the bookcases, her hum echoing against all the hard wood.

"I understand you and Petunia are considering

courting," the duke ventured.

Though Owen had tried to imply as much, he suddenly found the charade cloying. "Miss Bateman is delightful. I'm sure she'll find the right man for her."

The duke eyed him, but Belle returned lugging three leather-bound books stacked from her waist to under her chin. Owen hurried to relieve her of them.

"Tell him the good parts," she encouraged her father.

"I thought they were all good parts," her father said with a frown.

Belle laughed. "You know—the *really* good parts. Like where we fought off Romans. And how you met Mother."

"Romans it is," her father said, but Owen thought he saw a little color climbing in those sculptured cheeks.

They were so cute together. Belle couldn't help admiring how Owen hung on every word from her father's mouth. His dark eyes lit, and he leaned forward, as if cheering on the early Drydens as they fought to protect their little island from the encroaching hordes. When her father finished, he looked well satisfied with himself. She could imagine them becoming friends.

After Owen married Tuny, of course.

She was just glad that the storm blew itself out by dinner. Everyone seemed relieved, if the easy conversation around the table was any indication. Immediately afterward, the various teams moved to different rooms in the castle to plan their tableaus.

Belle had appropriated the Green Salon. Charlotte perched on one of the sofas, while Tuny dug through the pile of costumes Belle had moved to the other sofa. Owen leaned against the back of the sofa as Belle went to stand in front of the serpentine marble hearth.

"You will have heard by now that we are to depict the Judgment of Paris. I believe we all know the tale."

Tuny glanced up. "I didn't, but Charlotte was telling me about it at dinner. Some sort of beauty contest, wasn't it?"

"More than a beauty contest," Belle assured her. "Zeus, the father of the Olympian gods, was asked to name the most beautiful woman. Three goddesses were certain they should be given the title: Hera, queen of the gods and Zeus's wife; Athena, the goddess of wisdom and war; and Aphrodite, goddess of love and beauty. Not wanting to offend them, Zeus proposed a human known for his impartiality, a shepherd prince, Paris of Troy."

"Shepherd prince?" Tuny scoffed. "Leo may have pretended to be Fritz and Fritz Leo at times, but neither of them pretended to be a shepherd."

Belle waved a hand. "It's a long story. His parents thought he was cursed, so they gave him away at birth and later allowed him back in the family."

"I don't think much of his parents," Tuny said. "Who's playing them?"

"They aren't in the tableau," Belle said firmly.

Owen spread his hands and inclined his head. "And I will be playing the part of Paris."

Charlotte's mouth quirked. Belle had always admired her cool demeanor. It said there was little she could not handle. Now she turned her gaze on Belle. "And who did you have in mind for each of us?"

"You for Hera," Belle assured her. She hesitated only a moment before turning to her friend. "And Tuny for Aphrodite."

Owen blinked. Tuny went one further. She jerked upright and stared at Belle. "Me, as the goddess of love? You're mad."

"I believe," Charlotte put in smoothly as Belle drew herself up as well, "that what Petunia means is that she is known for her wisdom and would be better suited to play Athena."

Tuny nodded. "That's right."

Belle abandoned her post to move closer to her friend. "But, Tuny, you'd look so fetching in the costume I found for Aphrodite. I know it would be the making of our tableau."

Tuny crossed her arms over her chest. "I'd be the breaking of it, more like. What do you think your brothers will say when they see me next to you, pretending I'm prettier?"

"Oh, Tuny." Belle's face melted. "You're just as pretty."

"No," Tuny said, meeting her gaze. "I'm not. And there's nothing here that will change that fact. I don't mind most days that you have more than I do in everything that matters, Belle, but I won't stand up in front of my friends and family and pretend otherwise. Excuse me."

She hurried from the room.

"I've hurt her," Belle said, lower lip starting to tremble.

Charlotte rose. "That was never your intention, Belle. I know that, and so does Tuny. I'll speak to her, but I strongly suggest you rethink your plan for this tableau. Good evening, Mr. Canady."

He returned her nod before she swept from the room.

Owen could feel Belle's pain as she sank onto the nearest sofa. "Well, I made a mess of that."

He went to sit beside her. "As Lady Bateman said, we all know that wasn't your intention. You couldn't realize Miss Bateman would be so determined against the role."

"I should have known." She sighed, and it was all he could do not to pull her into his arms and promise everything would come out right.

"You mustn't think badly of her," she said, and he realized she was still determined to play matchmaker. "It was my fault. I see that now. I'll make things right. But I need your help."

Once more the desire to protect her rose up inside him. "I'll do whatever you ask," he promised.

Her golden lashes fluttered, drawing him closer. "That's a rather sweeping promise, but I'll accept it, with gratitude."

"So," Owen said, almost afraid to ask the question, "what is it you want me to do?"

"I want Paris to choose Athena," she said.

Of course she did. Those big green eyes were so hopeful, her face glowing as she turned it up to his. No man in his right mind would refuse.

"But Paris chose Aphrodite," he said. "Many of the people at this house party will know that."

She lay a hand on his arm, the touch warm. "But think of the impact of choosing Petunia."

He was. He'd thought he could have a harmless flirtation with her friend and leave with neither heart engaged. After seeing how Petunia had stood up to Belle, and hearing her reasons for doing so, he could not put the lady in that position. She deserved a man who loved her for who she was, not her relationship with the duke's family.

"I'm sorry, Belle," he said. "But it wouldn't be right."

Her pretty face puckered. "But why? You are courting Petunia. Surely no one would question you choosing her over Lady Bateman or me."

"You *want* me to court Petunia," he told her gently. "I begin to believe that Miss Bateman and I will never suit."

"No, no!" she protested, shaking her head so hard her ringlets bounced. "You've just seen her in an unflattering light. She is so much more than others give her credit for. She deserves a handsome, charming husband who loves her."

"I was just thinking the same thing," he said, taking her hands in his. "But I fear I am not that man." It was dangerous to admit as much, but he could not stop the words from coming out.

She pulled away and surged to her feet. "You're wrong. Petunia cares about you. I won't allow anything to come between you."

"Then perhaps," he said, leaning back so he could look up at her, "someone else should play Paris."

"Perhaps they should," she said, and she stalked from the room.

CHAPTER TWELVE

BELLE HAD ANNA take word to her sisters and Tuny that there was to be a meeting in her room that night. It was the best way to make amends. She and her sisters used to meet after everyone else was in bed, first in the middle of the schoolroom onto which their rooms had given and then in one of their bedchambers along the family corridor. Whenever Tuny had been staying with them, she'd join them.

She came in last tonight and so warily that Belle's heart turned over. She slid from her bed, where Larissa was cuddled near the white-lacquered headboard with Callie at the foot, and hurried to meet her friend.

"Please forgive me," she said, taking Tuny's hands in hers. "I can be perfectly beastly when I make up my mind about something."

"So we've noticed," Tuny said, but a smile edged into view, and Belle knew she was forgiven.

She led her friend to the four-poster bed, and Tuny gathered her blue flannel nightgown to clamber up beside Callie and lean against the footboard.

"What's happened?" Larissa asked, glancing between Tuny and Belle as Belle climbed back under the covers beside her.

"Tuny told Belle to stop pushing Mr. Canady on her," Callie supplied. She grimaced as they all looked her way. "Mrs. Winters was talking with Mrs. Lowry, the cook."

"That's not exactly what I said," Tuny put in. "But I will own I'm not sure Mr. Canady is the man for me."

"Why?" Belle asked. She held up one hand and ticked off his better qualities. "He's handsome, charming, kind to animals, and a gentleman."

"He's kind to his horse," Tuny allowed. "He's also handsome enough, and I agree he's a thoroughly charming gentleman. But he moves my heart not a bit."

Belle let her hand fall even as her frown gathered. "I don't understand."

Larissa tucked her white lawn nightgown close and edged away from her toward Tuny. "There are many handsome, charming gentlemen on the *ton*, Belle. But Leo was the one who touched my heart."

Callie nodded, hands rubbing along her own pink lawn gown. "I thought I wanted someone quiet and self-effacing, but I fell in love with Fritz."

"That's how it happens," Tuny explained. "Two people meet, find they are exactly what the other was looking for, and decide to spend the rest of their lives making each other happy. I know you tried, Belle, but Mr. Canady is not exactly what I've been looking for."

They were aligned against her. She'd never felt so alone. She tugged the covers to her stomach. "But he came here for you!"

Tuny cocked her head. "Did he? At times, it seems as if he came here for *you*."

Belle reared back, knocking her skull on the headboard. "What! Of course he didn't."

"I have heard him praise you," Callie pointed out. "He told Leo he found you beyond compare at Lady Carrolton's last soiree, and he told Fritz no lady had your grace on the dancefloor at Ivy's ball."

Larissa nodded. "And he appears to show a marked preference for your company."

"That's because I'm always trying to guide him in how

to become closer to Petunia," Belle protested.

"For someone being guided," Tuny said, "he doesn't seem to want to follow."

Tears pricked her eyes. "I was only trying to help."

All three of them crawled up the bed to her side. Callie lay her head on Belle's shoulder, Larissa put an arm about her waist, and Tuny patted her foot.

"We know you were trying to help, Belle," her oldest sister assured her. "But when it comes to the heart, sometimes even your abilities must bow."

She puffed out a sigh. "I won't give up. You can't ask it of me. You all promised we'd be married by harvest."

Tuny withdrew her hand. "Would it be so terrible if one of us didn't marry by harvest? Especially if marrying meant marrying the wrong man?"

Belle dashed away a tear. "I would never want you to marry the wrong man. Ever! I just want you to be happy."

"And I want *you* to be happy," Tuny told her. "Just not enough to make myself miserable."

"Very well," Belle said, another sigh pushing up inside her. "I'll stop trying to further an alliance between you and Mr. Canady."

"Thank you," Tuny said, settling back in her spot.

"But you must tell him," Belle warned. "Despite what you said, I truly believe he came here hoping to become better acquainted with you. You need to tell him the two of you will not suit."

She thought, she hoped, Tuny might argue. Owen might have come to the same conclusion, but perhaps, if they truly talked, they might find they had more in common than they'd thought. Marriages could be built on such a beginning.

But Tuny nodded. "Very well. I'll speak to him tomorrow."

And Belle could only hope it would be enough to bring them both to their senses.

Owen came downstairs early the next morning in hopes of checking on Jasper before any of the others were up. But he found the duke, duchess, Sir Matthew, Lady Bateman, and Lady Larissa there before him. They barely looked up long enough to nod a good morning before focusing back on their conversation.

"It's settled, then," the duke said. "Larissa, Leo, and I will see to the farms from the castle west to the lock. Jane, Callie, and Fritz will check the farms to the east past the main stables. We'll each take an Imperial Guardsman."

"And Charlotte and I will go into the village and report on any damage there," Sir Matthew agreed.

His wife nodded.

They did not ask for his help, but Owen felt compelled to offer. He wasn't sure why. For years, the only being he'd felt drawn to protect was Jasper.

And now Belle.

Had his time with the duke's family opened some unknown corner of his heart?

"What can I do?" he asked as a footman brought him a cup of tea.

The duke's cool green gaze swung in his direction. "A few cottages lie out along the Thames on the northern edge of the island. Perhaps you, Belle, and Mr. Roth can check on them."

"I'm sure Petunia will want to help as well," Lady Bateman told him.

"Then Mr. Canady can take her up with his group," the duke advised. "You'll need to ride. The roads could well be covered with debris. I've asked Mr. Quayle to send up additional horses from the main stables so everyone will have access to a mount. Report what you find to Mrs.

Winters if you can't find me."

"Of course, Your Grace," Owen agreed.

And so, a short time later, he found himself waiting at the castle stable as Belle, Petunia, and Mr. Roth of the Imperial Guard mounted the horses the duke had provided. Owen had to force his gaze away from Belle. He'd seen a lady or two in London attempt Cossack trousers for riding, a fashion brought about by the advent of the Batavarians to England, it was said. Certainly Mr. Roth was wearing a black pair of the puffy trousers tucked into his boots. Belle looked far more fetching in the ensemble.

Mr. Roth was a few years older than Owen, with coal-black hair and a solid chin.

"I am unused to being under the command of anyone except Count Montalban and Captain Wyss," he said to Owen as he settled into the saddle of a blood bay mare with long legs that probably ate up the ground. "You must tell me if I do not follow your lead."

Him, leading a party to rescue those who might have been harmed by the storm. He wasn't sure how he'd come to this, but there was a sense of satisfaction to it, as if his body had somehow grown.

"I'm sure you and I can come to an agreement," Owen told the guardsman. He tipped his head toward where the groom was cupping his hands to help Belle into the sidesaddle of her favorite horse, Unicorn. "It's Lady Belle who'll likely lead us a merry dance."

One corner of Roth's firm lips tilted up. "So I have noticed. Never have I seen a more interesting use for riding trousers." He schooled his face as the two women rode up to them.

Petunia was on the back of a rose-grey horse, likely a mare by the calm demeanor. The color complimented her dove grey riding habit, but Owen couldn't like the way the horse plodded along as if even crossing the stable yard was an effort. Petunia had claimed she wasn't a bruising rider. Perhaps the stablemaster had given her the most docile beast available.

"I can show you the quickest way to reach the northern shore," Belle offered, gathering her reins in front of her. The black riding coat with the braid crossing her chest and the Cossack trousers were similar to Roth's uniform, but no one would have mistaken her for a member of the Imperial Guard, especially not with that flashing smile and golden curls. And, for all the bold outfit, she had still chosen to ride sidesaddle.

"Follow me," she declared, directing Unicorn toward the gate as if confident they would be right behind. Roth cast Owen an amused look before dutifully following. Owen held Jasper back to allow Petunia to go next, then brought up the rear as the horses exited the castle courtyard.

Once off the castle mount, they could go two abreast, and Owen found himself riding with Belle's friend while Roth moved his blood bay up next to Belle's white mare. Everywhere, the passing of the storm was evident. Trees leaned or lay toppled, branches clawing at the sky. Shrubs barely clung to the soil, their leaves ripped from the stems.

The duke had been right about the roads as well. Owen and the others had only gone a little distance along a lane heading toward the river when they found a fallen tree blocking their way. Belle's Unicorn and Roth's mount were easily persuaded to jump a wide part of the trunk without any branches, but Petunia's horse shied.

"What's wrong with you?" she told the mare. "It doesn't even reach your belly. You could practically walk over it!"

The horse skittered back a few more steps, but it did not attempt to take the leap.

Jasper snorted as if unimpressed.

Belle and Mr. Roth had reined in and were waiting on the other side. Now Belle slid from the sidesaddle and handed the reins to the Imperial Guardsman before venturing back toward the tree.

"She's afraid," she called to Petunia.

"She's not the only one," Petunia told her. Indeed, her hands gripped the reins so tightly, Owen could see the kid leather stretched taut over her knuckles.

Only one way to solve this problem. Owen dismounted. Jasper eyed him, but he knew he didn't need to tie the horse. Jasper trusted him enough to stay at his side.

"Allow me, Miss Bateman," Owen told her. He came along the mare cautiously, murmuring words to calm. The rose-grey shuddered, but she allowed his presence. Owen held up one hand. "If you'd entrust me with the reins, Miss Bateman?"

She nearly threw the strips of leather at him. Owen caught them and held them at the ready.

"Can you dismount?" he asked.

She nodded shakily and managed to slip from the saddle to land unsteadily on her feet. Owen took her elbow with his free hand, and she smiled her thanks before righting herself.

Owen patted the mare. "Easy, now, girl. It's just a little jump. No different than taking a puddle. Come along."

Jasper shifted as if he didn't much like the idea of Owen interacting with any other horse.

"Only for a moment, old fellow," Owen called to him. He led the rose-grey up to the trunk. She hopped daintily over the obstacle. Owen tossed the reins to Roth, who caught them easily.

He had no sooner turned then he caught a flash of white, and Jasper vaulted the trunk to join the others.

"Putting on airs," Owen told him with a fond smile.

He answered with a snort and a toss of his head as if rather pleased with himself.

"It's all very well and good for the horses," Petunia pointed out. "But I could use a little help."

"I'll see to her horse," Belle promised with a smile to him. She moved to stroke the rose-grey's hide.

Owen went back to help her friend. The height of the trunk was easy enough for a horse to jump but not so easily handled for a lady in a riding habit with its long skirt. In the end, Owen swung her up into his arms.

Her eyes widened. They were a warm brown, reminding him of a fine leather saddle. Belle might be the one snorting if she thought that was the highest compliment he could pay the lady.

"This will be over quickly," he promised Petunia before setting her up onto the thick trunk. She held herself stiffly, as if waiting for a strong gust of wind to come calling. Owen vaulted over and lifted her down onto the ground.

"Well, that's a fine mode of travel," she teased him, cheeks pinking.

Owen sketched a bow. "Happy to be of service, milady."

He followed her to her mount and cupped his hands to allow her to push herself back into the sidesaddle. Roth eyed him, brow raised. Did he think Owen was flirting? Owen could only hope Belle didn't have the same impression. He'd thought he might finally have convinced her to stop trying to pair him with Petunia!

He turned to find Belle at his elbow. "If I might avail myself of your services as well, sir?"

Her Unicorn waited patiently. But the horse was easily two hands higher than the rose-grey, and Belle was inches shorter than her friend. Simply boosting her up might not do the trick.

Or perhaps he merely wanted to get closer.

Either way, Owen set his hands on her waist, and she sucked in a breath. Her gaze met his, as startled as that of a doe. As always, the green pulled him in, whispering of cool morning meadows and summer fields that stretched to the horizon. The color of home.

Perhaps he had a little of the poet in him after all. He

shook off the odd notion, lifted her up, and set her on the saddle.

"Thank you," she said, sounding almost breathless.

Or perhaps it was his breath that was faltering.

He stood there a moment, gazing up at her, tracing the arch of her brow, the curve of her lips.

Then Jasper snorted.

Right. Time to remember his duty. Owen made himself step back and went to see to his horse. He swung himself into the saddle, then bent closer to the horse's pearly grey ear. "Never fear, my lad. You will always be first in my heart."

Jasper all but pranced as he put himself next to Belle's Unicorn. Roth drew his horse beside Petunia's, and they set off once more.

Fortunately, all the houses along the northern end of the island had faired well in the storm. It was a testament to the duke's stewardship that all had sturdy slate roofs that had withstood the wind with only the loss of a tile here and there. A few outbuildings were canting, and water lay across yards from waves thrown up by the Thames, but the owners were already busy setting things to rights.

"Will you tell your father we'll come help the others?" one of the cottage owners asked Belle.

"Of course," Belle said. "And I'm sure he'll be as thankful as they will be."

She led them back a longer route to return to the castle.

"Fewer trees," she said to Owen as if she'd noticed him glancing around. "Less likelihood of obstacles."

It hadn't been the obstacles but the area he'd been studying. Everywhere he looked, people were out working—setting stones back into chimneys that had tumbled, gathering crops that had been crushed. But nowhere did he spy the man on the chestnut horse, watching his every move.

It was the same back at the castle. Everyone from

the kitchen pot boy to the duke was out helping their neighbors, and all with words of relief and thanksgiving. Even Dolph, the massive hound that belonged to Count Montalban, had been put to work, though Owen thought the dog was probably in his element rounding up cattle that had wandered through a broken fence. That, after all, had been why *Sennenhunds* had been bred, to herd alpine cattle, or so the story went.

Owen pitched in to help repair the stable door, which had taken the brunt of the battering nearest the castle. He thought someone might comment on a gentleman knowing his way around a hammer and turnscrews, but the stablemaster thanked him heartily for his help. It was one of the few times the things he'd learned under his great-uncle's forced employment had come in handy.

"Nicely done," Belle said, giving the door a swing. The newly oiled hinges didn't so much as squeak. She had come with her mother, her sisters, her friend, and Lady Bateman, bearing tea and biscuits to fortify the workers.

"Have to keep my lad safe," Owen said with a glance to Jasper. The horse took one look at Belle and turned his back on them both.

"I wish I knew what I could do for him to like me," Belle said with a frown, hand falling. "Unicorn likes apples."

"Jasper doesn't," Owen informed her. "And I wouldn't offer him a carrot unless I'm around. You might lose a finger."

She wrinkled her nose. "I should be going in any event. Mrs. Hornblum, the wife of the lockkeeper, lost their chicken coop, and Mother wants to send down some eggs to tide her over until the chickens can be found."

He'd never lived in such a place. Uncle Wentworth's servants had worked grudgingly, and most had left as soon as they had better opportunities. The duke and his family were part of the fabric of the island, working with the other inhabitants to protect the past, repair the present, and weave the future. The duchess and Lady Bateman had listed high criteria for the man who would marry into one of their families. It seemed they did their best to meet those same criteria.

What he wouldn't give to live in such a place, among such people. To be respected for what he could do rather than despised for who he had been born to, surrounded by those who truly cared for each other.

Did he have it in him to choose a different road, perhaps one that led to a place at Belle's side?

CHAPTER THIRTEEN

BY THE TIME Owen accompanied Belle, her father and family, and their other guests to services on Sunday, he was resolved to find a way to end his bargain with the spy from Württemberg. Every moment in Belle's company, every kindness that her family and friends showed him, told him he must change course if he was to count himself any sort of gentleman. If only he knew how to safeguard Jasper in the process.

The duke and his family attended the village church across the bridge. They made for quite the parade in the bright summer sun. The landau went first with His Grace, his wife, their sons, and Belle and Owen. He was cognizant of the honor of sitting beside her on the fine leather seats, even if it was the most expedient arrangement. The royal carriage that followed was already filled with the prince, count, Belle's older sisters, and two of the Imperial Guards. Mr. Roth was riding with Petunia in the Bateman coach. Behind all the carriages walked the servants, the men in their olive livery and top hats, the ladies in their best dresses and bonnets or feathered hats.

Owen had noticed the solid church of golden stone as he'd ridden through the village when he'd first arrived. The square tower with its bronze cross rose above all the other buildings in the area, except for the castle itself across the canal. Belle's father led his contingent through a private entrance on one side to the first three walnut box pews on the left of a center aisle, the doors of which held the bowing unicorn crest Owen was coming to recognize as the duke's. Stained glass windows cast colored patterns on the ladies' muslin gowns as they filed in after him, past the gilded finials that topped the doors.

Owen hadn't expected to see Mercutio or his servant in the chapel, so he wasn't surprised when he caught no sign of them among the villagers that filled the remaining pews. They all seemed so pleased to be there, smiling and nodding to each other. Perhaps they were still feeling thankful to have survived the gale.

He hadn't made a habit of worshipping regularly since his great-uncle had enforced the practice when Owen was younger. For Uncle Wentworth, church had been about judgment—God's judgment on sinners and Uncle's judgment on his neighbors.

"Giving herself airs," he'd say out of the corner of his mouth to Owen about Mrs. Polhurst, who liked to sing with animation. "The Lord won't listen to hymns like that."

"Thinks too highly of himself," he'd mutter after a particularly inspiring sermon by the vicar. "God sees through his posturing."

And Owen had seen through his great-uncle's posturing to the bitter soul within. The blood of his mother's family might have flowed through the fellow's veins, but Owen had resolved to be nothing like him, even to attending church.

Belle seemed to worship a different God. Her gaze was on the elderly, round-faced vicar as he spoke, her curls bobbing when she nodded at a particular point she endorsed. Her clear soprano trembled with joy as she sang a hymn of praise.

I wager You listen to her singing, Lord.

He nearly cringed at the thought. God might not be as condemning as Uncle Wentworth had implied, but

He likely didn't want His children wagering Him, on anything. And no matter how loving, He likely looked with disfavor on Owen's current activities.

I can't blame You there, Lord. I'm learning I've been wrong about a number of things. I hope You'll be patient while I correct my mistakes, and if You could see Your way to helping, I'd be forever grateful.

The closing hymn, about unmerited grace, was surprisingly easy to sing. His baritone melded with Belle's soprano in a way he thought rather pleasing.

As the others streamed through the churchyard for the waiting carriages at the end of the service, he touched Belle's arm, his convictions strengthening every moment. If he was ever to be a man worthy of standing beside her, he had to redouble his efforts to free himself and Jasper from Mercutio's clutches.

"I think I'll take a stroll through your delightful village," he explained when she glanced at him askance. "I'll return to the castle shortly."

She looked as if she might agree to accompany him, and he steeled himself to refuse, but Petunia caught up with her then, and the two were soon in conversation about the plans for the tableau, which they were to enact tomorrow afternoon. Owen slipped away through the side gate.

He ambled down the village lanes as if he hadn't a care in the world, but he watched carefully for Mercutio or his servant to no avail. Too much to hope the Italian had given up. And the threat to Jasper remained, regardless. He could walk up to the cottage and demand to see his nemesis, but he wanted more leverage before doing so.

Most of the village shops were closed on the Lord's Day, but the public house remained busy. It was a low-slung building roofed in slate, nestled along the Thames to the east of the island. Owen wandered in and took a table near the back of the wood-paneled room. The shutters on the windows had been thrown open, but the wood tables and chairs were dark enough that they swallowed the sunlight before it reached very far.

Normally, he'd have sat closer to the tall counter that divided the room from the kitchens, finding excuses to make the acquaintances of the locals, sniffing out who might have a horse he could pit against Jasper. Now, he wanted to go unnoticed, unless it earned him the information he sought.

A woman around the duchess's age, a few brown curls escaping the cap on her head, bustled up to this table, blue cotton skirts swinging under her tidy apron. "What will you have, sir?"

"I'd prefer conversation to ale," Owen said, laying a coin likely double the cost of a pint on the worn wood table.

Her grey eyes narrowed. "We run an honest establishment here."

Owen held up his hands. "I meant no disrespect. I'm visiting His Grace, and I merely hoped to learn a bit more about your fine village."

As he'd expected, the duke's name inspired confidence. Her shoulders came down, and she nodded, scooping up the coin. "Happy to oblige, my lord."

He didn't correct her on the use of the title. If Mercutio learned a visiting lord had been asking questions, he might not attribute those questions to Owen.

"Have you had much business from strangers?" he asked as she busied herself wiping down the table with a rag she'd pulled from where it had been draped along her apron tie.

"Little from His Grace's visitors. He's a good host. And we are far enough off the king's highway that we don't get many travelers. The only one lately is that foreign fellow what took Primrose Cottage."

That had to be Mercutio. "I'm sure he's happy for your

hospitality as well," Owen told her.

She snorted, reminding him of Jasper. "Not him. He didn't bring servants along, but does he hire any of the locals? Oh, no! He brings in a fellow from Walton-on-Thames, the next town over. I ask you. Who does that?"

Someone trying to prevent even a hint of his whereabouts from reaching the duke or the Batavarian contingent.

"Thoughtless indeed," Owen agreed. "Perhaps he doesn't intend to stay long."

"That's true enough," she said, stuffing the rag back into its place. "A fortnight only, Mr. Willard, the duke's steward, said when last he called upon us. I can only hope the next person who leases that pretty cottage intends to stay a while."

He thanked the barmaid for her trouble and headed for the door. She had given him little to go on, except the fact that the fellow on the chestnut horse hailed from a nearby town.

How else could he best the Italian?

He started for the castle, mind swirling, only to hear his name being called. Across the lane, Belle waved a hand at him, Petunia at her side.

Owen looked both ways, then crossed the rutted street to join them. "Ladies. I'm surprised to see you shopping today of all days, and with no chaperone or footman along." He made a show of glancing this way and that, all the while schooling his face to pleasantry.

Petunia colored as her gaze avoided his, but Belle smiled at him with her usual bright look. "We weren't shopping. We were looking for you. And we don't need a chaperone in the village. Everyone knows me."

And none would dare trouble the daughter of the duke.

"Well, you have succeeded in finding me," Owen said with a bow. He gestured toward the bridge. "Allow me to escort you back to the castle."

To his surprise, Belle picked up her frilly muslin skirts and swept ahead of them. He frowned after her a moment, until Petunia cleared her throat.

"That's her way of reminding me that you and I must have a conversation," she said.

Interesting. Surely if they had discovered him, it would be the duke or the prince who confronted him, not Petunia. Curious, he offered the lady his arm, and they set off after Belle, who was walking a few feet ahead of them.

Close enough to overhear, the minx.

"Is this about the tableau?" Owen asked when Petunia seemed to have trouble beginning.

He glanced over in time to see her swallow. "Not exactly. It has come to my attention, Mr. Canady—"

"Owen," he offered.

"Owen," she corrected herself with a grimace that did not bode well for this talk. "It has come to my attention that you might harbor feelings for me."

She glared at Belle's back as if the words had been coerced out of her. Owen felt a similar tension. He hardly wanted to make Belle's friend his enemy, but he could not tell her that he held affections for her when he didn't.

"And this discomforts you," he said instead.

"A bit," she admitted, sunlight turning a dark blond curl to bronze. "You're a fine fellow, and I enjoy your company, but I don't think we'd suit as husband and wife."

"I also enjoy your company," Owen told her, relief palpable. "And I have reached a similar conclusion."

She sagged against his arm. "Oh, good." She straightened. "I hope there will be no hard feelings between us, then."

"None," Owen said, gaze going toward Belle's swaying skirts. "In fact, I begin to believe there might be another lady in my future."

Belle had never noticed that skirts and petticoats made such an infernal racket against the ground. She could scarcely make out what Owen and Petunia were saying to each other with all that swishing. And the occasional wagon or carriage rumbling past didn't help. She couldn't walk any closer without making herself obvious. However did Callie manage being invisible and still hear everything!

Petunia hurried to catch up to her as the lane debouched onto the main road across the bridge. "There, done. You should be pleased."

Belle perked up, plumed hat tilting with her head. "Should I be? Did you two come to an understanding, then?"

Petunia glanced back to where Owen was beginning to close the distance between them as well. "We did. We shall continue being friends, with no expectation of more."

It was as she had feared. Poor Owen! How disappointed he must be to have had his suit refused. He'd intimated he'd feared this would be the outcome, but he had to have harbored some hope.

She cast him a look as he moved in beside them. His gait was jaunty, his smile its usual charm. Perhaps he wasn't so devastated after all. Still, she was the one who had brought him to this pass by insisting that he court Tuny. She must do her best to see that he enjoyed the rest of the house party.

They returned to the castle to find that plans were being made to go rowing. The Thames had sufficient traffic from barges and boats moving past the island that it was not generally congenial for a leisurely boat ride, but the side branch her father had widened and installed with the lock could be as still as a lake. Though the water was rather lower than usual with the heat of the summer, the expanse made a very pretty setting with the shadow of the castle and trees lining one side and village cottages the other, the stone bridge crossing the center of the length.

They owned several small boats, and soon everyone was pairing up for the outing. The governess Miss Winchester, Petunia, and the children would take one of the bigger boats, with Mr. Huber and Thal at the oars. Her mother and father were content to watch from the shore with the other Imperial Guards, one of whom was given charge of Dolph. Leo and Larissa, Callie and Fritz, and Sir Matthew and Charlotte ventured out on the water, each pair in their own boat. It was the work of a minute for Belle to convince Owen to partner her.

The blue-green waters parted silently as Owen set off from the shore. Belle could see her reflection, framed by the white puffs of clouds above, as the boat glided along. Not far away, Fritz brought his oars down hard enough that they splashed. Larissa, in the other boat, huffed. Both Leo and Owen angled their strokes to widen the distance between the boats. That suited Belle just fine.

"I'm terribly sorry about Petunia," she said as they floated west along the waters. "But I'm glad you were able to cry friends."

He nodded, angling the boat to follow the shore. "So am I. I admire her greatly."

"If only that admiration could grow into more," Belle lamented.

He gave a mighty heave on the oars, and the boat shot down the water. Was he more disappointed than she'd feared?

"Is there anything I can do?" she asked as they slipped around a little bend in the shore and lost sight of the others.

He shipped the oars. "Thank you, Belle, but I'm fine. There's another lady out there for me."

What a positive outlook! "Of course there is," she

assured him. "Why, she could be right around the corner, at the very next ball you attend."

"At the opera, perhaps," he said, smile widening.

"Or Almack's," she agreed.

"Or in this very boat."

Belle blinked. He was watching her, smile slowly fading into something that set her pulse to climbing.

"Owen, I…" she started.

Then he leaned toward her, and she found herself meeting him halfway. His lips brushed her softly. Her eyes fluttered closed. Oh, the sweetness! The tenderness, as if she was made of something fine and good and impossibly precious.

Belle pulled back to stare at him. A smile was curving his lips, as if he knew exactly the effect he'd had on her. More, there was a tremulous quality to that smile, as if he had been equally affected.

This couldn't be right! She'd been so certain he was meant for Tuny. She was waiting to find her perfect husband, one who would make her family proud and her heart sing.

Even if he set her heart to singing as no man ever had.

CHAPTER FOURTEEN

OWEN WATCHED THE realization spread across Belle's pretty features. Her eyes widened, and her breath caught. He hadn't intended to kiss her, but that sweet look and his own longings had combined to make it difficult to do anything else. If she hadn't met him halfway, he'd have been willing to sit back. Now, he wanted only to gather her closer.

Funny how boats prevented that.

Just their movement had set it to rocking. She grabbed the edge as if to steady herself. He rather needed to clutch at something himself. He had kissed a few ladies along the way, always by mutual agreement and always with the understanding that the moment would go no further.

Why did he find himself wanting more from Belle? He could envision a marriage, a home, family. All things he had once considered impossible. Yet, were they any more possible now?

Her color was climbing, so he set his hands to the oars.

"Forgive the impertinence," he said as he bent his back to turn the craft. "You are in all ways to be admired."

She lowered her gaze to her hands, clasped tightly in her lap. "I'm sure it was merely an aberration brought on by the moment."

It was an easy excuse, but he doubted the truth of it. Something more was happening inside him, changing his outlook, his goals. Still, she deserved far more than a half-thought-out declaration.

He managed to find benign topics of conversation until he had brought them back to the shore. One of the footmen took charge of the boat, and Owen helped Belle out beside her parents. The duchess sent him a wink, as if she suspected something more than a boat ride had just occurred. The duke regarded him as he always did, with a studied look that seemed to pierce Owen's carefully erected shield. He offered them both a smile.

But he could not forget the kiss.

Truth be told, it wasn't just the kiss. Everything about Belle called to him—her glowing smile, her dulcet voice, the curve of her hip, the light in her eyes. She was uniquely focused on her goals, and even her goals—to see her sisters and friend settled happily—were admirable. He'd once thought few ever refused her anything, and now he knew why. How could any man argue with perfection?

If he was forced to continue in her company all afternoon, he would likely find himself staring like a moonstruck calf. Better to master these emotions. So, when they all returned to the castle, he excused himself to go riding. Belle's light seemed to dim a little, but she accompanied her friend into the withdrawing room with hardly a glance in his direction.

Owen strode for the stable, then called for his horse to be brought out.

Jasper lifted his head at the sound of Owen's voice, whickering a greeting.

"I took him out this morning, sir," Walters told him.

"I'm sure you did," Owen replied. "But another ride wouldn't be amiss."

A short time later, he and Jasper were heading down from the castle mount. Though the road was smooth, Owen kept the stallion at an easy pace until they reached the flat. He'd taken the measure of the land now, and he knew where to direct the horse so that Jasper could stretch his long legs.

"Eager to run, are we?" he asked with a pat on the grey's neck. "I know we generally take our winnings and bolt, but it might surprise you to learn that I'm not so inclined to quit this place."

Jasper snorted, and Owen eased up on the reins. The horse broke into a canter.

"Can't you see it?" Owen urged. Gathering the reins in one hand, he pointed to a cottage surrounded by waving grain. "A pretty place to live, a pasture where you can run as often as you like, lanes like this to amble along, and people who love us."

Jasper bobbed his head as if in agreement.

"Aye, a pretty dream, but I fear that may be all it is," he confessed as they headed for the north of the island, past more farms and copse of trees toward the blue-grey ribbon of the Thames. "I might have just enough money from our winnings to purchase a small estate in the area, but would breeding fees be enough to maintain it?"

As if Jasper heard the frustration creeping into Owen's voice, he stretched out, legs pumping. They flew down the lane, the warm air brushing the hair back from Owen's face. The island's fields passed in a green-gold blur. Owen's entire life had been a blur—never settled, never fixed.

Belle was the North Star, orienting him to where he was and where he wanted to be. She brought everything into clarity—his admirable qualities, his faults. A man might be willing to work his entire life to be the best for her. Whatever it took to make her happy.

Could he be that man?

Jasper slowed to a canter, a trot, a walk. The horse blew out a breath and shook his mane as they turned along the shore, following the curve of the island past the river.

"Good lad," Owen said, patting his shoulder. "I wish I could outrun my thoughts so easily. We came here to keep you safe, but I begin to believe there's a higher purpose involved. Belle."

Jasper twitched his ears as if giving the matter thought as well.

"I flatter myself to think I have some chance of convincing her to allow me to court her," Owen told him, "but I doubt her duke of a father would be so willing."

Jasper bobbed his head as if insisting on the matter.

Owen eyed his grey ears. "Do you know something I don't about the duke?"

Jasper pawed at the ground with one hoof before stepping up his pace again.

"No, not the duke," Owen mused, rubbing his gloved hand against his beard. "Belle. No one refuses her, not even her father, I wager. All I have to do is convince Belle, and she'll win over the others."

Jasper gave a little kick and allowed Owen to turn him back toward the castle. Owen felt the same urge to caper. For the first time in his life, he could see the finish line.

And it was glorious.

Belle found it impossible to concentrate that afternoon. She knew what she must accomplish. Tuny and Charlotte had already chosen their costumes for the tableau, and she had approved as director. She had to choose her own costume, then meet with everyone one more time after dinner to ensure positioning was optimal as well as search out any props.

But as she went to fetch the gilded, flat-bottomed sphere her father used to hold down papers on his desk, she caught herself remembering how the sunlight had glinted on Owen's dark hair, how his muscles had rippled under his coat as he'd plied the oars.

No, no! This would never do. She snatched up the sphere to be used for the golden apple Paris would offer. Paris, who would be played by Owen. How could any lady refuse his attentions? Helen of Troy certainly hadn't.

Humph! She left the sphere in the Green Salon, gathered her skirts, and climbed the stairs for the schoolroom, where she knew there was a small, stuffed owl Tuny could use to symbolize Athena. Miss Winchester was in the middle of reading a story to her charges. Belle wasn't sure why Mr. Huber was there. Certainly neither Leo nor Fritz was in evidence, but the Imperial Guardsman seemed to be watching the governess as avidly as the children.

As avidly as Owen had watched Belle.

The memory sent a shiver through her, but she marched to the corner, picked up the owl, and left.

The process of selecting a costume didn't help matters. She'd had Davis bring one of the trunks to her bedchamber. But as she picked up an older silk dress from among the choices, she remembered the silken feel of Owen's lips against hers. Shaking her head, she dropped the gown back into the trunk and selected a crimson overdress with gold fringe. Topping a white muslin gown, perhaps? She held it up against her frame and studied herself in front of the mirror, only to see the tender look in Owen's eyes as they'd disengaged.

Oh, but she was in trouble!

She could feel the emotions swirling inside her—elation, anticipation, and something even warmer, whispering of forever. But she wasn't ready for forever. She'd promised she would see Tuny safely settled first. And Owen, for all he was handsome and charming, was not the sort of gentleman generally accounted a good catch for the daughter of a duke. He had no title, no distinguished family, no lofty estate, no impressive fortune.

Not that those things had ever really mattered to her before. Some titles were merely gilding—there was no history or endeavor behind them. Look at the many baronetcies granted by the king every year for "services rendered." She had a distinguished family of her own. She had a dowery as well, which could go toward building a fortune and buying an estate.

If she could persuade Owen to take her money. Some men could be prickly about such things, she'd heard. But he had never seemed a fortune hunter to her.

So many thoughts danced in her mind that it was a wonder she made it through dinner and managed to join Tuny and Charlotte in the Green Salon for the rehearsal a short while later. Owen must be still changing into his costume.

"I thought we were all to wear our costumes for this rehearsal," Tuny said, glancing from the drape of the white muslin gown she'd found for her character to the gilded gown from an older age Charlotte was wearing, then back to Belle's evening gown of celestial blue.

"I have yet to determine my costume," Belle told her. "I'm leaning toward something red, over white muslin, with my hair about my shoulders."

"Very fitting for Aphrodite," Charlotte said with a nod.

"I merely want to be sure we are positioned to most advantage," Belle went on. "Charlotte, if you would stand here, by the hearth, with the fire behind you?"

Charlotte went to the spot Belle had indicated, then drew herself up, chin high and gaze haughty, like the queen of the gods she was supposed to be.

"Very nice," Belle said with a grin. Then she cocked her head. "Do you think it will be too warm tomorrow for a fire in the hearth? It would silhouette you magnificently."

"Much too hot," Charlotte told her, breaking her pose. "That storm tempered things a bit, but it's still unreasonably hot for August."

Belle straightened. "You're right. The only other thing I'd change is your hair. Mother has a gold coronet. I wonder if she'd let you borrow it. As queen of the gods, Hera would appear to need a crown."

"I'll ask Jane tomorrow," Charlotte promised.

Belle turned to her friend. "Tuny, you'll be here, just to the left of Charlotte and a little in front of her."

Tuny frowned at her sister-in-law. "Your left or hers."

"Hers," Belle clarified.

"I believe that's called stage left," Owen said.

Belle turned to find he had come into the room, and her breath caught anew. He'd located flesh-colored stockinet trousers that proved he had no need to pad his calves and paired them with Moroccan leather boots and a long brown wool coat embroidered with leaves along the cuffs. Lace peeked out at his throat and wrists, and a hat with a peacock feather in the band rested on his head.

"Nicely done," Charlotte said. "The impartial prince-shepherd."

Tuny made a face. "I still can't believe he was a shepherd and a prince. Who wrote this story?"

"Homer," Charlotte supplied. "A very respected ancient poet."

"Required reading at university, I hear," Owen agreed, moving to their sides. "Even for those going into the church."

"Ministers have to read about Greek gods?" Tuny shook her head.

"At the moment, we just need to look like Greek goddesses," Belle reminded her. She turned to Owen. "Charlotte is going to be in the middle, with Tuny and me on either side. I'd like you to stand facing us."

He positioned himself, but now he wore a frown. "Won't my back be to our audience?"

"Not if you stand where I'm thinking," Belle said. She went to put both hands on his shoulders and pushed just the slightest against the muscle. He pivoted. She glanced down at his feet. "There. Better."

"Much better," he said, voice warm in her ear.

She glanced up to find him inches away. The glint in his eyes warned her he too was remembering their kiss. She dropped her hands and scurried back so fast she bumped into Tuny.

Her friend caught her before she tumbled to the carpet.

"Thank you," Belle said, face flaming.

Tuny shrugged as she let go. "Well, I am supposed to be the goddess of wisdom."

Belle made herself focus on their rehearsal. She and Tuny found a way for the stuffed owl to sit on one hand, then she repositioned Charlotte and Tuny until she was satisfied with the picture they made. After some wiggling, she had found the right place for herself as well. If that brought her a little closer to Owen, it was only because of the role she would play.

"I think we're ready for tomorrow afternoon," she told them as they relaxed back onto the sofa and chairs. "Father's group will set up first. Mother's group will view his, and then set up. We will view both, then set up our tableau. Mother's group will tour through when everyone else has seen theirs, and Father's group will come last."

"But Miss Winchester, the children, the Imperial Guards, and Aunt Meredith and Uncle Julian will be our primary audience," Tuny reminded everyone.

Belle nodded. "They'll tour through the three tableaus, and then vote on which they found most inspiring. I'm not sure what Father intends for the winners, but I've no doubt it will be wonderful."

"Just don't break your pose," Tuny warned. "If I know Rose and Daphne, they'll say something sure to make you laugh."

"Thal and Peter too," Belle told them.

"And I would not put it beyond the Imperial Guards

to want to discredit us to give the prince and the count a greater chance of winning," Charlotte added.

"This should be interesting," Owen said, mustache curving up with his smile.

As if to belie the point, Charlotte covered a yawn with her hand. "I'm for bed. See you all in the morning."

Tuny followed her out.

Belle started after them, and Owen stepped into her path.

"I've discomfited you," he murmured, watching her.

She should deny it. It wasn't wise to give a gentleman the upper hand. Larissa had taught her that. But he was as much friend as potential suitor. He deserved her honesty.

"Perhaps a little," Belle admitted. "That was my first kiss. I wasn't expecting it."

He inclined his head, mouth twitching. "Forgive me for not living up to your vision."

"Oh, it wasn't that. You were marvelous. That is…" She was blathering! She knew how to speak so as to give greatest impact. She squared her shoulders.

"That is, I had thought my first kiss would come after a declaration, not before," she continued, only to cringe at the words. She'd all but told the man she expected him to propose!

But he didn't go down on bended knee. Instead, he rubbed his bearded chin with one hand.

"I've never been one to follow the rules," he murmured. "But I had thought a declaration came *after* a courtship, so the lady is assured the gentleman will suit. I haven't been courting you, Belle."

She could not look at him. "No, of course not."

"But I expect that to change shortly."

Her gaze jerked toward his, but he was already striding from the room, leaving his tantalizing words hanging like a clump of mistletoe in a kissing bough.

CHAPTER FIFTEEN

BELLE HAD A hard time sleeping that night. Had Owen really meant he intended to court her? She'd had any number of gentlemen in her train during the Season. They could be counted on to petition her hand for a dance at every ball, carry on conversations at soirees, and applaud wildly to her singing at each musicale. They stopped by at least once a week to call. Some brought tokens of their esteem—a rose from their father's hothouse, perhaps, or a poem composed in her honor.

None had risen above the others. None made her heart beat faster just by glancing in her direction.

Owen did.

But did that mean she was ready to consider him as a husband?

She was certain she'd be heavy-eyed by morning, but she seemed to have taken no ill effects. She patted her curls into place before rising from the dressing table.

"I'm afraid you'll have your hands full helping everyone change into their costumes this afternoon," she told Anna, who was putting away Belle's night things.

"It will all come out right," the maid assured her. "I've already enlisted Sally from the kitchen and Marylynn from the laundry to help. And there's Lady Bateman's maid to join us for the ladies, and your father's valet and the ones for the prince and the count to help with the gentlemen. We'll get you all squared away in time to perform. And your father said we could watch too." She beamed at the idea.

"Then I'll look for you in the audience," she told the maid. With a wave of her hand, she sailed from the room.

Her steps didn't falter until she reached the breakfast room. What if Owen was there ahead of her? Her hand went to her curls, and she forced it down. She had no reason to primp! Owen knew exactly what she looked like and seemed to find it quite acceptable.

She sashayed into the room and went to take her usual spot overlooking the garden window. It was another lovely day, and the flowers stretched out below in a riot of color. Easier to gaze at them than at Owen, who, a quick glance told her, looked rather fine in a bottle green coat. After all, she didn't want him to think she was ogling.

But as she reached her chair, he rose and came to hold it for her. She wasn't the only one surprised, for their footman, Davis, had to jerk to a stop, then turn and pretend the sideboard had been his intention all along.

"Good morning, Belle," Owen murmured, her name like a caress as he slid the chair under the table. His arms temporarily bracketed her, and she had to force herself not to lean into the embrace.

He straightened to return to his seat down the table from her. The others must have breakfasted before them or were sleeping late, for they were the only two at the table at the moment.

"Is there any more of the salmon, Davis?" she asked as the footman brought her her usual cup of melted chocolate.

"Mr. Canady has the last piece, your ladyship," he said with a recriminating glance down the table at Owen. "But we have some nice kippers this morning."

Once more Owen rose. "I haven't taken a bite. Please, Belle, I would rather you had it."

As Davis backed away, Owen set the dish of rosy fish

down on her plate.

Belle glanced up at him. "As Tuny would say, bit much."

"Wait until this evening," he murmured.

A shiver went through her that was all pleasure. She could hardly wait to see what else he would do.

Charlotte and Sir Matthew came in then, so conversation turned more general. It wasn't until Belle had finished eating and risen that Owen took his place at her side.

"Would you care to go riding this morning?" he asked as they left the room together. "It's a beautiful day, and the temperature is still cool."

Oh, for a moment in the saddle, pelting down the lane, the wind in her face! She sighed. "That would be lovely, but I really should settle on a costume."

He opened his mouth, and she held up her hand. "And no, I don't require assistance. I will see you in the Green Salon at noon."

He inclined his head, and she hurried for the stairs.

Was this what courting entailed? She hadn't really considered the matter before. All this attention, this admiration, it was rather… gratifying? Invigorating?

Cloying?

She wasn't sure what to make of her feelings, so she spent the morning trying on one costume after another, until she finally settled on a purple velvet gown with a white silk underdress and gold braid crossing the bodice and edging the hem. Anna brushed out her curls into a single heavy fall that draped over one shoulder and was held in place by pearl-studded combs. Too late to look for a crown for herself, though the style cried out for something circling her brow.

There was a rap on the door, and Anna went to answer it. A moment later, and she returned to Belle's side bearing a wreath.

"For you, your ladyship," she said, holding it out. "That's bilberry, that is."

Belle took the wreath gingerly. Long stems holding tiny, dusky green leaves and rounded, blue-black berries had been woven together to form a crown. A card was tucked among the greenery.

"The myrtle plant belonged to Aphrodite," it read. "May this one crown the fairest of them all. With all my admiration. Owen."

"It's just the thing for your hair," Anna marveled.

"So it is," Belle said, smile feeling shaky.

Anna settled the coronet onto her hair and pinned it in place. She tied purple ribbons to the ends and let them flow down Belle's back and mingle with her hair.

"Perfect," Belle breathed.

"It's almost time," Anna warned her, stepping back.

Belle rose and headed for the salon.

The others were there before her. Charlotte was her usual serene self, but Tuny was pacing, her muslin skirts flapping more than the stuffed owl on her hand ever had.

"There you are!" she declared, stopping in the middle of the carpet. She eyed Belle from toes to top. "Very nice."

"Worth the wait," Owen said, moving out of the shadows along one wall.

The sight of him pressed against her, pulling her closer and pushing her back at the same time. She drew in a breath and forced herself to focus. "Leave your accessories here. We'll be viewing Father's and Mother's tableaus first."

Charlotte and Tuny followed her out of the room. Owen moved to walk beside her.

"Nervous?" he asked.

Yes, but not for the reason he thought. "I'll be fine," Belle assured him. "You?"

"Never with you at my side," he vowed.

She was sure her cheeks were pink as they walked into the library.

Her father, Callie, and Fritz had been given the task of

depicting a scene from the tales of Robin Hood. Callie, in a low-waisted velvet gown and with a tall, pointed hat on her hair, was clearly Maid Marian. Fritz in doublet and hose, with a bow in one hand and a quiver on his back, must have been Robin. Her father wore a rough brown robe belted with a rope.

"You thought it odd to find a shepherd-prince in our story, Petunia," Owen said aloud. "I find it just as odd to see a friar-duke."

Belle's father, who was standing just behind Callie, narrowed his eyes at Owen, but otherwise, he did not destroy the tableau.

"Very nice," Belle told them all before herding her own group on to see the next.

Her mother's group were supposed to depict King Alfred defeating the Norsemen. Leo made a very convincing king, standing with chin up and sword raised. Larissa next to him held a long bow drawn, prepared to repel the invaders. In a tunic trimmed with fur, axe in one fist, Sir Matthew looked every inch the fierce fighter. So did Belle's mother, in a fur-trimmed gown, hair braided and wound round her head. Belle wouldn't have wanted to face her with that hatchet and such a look of fury on her face.

"I see I was wrong," Owen murmured to Belle. "I thought your father was the one to fear."

Belle bit back a smile. So did her mother, by the way her cheek was twitching. Still, Belle had to haul Charlotte out of the room, so fixedly did she gaze at her husband.

"Hurry," Belle urged, motioning them back toward the Green Salon. "Our first audience will be here any moment.

They streamed into the room and took up their places. Belle glanced around at them all. "Does everyone have everything?"

Charlotte waved a peacock feather fan before her

gilded gown. "Yes."

Tuny righted the owl and nodded.

Owen tossed the globe in the air and caught it. "Ready."

"Good luck," Belle said. She took up her pose. But she didn't have time to feel nervous before Anna and the staff trickled through the door. Mrs. Winters and Mrs. Lowry were in the forefront, the outdoor staff like Mr. Quayle farther back. They clustered around, some glancing as much at the room they had probably never entered as at the tableau.

"Lady Belle is beauty," Anna told them all. "Miss Petunia is wisdom. And Lady Bateman is their mother."

Close enough. Belle refused to comment. Out of the corners of her eyes, she saw Tuny's lips wiggle.

"What's he doing, then?" someone asked, pointing at Owen.

"Getting ready to make a pie, looks like," the kitchen girl said, eyeing the gilded sphere Owen held out toward Belle.

Mrs. Lowry, their cook, snorted. "Not with one apple, he isn't. Looks to me like he's sweet on her."

Belle clamped her teeth together, but she couldn't help the heat rising in her cheeks, particularly when Owen winked at her.

"A very nice tableau," Mrs. Winters assured them before shooing her staff out.

"Clever lady, your cook," Owen murmured.

"Shh!" Belle warned. "The next group will be on their heels."

The three Imperial Guardsmen marched in as her words were fading. They wore their everyday uniforms, black against the greens of the room, and they stopped right in front and eyed the ladies.

Mr. Keller, who was one of the younger members, cocked his blond head, then nodded. "Nicely done."

"We do not speak to them," Mr. Roth ordered.

"Except to tell them they are very fetching," Mr. Keller protested.

"You can do that silently," Mr. Huber told him. He swept them all a bow.

Mr. Keller followed suit, and Mr. Roth pointed toward the door and ordered them all out.

"At least they didn't try to make us forget ourselves," Tuny said. Then she snapped back into character as Miss Winchester, Thal, Peter, and her nieces came in.

"There's Mama!" Rose proclaimed. She waved her hand. "I'm here, Mama! See me?"

Belle couldn't turn to look at Charlotte behind her, but she must have let her daughter know she saw her, for the little girl grinned.

Daphne was focused on Petunia. "You look funny, Aunt Tuny. Do you need to use the necessary?"

Petunia gave a quick shake of her head, but Belle was certain she heard her teeth grinding.

"Once upon a time," Miss Winchester told her charges, "there was a contest between three ladies as to who was the most beautiful. This young man is giving the prize to the one he believes meets that standard."

"Belle," Peter said, as if it were a foregone conclusion. "She always talks people into doing what she wants."

He didn't sound displeased by the fact, but Belle's cheeks were heating once more.

"I don't know," Thal said diplomatically. "Lady Bateman and Petunia are nice looking too."

"Old," Peter said with a shake of his head.

Charlotte choked.

"We should see about our voting," Miss Winchester said, ushering her charges toward the door.

"This is harder than it looks," Owen murmured.

Aunt Meredith and Julian came in next, and, if Belle had counted correctly, they were the last group they must attempt to impress. Her mother and father's groups would come through too, but they did not have a vote.

Her aunt and uncle stopped and looked over the tableau, Fortune trotting along with them. At least Aunt Meredith and Uncle Julian didn't say or do anything that might make Belle break the pose.

Fortune was something else entirely. She wound around Petunia's ankles, gaze up as if hoping for a pet, then moved on to Charlotte and finally Belle. Belle stood perfectly still as the silky fur pressed against her stockings.

Then Fortune approached Owen. She stopped to sit in front of him, and Belle found another reason entirely to hold her breath. The cat eyed him, tail swinging back and forth against the carpet. He did not move a muscle.

She rose and twined herself around his legs twice before returning to Aunt Meredith, who looked more surprised than Belle had expected.

"And here's the final tableau, my lord," Mrs. Winters said.

Belle nearly frowned before remembering to school her face. Her father would have been addressed as His Grace, and he and Fritz were in other tableaus. What other lord did they have in residence?

Lord Ashforde stepped around their housekeeper to take in the tableau, nodding to Owen, Belle, and Charlotte before his gaze hit Petunia. Then he merely stood and stared.

Owen had never seen a man look more stunned. By the color climbing in Petunia's cheeks, she saw it too. But if anything, her head only rose a little higher, and she maintained her pose as Athena, goddess of wisdom.

"The Judgment of Paris, I see," Lord Ashforde said in his cool voice. "I always thought the fellow should have awarded the prize to Wisdom."

He suffered the housekeeper to lead him out.

As soon as he disappeared from view, Tuny whirled. "You promised me he wasn't going to be here!"

Belle held up her hands. "I didn't promise, exactly."

"Abelona Dryden, I wash my hands of you." Tuny dusted off her hands and stalked from the room.

Belle stared after her, washing white.

"A bit of warning might have helped," Lady Bateman said, easing around her. "I'll see you at dinner." She swept from the room.

Belle stood alone, lower lip trembling. Owen set aside the golden globe and went to her side. "Matchmaking?" he ventured.

She nodded. "I thought it might go one of two ways. Either you and Tuny would be betrothed when he arrived, and she could show him what he had missed. Or she would have decided you were not what she wanted and run to him instead." She cast him a quick glance. "I was hoping for the former."

He was just as glad he hadn't given it to her. "Her antipathy seems to be deeper."

"Yes, and I've never been entirely sure why. He's rather presentable."

Hard to argue. Ashforde had everything Owen didn't—respected family name, wealth, position, power.

And apparently Belle's admiration.

"He's a fine fellow," he allowed. "But not what Petunia wants."

She blinked, then her hand went to her mouth. "Oh, Owen! That's it entirely. I should have known what Tuny wants, only I never thought to ask. I just assumed she'd want what I want."

And she'd chosen him for her friend. Owen's heart thudded in his chest. "And what do you want?"

It was an impertinent question, one he had no right to

ask. She didn't look at him, gaze fixed on the door her friend had stormed out of.

"I had a vision for my true love," she murmured. "He would ride brilliantly, dance divinely, and be able to converse on any number of subjects with ease."

He drew in a breath. "I have a chance, then."

She met his gaze at last, tears shimmering on her lashes. "Yes, yes you do."

Slowly, giving her every chance to pull away, he leaned closer, until he could brush his lips against hers. This was better than winning any race, more real than any persona he'd had to put on. This was true.

"I think you won, Belle!"

Owen pulled back as her brother Peter galloped into the room. The boy jerked to a stop and made a face. "You too! Ug!"

Belle opened her eyes, looking a bit dazed, then turned to face her brother. "You will say nothing about this, to anyone. Do you understand?"

Some of the urgency in her voice must have convinced him, for he swallowed and nodded. "Fine. But you owe me a game of charades."

"Fine."

He stomped out of the room.

"You don't want your family to know," Owen said, spirits deflating.

"I don't want anyone to know," she said. "Until I know."

And she followed her brother out the door.

CHAPTER SIXTEEN

JANE HAD ASKED Meredith and Julian to make themselves comfortable in an upper sitting room until the tableaus were completed, but Meredith found herself pacing the floral carpet, Fortune following as if determined to catch the lace on her skirts. Normally, she relied on her pet's intuition when it came to knowing a person's character, but she could not shake the feeling that Fortune had been wrong about Mr. Canady.

"The news wasn't that bad," Julian mused as he sat on one of the rose-colored sofas, arm draped along the curved back. "He isn't a hardened sinner."

"He isn't a saint either," Meredith argued. Her head came up as Jane entered, still costumed as a Norse invader. Somehow the fur suited her. Fortune hurried to greet her, and the duchess bent to run a hand along the arched back.

"Forgive me," she said, glancing up at Meredith and Julian. "Lord Ashforde has arrived, and I had to see him settled first. Would you like tea before dinner?"

"No, thank you," Meredith told her, "but I hope you can spare me a moment. It's about Mr. Canady."

Jane had learned enough about being a duchess that she didn't stiffen. Instead, she straightened, went to join Julian on the sofa, and looked up at Meredith expectantly. "You have my complete attention."

Fortune sat at Jane's feet as if prepared to listen as well.

Meredith perched on the nearest chair. "Julian and I were sufficiently concerned about his courtship of Petunia…"

"Or Belle," Jane put in.

Meredith sat back. "Indeed. Then I'm even gladder Julian asked his staff to look into the fellow."

Jane glanced at Meredith's husband. "Is he a fortune hunter?"

As if she recognized the sound of her name, Fortune jumped up beside Jane and looked up into her face.

"No," Julian allowed, hands braced on his thighs. "But he does appear to have lived by his wits for some time."

"And only his wits," Meredith reminded him before turning to Jane. "He has no inheritance, no estate, no property of any kind to his name."

Jane frowned. "How's he paying for the clothes, his lodgings in London, then?"

"He appears to have had some luck racing his horse," Julian explained.

"That I can imagine," Jane said, frown easing. "I've seen the horse. He's a prime goer. Mr. Canady likely wins every time."

"So it would seem," Julian agreed.

"We surmise that he's amassed a nest egg with his winnings," Meredith told her. "But we fear it would not be enough to support a wife, either Petunia or Belle."

Jane nodded. "That might explain his reticence to court either. He may be wondering what he has to offer a lady."

"Meredith and I wonder the same thing," Julian admitted.

"Though I took some satisfaction that Fortune behaved approvingly toward him just now," Meredith added.

Fortune cocked her head and continued to eye Jane, as if waiting for some sort of pronouncement.

Jane smiled at them all. "Well, many wondered what a cavalry officer's widow had to offer a duke, and we all know how that turned out. I say we keep a closer eye on Mr. Canady. I'm hoping he'll show his true colors soon."

Belle had wanted to apologize to Tuny straight away, but her mother and father and their teams had found her first, and she had had to invent an excuse as to why they would not be viewing her tableau.

"Overcome by the emotion," she told them, fanning herself with one hand. It was only the truth. Between Owen's kiss and Tuny's reaction to Lord Ashforde, Belle could hardly think.

She next went upstairs to see her friend, but Tuny's maid refused to allow her entrance.

"Miss Bateman is resting," she said, blue eyes narrowed and face hard, as if she knew Tuny's weariness was all Belle's fault.

Dinner was worse. Tuny sent word she would be taking a tray in her room. Charlotte had mentioned that she knew her sister-in-law had hard feelings toward Lord Ashforde, and Sir Matthew must have known as well, for they both were cool to him. They must also have known Tuny had told Owen they would not suit, for Sir Matthew, who was seated on one side of him, spent more time talking to Belle's mother than to Owen.

At least Callie and Aunt Meredith, on either side of Lord Ashforde, attempted to engage him in conversation, but everyone seemed to feel the tension. Her mother and father kept glancing at each other down the long table, and even the combined charm of Owen, Leo, and Fritz couldn't quite restore the good humor that had been so prevalent previously.

Belle wasn't sure whether to be relieved or disappointed that Owen did not resume his campaign of courtship. He kept his conversation easy and his smile at the ready. Even so, the leg of mutton with cauliflower and spinach they were having as part of the main course was one of Belle's favorites, but she barely tasted it. She'd been so intent on matching Tuny that she'd failed to take her friend's desires into account. If Owen hadn't made her realize as much, who knows how long she might have persisted!

"I'd like to thank everyone for the marvelous tableaus this afternoon," her father said as the footmen began to clear the platters. "The results are quite close, within a vote or two of each other. You are all to be commended."

Her mother nodded. "And the winner?" she nudged.

He smiled. "The Judgment of Paris. I am having golden apples cast for all four of you."

Belle smiled her thanks, but all she could think about was how much sweeter the victory would have been had Tuny been beside her.

"Good," Owen called after the others had expressed their appreciation. "Because then I won't be put in the impossible position of choosing the fairest of the fair."

Charlotte unbent enough to raise her glass in toast to him, and Sir Matthew cuffed him good-naturedly on the shoulder, nearly oversetting him.

Owen offered Belle his arm as everyone rose from the table to adjourn to the withdrawing room for games. She shook her head.

"I must make things right with Tuny," she murmured.

He took her hand and brought it to his lips, setting her knees to wobbling. Then he followed the others.

Belle caught her mother's arm to keep her in the dining room a moment. "Would you mind if I went upstairs early, Mother? I'd like to talk to Tuny."

Her mother regarded her, a light in her deep brown eyes. There was a legend in the family that she could get rocks to confess their misdeeds. Certainly none of her children had ever been proof against her. "Put your foot in it, did you?"

Belle dropped her gaze to the carpet. "It seems I am not a very good matchmaker."

"Bringing in Lord Ashforde last minute was a gamble," her mother allowed. "But we mustn't allow him or Petunia to suffer for it. And how does Mr. Canady figure into the matter?"

Belle swallowed. "Tuny and Owen have decided they will not suit. He seems to be interested in someone else entirely."

"You," her mother surmised.

Belle's head came up. "You knew?"

Her mother shrugged. "Your gentlemen friends tend to get that moony look in their eyes. You have a talent for making people feel valued, Belle. Some hunger for that."

Belle shook her head. "It's not a very good talent, or Tuny wouldn't be so angry with me."

"Maybe it's not the talent but how you use it," her mother suggested. She patted Belle's arm. "Go on then. Make your amends. Give Tuny my love as well."

With a nod, Belle picked up her skirts and hurried upstairs.

Constance opened the door to Belle's knock. At the sight of her, the short, blond maid drew herself up and fixed her blue gaze on the other side of the corridor. "I am to say that Miss Bateman is not receiving."

"And I am to say I'm so, so sorry," Belle answered. "Please, may I see her?"

This time, Constance wilted. "It's not my choice, your ladyship, but I'll ask." She shut the door gently.

Belle waited, fists pressed against the blue of her skirts, and heart pressed against her chest.

The door swung open, and Tuny faced her. The set of her face was bad enough, but the red rims of her eyes, proof of tears, cut into Belle.

"I'm not willing to hear another apology unless it

comes with a change in behavior," her friend declared.

Belle puffed out a breath, hands falling. "I'll try, but it's clear I will struggle. I care about you, Petunia, and I want to see you happy."

"Then maybe," Petunia said, "you could allow me to see to my own happiness."

Belle swallowed the lump in her throat and nodded. "You're right. I'm so sorry I interfered. I asked Lord Ashforde to come late like that because I was sure you and Owen would be betrothed by then, and you could show him what he had missed."

Petunia's angular face softened. "Much as that might have been pleasing for the moment, I would have far preferred to have been consulted in the matter. We spoke of this, Belle, before the party. I told you I didn't want him here."

"Yes," Belle agreed, "but you never said why, precisely."

Tuny put her hands on her hips, tightening her blue flannel dressing gown against her body. "Must I tell you everything? If you're truly my friend, you'd listen to my wishes, not your own."

The words pinched her heart. Belle hung her head. "I can see that. I let my own wishes take over. I won't do it again."

"Good," Tuny said.

Belle shifted on her feet. "I would like to know, however, what it is you do want in a fellow. I promise not to thrust him on you, but I could at least point him out if I knew."

Tuny's sigh was audible. "What I want, Belle, is a fellow who values me so much it doesn't matter I wasn't born to good Society or that I'm not as beautiful or wealthy as some. I want a man I can admire for his character and good sense, a man who stirs my heart. Owen seems to enjoy my company and he appears to have a fine character, but there's no spark."

"And there's no spark with Lord Ashforde?" Belle dared

to ask, glancing up.

A fire seemed to be simmering in the dark brown of Tuny's eyes. "There was a spark, but he snuffed it out right and tight. So, you'll understand when I say I feel the need to keep him at a distance."

"Of course," Belle said. "I'll do whatever I can to help."

"I'll hold you to that," Tuny told her. "You keep him busy. I'll latch onto Owen and never let go until I've seen the last of Lord Ashforde."

Belle opened her mouth to protest. Owen had decided to court her, and she was becoming quite content with the idea. She didn't want him hanging on another lady's arm, even if it was only pretend. And how would he feel if she turned all her attentions on Lord Ashforde?

But she loved Tuny like a sister, and if her friend needed a shield in Owen, Belle should allow her that. After all, it was entirely Belle's fault Tuny and Lord Ashforde were in this predicament in the first place. A shame she simply couldn't send him away, but her mother was right—he shouldn't be made to feel slighted because of Belle's mistake.

"Excellent plan," she told her friend. "We'll enact it first thing tomorrow morning."

It had been a difficult evening, despite the duchess's attempt to rally everyone in games. Owen had felt the mood shift, but he wasn't entirely sure of the reason. Petunia had obviously taken Lord Ashforde in dislike. It seemed as if most of the other guests felt the same way. At least Lord and Lady Belfort left shortly after dinner, with their canny pet, and Fortune did not have an opportunity to provide her opinion on Lord Ashforde's character, for it would likely have been as dismal as that of the other guests.

Owen could not imagine what his lordship could have done to warrant such a response. He had only met the baron a few times in London, but the raven-haired, clean-shaven Ashforde had always seemed calm, contained, like fine tea kept under lock and key. The only time the two of them had run afoul had been at a benefit dinner to raise money for the Society for the Prevention of Cruelty to Animals.

Owen had been trying to inveigle his way into the good graces of the duke's family by bidding on one of the pieces of art being auctioned. Ashforde had decided to bid on the same piece. By the way his look kept brushing Petunia's, it had been clear to Owen the fellow wanted to impress her. So, he'd allowed the bid to go quite high before bowing out and leaving the purchase to the baron's deeper pockets.

But that had been more than a month ago, and Owen had heard no rumors about Ashforde, let alone anything troubling enough to cause the level of tension in the room tonight. By the way Ashforde glanced among the other guests, blue eyes narrowed, he was no more sure of the matter.

Even worse was Belle's absence. Owen could hardly pursue his quest to convince her to take a chance on him if she was nowhere in sight. And, without her beside him, the games the duchess led them though lost their sweetness.

But worse yet was the note he found shoved under his door.

You are wanted in the village.

The hand was flowing and gentlemanly. Anyone else who stumbled upon it might think he had a friend or at least an appointment with the local tailor. But he knew the source. Mercutio was calling him in to report. Time was growing short. Somehow, the spy had gained access to the castle again. The thought chilled Owen further.

But not enough to obey.

He crumpled the note in his hand and went to burn it in the hearth. He was done with groveling, done with hiding in the shadows. Nothing would have made him happier than to tell the duke all about the villain in the village, but any chance to win Belle's affections might be lost in the process. He would find a way to protect Jasper without betraying Belle or informing her father. He just had to think of a plan.

He had little chance the next day. He came down to breakfast early, hoping to take Jasper out for a ride, which was always where he did his best thinking. Petunia was there ahead of him.

"Good morning, Owen," she heralded. "Dressed for riding, I see. I'd be delighted to join you."

So delighted she was already wearing her dove-grey riding habit, a grey top hat with net veil waiting beside the plate. Had she been intending to ride out alone? That couldn't be safe. She was too inexperienced.

"Of course," Owen said. "Always happy to ride with a pretty lady at my side."

She smiled at him, but the brightness didn't quite reach her eyes.

He tarried as long as he could in hopes of asking Belle to come with them, but she must have been sleeping late. After his fourth cup of tea, he really couldn't delay another moment, especially since he could hear a dull tapping that was likely Petunia's foot against the carpet.

He rose, and she joined him, and together they headed for the stable.

A short time later, they were trotting down the mount from the castle on a cool summer morning. She seemed to be giving all her attention to her horse, the rose-grey again, so he didn't speak to disturb her. Jasper fretted at so sedate a pace. Owen gave him a pat in commiseration, but he couldn't very well talk to the horse in company.

He knew how odd others would take it, even if Jasper had ever been the only one who really listened to him.

It wasn't until they'd ridden out along the lane toward the bridge to the village that Petunia looked his way.

"I need your help."

Owen raised his brows. "Of course. What's happened?"

She gathered the reins a little tighter, and the horse obediently slowed further. She must have realized her mistake, for she gave the horse its head, and the rose-grey fell into step alongside Jasper.

"You may have noticed that Lord Ashforde and I do not get on," Petunia said.

Impossible to miss. "Indeed," he said. "Though, in his defense, I have always found him logical and straightforward."

"And arrogant and full of himself and…" She shook her head. "Don't get me started. Suffice it to say, Belle encouraged him to come with the idea he might want to court me. He doesn't. He's made that clear."

How could she have missed the look in the fellow's eyes when he'd first seen her as Athena? Or his determination to pay an extraordinary price for a painting, merely in the hopes of pleasing her? Ashforde showed every sign of a man on the verge of succumbing to the lure of matrimony.

"Is it possible you've mistaken him?" Owen asked carefully.

"Not in the slightest," she assured him. "Please believe me. He was given the opportunity to court me and turned it down most emphatically."

Had the fellow insulted her with an offer of something other than a courtship? Owen knew some aristocrats who sought mistresses from the daughters of tradesmen, but Sir Matthew and Lady Bateman were well thought of among the *ton*, despite the Bateman family's antecedents. And surely Ashforde was too honorable to offer Petunia a *carte blanche* to be his mistress.

"Then he's a fool," Owen said. "And you are well shed of him."

Her smile warmed him as much as the morning sun. "Thank you. But you must see that his presence here puts me in a difficult position. Belle thinks he's come to further an acquaintance. I doubt it, but I can't take that chance. That's why I need your help."

Owen frowned as they passed the entrance to the bridge and headed east along the canal, the water still and green-blue in the morning light. The scent of hay rode on the breeze.

"What exactly do you want me to do?" he asked. "Lord Ashforde is a guest of the duke and duchess. I can hardly order him to leave."

"He might leave on his own, if he thought I was in love with someone else," she countered.

Realization dawned. Owen reined in Jasper, and she managed to bring her horse to a stop as well.

"You want me to pretend I'm courting you?" he asked. Though he'd been doing just that for weeks, now that he knew his feelings for Belle, it felt a sacrilege. And what would Belle think to see him fawning over her friend days after he'd kissed her not once but twice!

"Yes," Petunia said, voice calm even though color was climbing in her cheeks. "We both know it's a humbug, but he won't. I can let Matty and Charlotte in on the ruse. You don't have to go so far as to kiss me, but a few longing looks and your presence at my side will help to stifle whatever interest he thinks he might have in me."

Owen cocked his head. "But I thought you said he wasn't interested in courting you."

"He's not!" she insisted. "But Belle will have put a flea in his ear, and you know no one refuses her."

All too true. "Have you spoken to her about this?" he asked.

"Last night," she informed him. "She agreed it was the best course."

Had she? That doused his hopes. If he had made any headway, surely she would have refused to share his attentions.

On the other hand, if she were sure of his intentions, perhaps she didn't worry about a little subterfuge, if it helped her friend. And if helping her friend endeared him to Belle, it was all to the good.

"Very well," he said. "But only until the ball on Wednesday night."

She frowned. "What happens at the ball?"

"I intend to make my feelings known to the lady I care about," he said. "You can understand why giving all my attentions to you might make that difficult."

Her eyes widened. "You're in love with Belle. Of course you are. Who wouldn't be?"

Much as he didn't like the idea of being one of the herd, he could not deny it. But Belle deserved to hear it first. "I will leave the matter between myself and the lady."

Petunia nodded. "Bright lad. I'll say no more on the matter, for now. And thank you. This is a greater sacrifice than I thought."

"It is never a sacrifice to help a friend," he assured her.

He could only hope the sentiment would prove true.

CHAPTER SEVENTEEN

OWEN MUST HAVE agreed to Tuny's request, because he lived in her pocket most of the day Tuesday and Wednesday. Lord Ashforde remained his usual cool, polite self, but Belle caught him gazing after them a time or two as if trying to understand.

Belle understood, but still she felt as if a burning coal had lodged in her chest. She'd started to think Owen might be the man for her. Though she knew his attentions to Tuny were only pretend, she couldn't help wondering whether something more was at play.

She had to put aside any concerns Wednesday afternoon, however, as more guests began arriving for the ball that evening. Petunia's sister, the Marchioness of Kendall, showed up first, with her husband; their thirteen-year-old daughter, Sophia; and their sons, Larch and Oleander, who were closer to Thal and Peter's ages.

"Please may I make my debut, Papa?" Sophia begged after they had all been welcomed by Belle's parents, sisters, and her. The black-haired beauty gazed up at him from thickly lashed blue eyes.

He glanced at Ivy, who cocked her blond head and returned his look with eyes as warm a brown as Petunia's.

Lord Kendall squared his shoulders. "A few more years, Pet. That's all I'm asking."

Sophia sighed as if much put upon and suffered her mother to lead her away.

"I'm not sure I'll survive it even then," Lord Kendall confided to Belle's father before following.

Shortly after, the Earl of Carrolton, who'd known her father since they were in school together, arrived with his wife, Yvette; their three sons, Eric, Harry, and Spencer, who ranged in age from ten to six; his sister, Lady Lilith, and her husband, Beau Villers; and their aged mother.

"Lady Quarrelsome in the flesh," Belle whispered to Callie, who forced her mouth into a smile.

The dowager Lady Carrolton had been their grandmother's dearest friend. She had visited often over the years and always with complaints about the girls' health, demeanor, or intelligence. Although the lady herself was prone to imagine every illness, she seemed determined to outlive them all. At least the good advice and taste of her daughter-in-law was evident, for she'd finally foresworn funereal black and was wearing a rosy pink that lent color to her cheeks. Leaning heavily on a cane, she surveyed the group waiting to welcome them.

"You were always too thin," she said to Belle's father, who had already greeted the Amazon Lady Lilith and her obsequious husband. "Tell your governess wife to hire you a better cook."

Her son, a mountain of a man, went so far as to grimace. Belle's father's face took on the polite mask he often wore in company, and Belle would not have been surprised if he wasn't biting the inside of his mouth to keep from answering.

Her mother answered for him. "We have a very fine cook, which you'll discover at dinner tonight," she said with a smile. "And as a former governess, I know just what to do with your grandsons." She tipped her head to the stairs. "Peter and the others are waiting, my lads. Have some fun."

With a look to their father, they fled up the stairs.

"You always were good with her," the countess

murmured, her French upbringing still evident in her voice as she leaned in to give Belle's mother a hug.

Undeterred, the dowager countess had moved on to eye Larissa, Callie, and Belle, and Belle readied herself for a scold.

"Tolerable," she pronounced, before sweeping past them for the stairs.

Callie blinked.

"I feel honored," Larissa admitted, and the three of them started laughing.

The Carroltons had scarcely made their way upstairs before Aunt Meredith, Uncle Julian, and Fortune arrived. Her aunt had affixed a jeweled collar and leash to her pet, but Fortune was already making her displeasure known by rubbing her cheek along the carpet and suffering herself to be edged along.

"Perhaps I can take charge of her," Belle offered. She bent and wiggled her fingers, and the cat stopped to consider her.

What was this? She'd never had the least trouble turning Fortune up sweet! Had all her matchmaking actually affected her own character?

Fortune wandered to her mother instead, brushing against her skirts and asking for a pet.

Belle rose, eyes stinging.

"She's likely just tired from traveling," Larissa told her, putting an arm about Belle's shoulders. "We shouldn't be surprised she'd go to someone she's known the longest."

"And maybe she knows something I have overlooked," Belle murmured.

Callie glanced from where their parents and the Mayes were talking to Belle, blue eyes troubled. "It appears your attempts at matchmaking are working, at least."

"I've never seen a more devoted suitor than Mr. Canady," Larissa agreed.

Those tears were going to fall any second. "It's all an

act. Tuny asked him to pretend he was smitten to fend off Lord Ashforde. I had thought Owen might want to court me instead, but now I can only wonder. Is he such a good actor? And if he is, what else has he been pretending?"

"Mother," Larissa called, "we're going upstairs to change for the evening."

Their mother nodded before her sisters urged Belle toward the stairs.

"So, it's to be Mr. Canady," Larissa mused as they started down the corridor of the chamber story. "He is a most presentable gentleman. But you're right that we know little about him."

"I know enough," Belle said, feeling compelled to defend him. "That is, enough to be certain he is a gentleman."

"But not the gentleman you expected," her sister guessed.

"No," Belle admitted. "And will Father and Mother be pleased with the alliance? You're marrying a prince, and Callie, you're marrying a count."

"And you know I would have married Leo even when I thought he was merely the captain of the Imperial Guard," Larissa reminded her.

Callie nodded. "And I began to fall for Fritz when he *was* the captain of the Imperial Guard."

Belle put on a smile as they neared her door. "Well, I may not have the option of marrying him. He hasn't proposed or showed the least interest in proposing. I made you all vow to be married by harvest, but it very much looks as if Tuny and I will fail."

"There's still a few weeks until harvest," Larissa said.

And her smile told Belle her sister was not content to leave it at that.

Belle stopped in the corridor. "Don't."

Larissa froze. "Don't what?"

Oh, but her sister could sound regal when she wished.

"Don't step in the middle," Belle told her. "I tried that with Tuny, and look where it's led us. I begin to think that, sometimes, the best course is allowing those we love to figure things out for themselves."

"Very wise," Callie said, sounding both surprised and impressed at the same time.

"In general, I agree," Larissa allowed. "But nothing says we cannot nudge Mr. Canady toward that end. You helped us, Belle. Now Callie, Petunia, and I can help you."

Owen had spent much of the afternoon with Jasper. It was one way to avoid having to lavish his attentions on Petunia. Belle's friend had been busy in the schoolroom in any event. With so many more children arriving for the next couple of days, Miss Winchester could use all the help she could get. No doubt that was why Mr. Huber had volunteered his free time as well.

But Owen could not go to dinner much less the ball smelling of horse. He was just passing the withdrawing room, heading for his room to change for the evening, when Petunia stepped out into the corridor and blocked his way. "Come with me, now," she ordered, pointing him toward the withdrawing room.

He was prepared to refuse if it ended up only the two of them in the space. He was willing to help a friend, but not to the point where her bruiser of a brother demanded a marriage for a supposed compromise. He was more than a little relieved to find Belle's sisters there ahead of him, all clustered near the door, as if lying in wait.

"Belle's still upstairs changing," Callie told them all as Larissa shut the door behind Owen and Petunia. "We should be safe for a little while."

Owen glanced around. Petunia was still in her cotton

day dress with the plaid scarf at her throat and around her waist, but Belle's sisters were already in their evening finery, satin shining in the light from the windows. All three of them had a tight look to their faces, as if they had come to a decision, one that did not bode well for him.

They could not have guessed his purpose. He'd left no trail that could be followed.

Owen swept them a bow. "Ladies, I am ever at your service. How might I be of assistance?"

"I understand you are interested in courting our sister," Larissa said.

"We thought we could offer some advice," Callie added.

"Playing matchmaker runs in the family," Petunia explained.

Owen couldn't help his chuckle. "So it appears."

Larissa raised her chin, making her look every bit the princess she was soon to become. "Belle is used to the best, Mr. Canady. You must take the courtship seriously."

"But not too seriously," Callie cautioned. "Belle likes to have fun."

"But not too much fun," Petunia put in. "You don't want to get on the duke's bad side."

"He's rather protective," Callie agreed.

Did they think him a novice? Perhaps he'd played his role too well.

Owen held up his hands. "Peace, ladies! Thank you for your trouble, but I know how to court a lady."

"No," Petunia said. "You don't."

Owen raised his brows.

Callie stared at her. "That wasn't very nice."

Petunia colored. "It's only the truth. He didn't move me in the slightest."

Much more of this, and he would begin to question his skills. "Perhaps that's because neither of us was in love," he suggested.

"True," Larissa said. "Any number of gentlemen showed interest before Leo, but they didn't move me either. Still, Mr. Canady, you have been inconsistent in your attentions."

Petunia raised her hand. "That would be my fault. I was trying to stave off any interest from Lord Ashforde."

"Before he arrived?" Callie asked with a puzzled look.

"Ladies," Owen said, "please believe me. You will see a new man tonight, and so will your sister. If she has any complaints, you have only to let me know, and I promise to rectify all."

Callie and Petunia looked to Larissa. Larissa studied Owen with equal intensity to Lady Belfort's famous cat. He tried not to squirm.

"Very well," she said at last. "Let's see how tonight goes. But we will be watching you, Mr. Canady, and we expect a very fine showing indeed. Belle deserves no less."

Belle took even more care in dressing for the evening than she usually did. In London, she'd attended balls with as many as six hundred people, most of them unknown to her. This was to be much smaller, only thirty people, the majority of whom she'd known since she was a child.

Every ball and event in London, she'd gone hoping the man of her dreams might be waiting for her. Now she *knew* he was waiting. The fact couldn't help but set her nerves to fluttering.

Her mother had had a little-used salon on the first floor aired, cleaned, and refurbished to hold the event. Now the parquet floor gleamed, and the crystal chandeliers glowed. The tall doors along the back that let out into the garden showed the smoky twilight of a summer's evening. At one end, a group of musicians on a raised dais were already tuning their instruments against the sound of voices in warm conversation.

Belle had to stand in the receiving line with her parents and sisters in the anteroom next to the salon as all twenty-five of their guests moved past. Besides those they had already greeted on their arrival, families from the neighboring estates were also in attendance. Mr. Godwin had grown up with Uncle Julian and Aunt Meredith. A tall fellow, all arms and legs, he was joined by his wife, another dark-haired lady of considerable stature. Jonathan Garvey, who had taken over his father's estate to the west of them, escorted his sisters Sarah and Amelia, who were Larissa and Callie's ages. And the flame-haired Julia Hewett, heiress to her father's considerable holdings beyond Weyton, came with her companion, a tiny, nervous-looking white-haired woman with the improbable name of Mrs. Daring.

As all of them filed past with kind words about her father's generosity, Belle kept looking for Owen, but he wasn't with Petunia or Leo and Fritz in their scarlet coats, or the Imperial Guards in their dress uniforms trimmed in gold braid. In fact, he was the very last person to greet them, as if he had been loath to attend at all.

Her nerves were fluttering again, like the butterflies that hovered over the summer wildflowers, as he approached and bowed over her hand. His evening coat was so dark a blue as to be almost black, but the color set off the blue of his eyes as he took her in. She was very glad she had decided upon her pearl-colored satin with the net overskirt embroidered with flowers, with gold satin ribbon under her bodice, along the modest neckline, at her wrists, and in cunning gathers three deep all along the hem. Together, they were the best of day and night.

As if he agreed, he took Belle's hand and bowed over it. "Dare I ask for the first dance?"

Belle's heart swelled. "Done."

As her father led her mother into the salon, Owen followed with Belle on his arm.

Her mother had chosen a country air for the first dance, and couples happily lined up down the center of the floor, while a few took seats on sofas and chairs along the wall opposite the windows to watch. Owen settled himself across from her with a wink that made her giggle.

He was the perfect partner, there to take her hands when she came around the set, making the little flourishes with his toes and his hands that set apart the master from the dilettante. Ladies smiled and nodded in approval. Gentlemen attempted to copy him.

Why did they bother? He had no equal.

Oh, but she was lost!

She would have liked nothing better than to spend the rest of the night dancing with him, but as the daughter of the host, she knew her duty. As if he knew as well, he kissed her knuckles and promised to return for a second dance soon before melting into the crowd.

She had to own her other partners could not measure up. Blond-haired, blue-eyed Jonathan Garvey had an easy grace, but he lacked Owen's polish. Mr. Roth danced as if he thought he must single-handedly defeat his partner in combat. Uncle Julian had a more congenial presence, but he kept beaming at her as if he couldn't quite believe the lady she had become but was tremendously proud of her nonetheless.

She thought Owen might look for other young ladies to partner, but he took to the floor with Yvette, Charlotte, and Ivy before Belle caught him partnering the dowager countess.

"I didn't know she could dance," Callie commented as she passed Belle on Fritz's arm.

"Let me know what she says," Belle whispered.

Callie nodded.

"Care for a dance, daughter?" their father asked,

offering Belle his arm.

"Of course," Belle said, smiling.

It was a rather sedate air, and Belle could only wonder if her mother had asked for it in consideration of the dowager countess. Lady Carrolton was too far down the line for Belle to make out anything. The few times she caught sight of the lady's face, it was pinched and puckered.

In other words, her usual look.

"Well?" Belle asked after her father had left her along the wall and Callie had joined her, having sent Fritz for refreshments.

"She criticized the music, the musicians, and the other dancers," Callie reported. "But she thanked Mr. Canady and said she would be willing to favor him with another so long as he did not lean so close as to peer down her décolleté."

That set them both to laughing again.

Larissa joined them too, ivory-handled fan swaying. "Nearly supper. Do you know who's leading you in?"

"I had hoped to request that honor," Owen said, appearing beside her. "Would you favor me, Belle?"

Belle beamed at him. "Delighted, sir."

And she could only thank her mother's cleverness in ordering the dances. The one just before supper was the waltz. Owen took her in his arms and twirled her around the floor, her skirts belling with each turn. So easy to lose herself in the blue of his gaze, to know herself admired by the wonder on his face. To feel protected, cherished, by his touch on her waist and hand. She clung to his fingers as the music ended, then strolled arm and arm with him to supper.

She took her place at the long table her mother had had set up in the room on the other side of the salon. Draped in figured damask, the table could hold at least forty, so there was plenty of room for all their guests. Footmen moved up and down the line, serving the pheasant in mushroom sauce, compote of berries, and dilled potatoes that were the first course. Goblets gleamed, and silverware sparkled.

So did the conversation. Laughter rang up and down the table. Fritz was on Belle's left, which was all to the good, as he only wished to talk to Callie on his other side. And Charlotte, on Owen's right, was more interested in her handsome husband.

And that meant, for once, she had Owen all to herself. What might she learn if she asked? Did she dare to demand to know his intentions?

CHAPTER EIGHTEEN

BELLE SMILED HER best smile at Owen as one of the footmen they'd hired for the ball refilled her goblet. All the while, her mind sorted through gambits.

"Enjoying the evening?" he asked as the footman refilled his glass as well.

"Very much so," she assured him. "Are you enjoying yourself?"

He smiled. "Any night is a good night with you beside me."

It was a good response, a very good response, actually, but he might have said that of any lady, at any event.

"And what about having me beside you do you enjoy most?" she asked.

His brows went up, but whether he was surprised by her question or thought she might be seeking praise, she wasn't sure. He reached for his goblet, likely to give himself time to think of an answer.

That he had to think that hard was not good.

"I appreciate the way you look at life," he finally said, setting the goblet back into place. "You show sincere care for friends and family, and they reciprocate. Both are rare."

"Surely not that rare," Belle protested, waving at the footman to move along when it appeared he thought he should hover. "Look at the Marchioness of Kendall and her family and Lady Carrolton and her family. More devoted couples you will not find."

He glanced down the table at their guests. Everyone was engaged in conversation, faces glowing. The Dowager Duchess of Carrolton sent him a look, and he inclined his head in acknowledgement. She smiled.

Smiled!

Belle shook herself out of her shock as he returned his gaze to her. "This visit with your family and their friends has given me an entirely different outlook on the aristocracy," he admitted.

"Your great-uncle does not seem to have been kind," she allowed.

"Indeed not. I was raised in a house where everything was questioned—from the cost of a purchase to the motivation for purchasing something in the first place. Standards were high and expectations that anyone would meet them low. I envy your expectation that things will go well."

Belle shrugged, though his words warmed her. "I am the daughter of a duke. Things generally go well for me."

He chuckled. "So I've noticed."

"Do they not go so well for you?" she asked, digging into the savory meat at last. "You may have been orphaned, but you seem to have made a good life for yourself."

"Things are not always what they seem."

She lowered her fork to glance at him askance. He was toying with the meal, but she didn't think he even saw it.

"And why is that?" she murmured.

"I have not always lived up to the expectations my mother would have had for me," he allowed, addressing himself to the plate rather than her. "Then again, neither did my great-uncle. I like to think I've done more with what I have been given than most would have. It seemed enough, until I met you."

Now *she* couldn't take a bite. "And now you want more?"

He looked up and met her gaze at last, and she sucked in a breath at the emotions blazing in the blue. "Now, Belle, I want you."

Goodness! She reached for the goblet and realized she was doing the same thing he'd done. "Owen, I don't know what to say."

He took her other hand and held it a moment. "Tell me that you'll dance with me again tonight."

That would be making a statement. Three dances and supper? No, she wasn't ready to go so far.

She removed her hand from his. "I can't. You know that."

He nodded. "I know. Very well. Perhaps a promenade later?"

That she could do within the rules of Society. "With pleasure," Belle told him.

The dinner over, Owen watched Belle walk away, the skirts of her pearly ballgown swinging. Not for the first time he wished Society's rules were less stringent. Would it truly set the world on fire if he danced more than twice with her?

It would likely set her father's hair on fire. Several times during the evening Owen had felt the green gaze on him, studying, weighing.

He refused to be found wanting again.

He was turning to see what other lady might like to dance when he noticed Lord Ashforde bearing down on him.

Well, bearing down might be too strong a phrase. The baron moved with his usual considered pace, but his gaze was fixed on Owen, as if everything turned on their meeting. Owen considered leading him a merry dance but decided against it.

"My lord," he greeted as the baron drew near.

Lord Ashforde's evening black only served to make his slender form look harder. He inclined his head, shirt points bright in the candlelight.

"Canady," he acknowledged. "I am finding it rather warm. I believe there's a terrace along the back. Would you join me for some fresh air?"

As far as he knew, when a gentleman suggested adjourning to the terrace, it was because he wanted to spend time alone with a young lady or he intended to call a fellow out in a duel. He eyed Ashforde. A muscle was working on his lean jaw, and there was a glint in his eyes that did not bode refusal.

"Fresh air would not be unwelcome," Owen said.

They both turned for the nearest doors. Owen put his hand on the latch, only to have it shoved toward him. He stepped aside to allow a young woman with fiery red hair past him. She cast him a startled glance, then lifted her skirts and disappeared among the crowd.

"Do you know her?" Owen asked the baron.

"A local heiress," Lord Ashforde allowed. "Likely seeking fresh air as well."

Or an assignation away from the chaperone who was even now coming to collect her. With a shake of his head, Owen followed his lordship out of the ballroom.

The sun had set at last. Lanterns cast pools of golden light on the stones of the terrace. The first stars were appearing in the velvety sky, and the last perfume of the garden blooms lingered in the air.

Lord Ashforde strode to the balustrade and stared into the shadows.

"Expecting an assassin?" Owen asked. "Or perhaps the fellow the heiress was meeting?"

He straightened and returned to Owen's side. "No. Making sure Lady Calantha is nowhere in hearing. She has the uncanny ability to remember what is said."

Insightful of him to have noticed. "Then I take it you have something you wish to say to me that should not be overheard."

"Indeed." He widened his stance. Was the fellow about to challenge him to a duel after all? He couldn't imagine what he'd said or done to warrant such a response. Or could it be that the baron was the one in Mercutio's employ? No, the note had arrived before Ashforde had, and Owen could not see him sneaking into the duke's library, even if he had been in the castle at the time.

"I realize this isn't my place," the baron said, "but I must know. Are you playing Miss Bateman false?"

So, he did care after all. Could the course of true love never run smooth?

But his lordship's feelings put Owen in a difficult position. Very likely, Petunia would want Owen to claim undying devotion, but Ashforde would never believe it after the way Owen had followed Belle about all evening. And he didn't want word getting back to Belle that he had claimed himself in love with Petunia. Even though she knew he had been pretending, such a declaration could only cause trouble for them both.

Caught in his own web. And he'd thought himself so clever. Owen swallowed the laugh that bubbled up.

"I'm not trifling with Petunia Bateman's affections," Owen told him. "I'm doing exactly what she asked."

The baron frowned. "Why would she ask you to lavish your attentions on her friend, Lady Abelona?"

"She didn't," Owen said. "She asked me to lavish my attentions on her, and I agreed to do so, until the ball."

His frown only grew. "I don't understand. What are your intentions toward the lady?"

"I have none whatsoever." Owen waved his hand toward the ballroom door. "The field is open, my lord, but I feel obliged to tell you that it will make for rough riding. The lady seems to have taken you in dislike."

Ashforde's brow cleared. "I had surmised as much, and I can only blame myself. Thank you for your candidness, sir. I can see I have much to think on."

Lord Ashforde's need to think might be entirely the problem, but Owen had interfered enough in Petunia's life. Besides, he had his own plans for the evening, and he could only hope that by the end of the night, Belle would have no reason to wonder where his intentions lay.

Belle could not be displeased by the night. Even though she'd had to refuse a third dance with Owen, he had confirmed he had feelings for her. He had appeared at her side toward the end of the evening, and they'd had a perfectly lovely promenade around the edges of the ballroom, talking about the future.

"Where do you go when the Season is done?" she had asked him as they passed the doors to the garden. "Back to Yorkshire?"

"Bath or Grace-by-the-Sea, more likely," he answered. "Somewhere Jasper and I can find company even in the middle of winter. I don't have a castle like this one waiting for me."

"Wey Castle is a bit draughty in winter," Belle admitted, nodding to the heiress, Miss Hewett, who had stopped dancing at one point in the evening and appeared to wish to sit quietly with her companion. "I always thought a cozy cottage would be more congenial. Father has several in the village. My favorite is Primrose Cottage, off the High Street."

He flinched, and she glanced at him to see what might concern him, but he merely sent her a smile. "I find it hard to imagine you in a less glittering setting than the castle or London."

"I was born and raised on the island, sir," she reminded him. "And my father is known as the Hermit Duke. I can be quite content in calmer spheres."

The final dance of the evening started. Owen had glanced her way. "Sure you won't dance with me again?"

Belle had shaken her head, and she shook her head now at the memory. Silly rules! Then again, spending so much time with one gentleman did raise expectations that something more than a dance was in the offing. Did she hope for a proposal from Owen?

More and more every day.

She sighed happily as she entered her bedchamber. She'd have some time to wait before Anna came to her. Larissa and Callie took precedence. Another rule, but one she could not mind at the moment. Some time to herself would not be remiss.

She wandered to the dressing table and removed the pearls from around her neck. Owen was handsome, charming, and a joy to partner, whether riding, rowing, or dancing. But there were moments when she thought something else was percolating behind his eyes. And then there were the tantalizing glimpses of his childhood, which had not been kind. Did such darkness leave a mark?

And what of his affections for Jasper? She understood loyalty to one's mount. It was a special bond. Unicorn had been hers since she was a child. Unthinkable that they might be parted. He clearly felt the same way about Jasper. Would he be willing to share the horse with her? Would that prove his affections for her as well?

From outside came a sound, lyrical and compelling. The musicians had stopped playing more than an hour ago. Surely they had packed up and departed by now. Why was she hearing a song?

She ventured to her window, which overlooked the

gardens at the back of the castle enclosure. Someone was standing among the flowers, gazing up at her window. Moonlight glinted on dark hair. Heart stuttering, Belle pulled up the sash and leaned out.

"'But soft! What light through yonder window breaks? It is the east, and Belle is the sun.'"

"I've read Shakespeare too, you know," Belle called down with a smile. "And *Romeo and Juliet* ends badly, for them both."

"It is my joy and punishment to love a well-read lass," he lamented.

She could not believe the declaration, but she knew how to play the game too.

"And I to love a gentleman of uncertain past. Oh, the horror." She pressed the back of her hand to her forehead like the best tragedienne at Covent Garden Theatre.

"Any chance of Rapunzel letting down her hair?" he called up.

Belle relaxed her pose to tweak a curl. "It wouldn't reach past the sill. Sorry!"

"Then I suppose it must be a song," he said. His warm baritone sailed into a melody.

"We all to conquering beauty bow, its pleasing power admire.

But I never knew a face till now that could like yours inspire."

His voice wove through the summer night. The moon seemed to be smiling. The stars danced to the tune. She could imagine small garden animals drawing closer to hear more. She certainly wanted to.

"Now I may say I've met with one who amazes all mankind,

And like men gazing at the sun, with too much light am blind."

Belle pressed both hands against the window frame, half afraid she'd jump down into his arms if she didn't.

He finished the song and swept her a bow.

She let go of the frame and clapped her hands. "Bravo, sir. Dare I hope for an encore?"

He straightened. "Perhaps. If you agree to go riding with me after breakfast tomorrow."

"Done," Belle said. And then she could ask him about riding Jasper. She glanced around the room, then spotted one of her handkerchiefs. Darting to retrieve it, she tossed it out the window. It fluttered down toward the garden, and Owen dashed to capture it.

"A token for my knight," she called.

He pressed it against his chest. "I will ever keep it close. Parting be such sweet sorrow, that I shall say goodnight till it be morrow."

"No more *Romeo and Juliet!*" she warned with a laugh.

He bowed again and disappeared into the night.

She turned to find Anna just inside the door, staring at her.

"Lovely," Belle said, going to stand by her bed. "You're just in time to help me change. Will you set out my riding habit for tomorrow? I'm going out right after breakfast."

Owen was still feeling rather pleased with himself when he jogged down the stairs the next morning, Belle's handkerchief lodged inside his shirt. The light had been behind her last night when he'd serenaded her, but there had been a joy in her voice, a pleasure that told him he was making headway. Perhaps today would be the day he could suggest a proposal.

Once more, he was the first at table, but she came down to breakfast only a few minutes after he did, dressed in a more traditional riding habit of black wool with braid across her chest. He hurried to hold the chair for her.

A look from the corners of her green eyes told him she knew what he was about. He merely smiled.

But they both finished breakfast in a remarkably short time before heading for the stable.

"Sleep well?" he asked now that he knew they could not be overheard.

Pink warmed her cheeks. "Well enough. A certain song kept going through my mind."

"I meant every word," he promised her.

She flashed him a grin as they came into the stable.

Walters moved to meet them. "Your ladyship, sir, how might I help?"

Belle cast Owen a look before smiling at the stable hand. "Mr. Canady and I are going for a ride. With his permission, I'd like to take Jasper."

Owen stiffened. "Belle, I…"

As if she knew he would protest, she pivoted, put her hand on his arm, and gazed up at him with a flutter of her lashes. "Please, Owen? He looks like such a goer. You know I'm a good rider. I'll take very good care of him."

But Jasper might not take such care of her. He could not agree to her request.

"He can be a handful," Owen explained. "I wouldn't want to impose him on you."

"It's no imposition," she insisted. "I'll let you ride Unicorn."

By the way Walters' brows were climbing, Owen was being offered a rare gift indeed. How would it feel to ride a duke's unicorn? Yet to trust her with Jasper…

He squared his shoulders. "I will introduce you, but if he shows the least sign of being disagreeable, the bargain is off."

"Of course," she agreed. "Oh, thank you, Owen! You cannot know how much this means to me." She squeezed up her shoulders as if she had been awarded a great prize. Still, his own shoulders felt tight as Walters led Jasper up to them.

The grey tossed his head, nearly prancing. Owen took the reins, and the horse calmed, mouth working on the bit. Owen stroked the velvety nose. "There's a lady here who'd like the favor of a ride, old fellow. Will you allow it?"

Jasper blew into Owen's hand.

"Is that good?" Belle murmured.

Owen shook his head, unsure, as the groom brought Belle's sidesaddle. Jasper flinched as Walters set it in place, as if the horse could tell the difference in construction or material.

"Don't set out until I'm in the saddle," Owen advised. "So long as he can see me, we might be fine."

She nodded. Owen kept stroking the horse, whispering encouragement, as Walters cinched the saddle in place, then helped Belle up into it.

Owen looked Jasper in the eye. "The lady on your back is impossibly precious to me. You will behave for her."

Jasper yanked away from his grip, but he stood immobile as Owen stepped back and went to mount the white horse.

Unicorn wasn't as broad in the chest as Jasper, but she had the same long legs. Still, it felt odd to be seated on any other horse. Owen glanced over, and Jasper shook his head as if he'd never seen anything so strange either.

"Ride alongside me," Owen said to Belle. He urged Unicorn forward, and Jasper followed suit.

"He has a lot of power," Belle ventured as they cleared the castle gate. "I can feel it."

"So does your Unicorn," he admitted. "It would be interesting to see how they raced against each other."

"Oh, Owen, could we?"

Those green eyes were all hope as they came down onto the flat. He swallowed. "I don't think it's a good idea, Belle. Jasper isn't used to racing with anyone but me in the saddle."

She sagged. "Oh, of course. Well, he's still a dear." She stroked his mane.

Jasper stretched out his neck and bolted.

Owen clapped his heels against Unicorn's sides and pelted after his horse. He could tell Belle was trying to rein him in, but Jasper fought her, head lashing and tail swinging. If Owen could just get a little closer…

Jasper braced both feet and stopped, and Belle sailed over his head to land with a sickening thud on the dry summer grass.

CHAPTER NINETEEN

TIME STOPPED. BREATH faltered. Owen reined in Unicorn and leapt from the saddle to run to Belle. Head tossing and reins trailing, Jasper headed toward the river.

Another time, another life, he would have remounted Unicorn and raced after him. Jasper had been his future for so long. But the woman he loved was lying on the ground. Nothing was more important than making sure Belle was all right.

He knelt beside her and put a hand to her cheek. The pallor, the stillness sliced through his heart like a knife. "Belle, sweetheart, speak to me."

He nearly shouted a hallelujah when her golden lashes fluttered open to reveal the green of her eyes.

"I was thrown," she said, as if the matter were more surprising than finding pigs flying across the clear blue skies.

"You were, and it's all my fault," Owen said, pulse still pounding. "Can you move?"

She shifted, then winced. "I think so. The ground is entirely too hard. I shall speak to Father about the matter." She offered him a ghost of her usual bright smile.

"I'm sure His Grace will have it plowed immediately." He slipped an arm under her shoulders. "Here, let me help you."

She eased up and sat a moment, blinking as if the day

were too bright. She could not seem to gasp in enough of the warm air. Had she broken a rib? Punctured a lung?

"Where's Jasper?" she managed, glancing around.

"Mr. Jasper decided to find more congenial companions," Owen joked, though the familiar fear of loss clutched at him with greedy fingers. "I'm sure he'll be back when it amuses him."

"Oh, Owen, I'm so sorry!" She shifted on the ground as if even sitting hurt, then looked to him, the corners of her eyes dipping down. "You must go after him."

"Not until I know you are unharmed," he promised her.

"It's my pride that's hurt more than anything," she said with a grimace as she gathered her riding skirts about her. She pulled her legs under her, and Owen helped her to her feet. She took an unsteady step and bit her lip, but at least her pretty face was now a much healthier pink.

"Take Unicorn and ride for the castle," she told him. "Tell Mr. Walters to come for me, then you and the other grooms can find Jasper."

Her plaintive tone only added to the urge inside him. He would not give in. "I won't leave you." He glanced around, locating a rock not far away, then bent and swung her up into his arms.

Her eyes widened as he carried her toward the rock. "I'll be fine, Owen," she protested.

"I won't," he assured her. He positioned her carefully on the rock. Once he knew she had her balance, he went and mounted Unicorn, then rode over to Belle and offered her his hand. She gripped it with both hands, and he pulled her up and into his lap, positioning her carefully on the saddle with her skirts trailing along his left leg.

"Wrap your arm around my neck," he told her.

Her arm entwined around him. Her face was inches away, gazing up at him with such trust and hope he knew he could never disappoint her. Arms encircling her curves, he urged Unicorn back toward the castle.

Carrying two riders was never easy on a horse, so Owen was forced to hold Unicorn at an easy pace. Belle kept glancing up at him from under her lashes, but she seemed content to stay close and stay quiet. He was grateful. His thoughts were spinning furiously enough as it was.

He might be holding Belle in his arms at the moment, but, without Jasper and the income he brought in, Owen and Belle had little hope of a future together. He could only pray that someone would find Jasper and keep him safe until Owen could go for him.

It seemed she'd mistaken herself, again. Belle clung to Owen as Unicorn ambled up the hill to the castle. She'd thought she could prove Owen's feelings if he allowed her to ride his horse. In a way, she'd succeeded. Jasper clearly meant the world to Owen. And Owen was willing to sacrifice him, if that meant keeping her safe. But now Jasper might be in danger, because of her.

"I'm so sorry," she said again as he urged Unicorn toward the stable.

"It's all right, Belle," he said, hold as gentle as his tone. "I agreed to let you ride him. If anyone is to blame for this, it's me. I will never forgive myself if any permanent harm comes to you."

Mr. Walters was out in front of the wide stable doors, running a brush down the flanks of Meridien, one of her father's favorites. His gaze met Belle's, and he dropped the brush and came running. "Your ladyship!"

"Lady Abelona was thrown," Owen informed him, reining Unicorn to a stop. "Send someone for the physician, and help me get her down."

"Gem!" Mr. Walters shouted, and one of their younger stable hands came running. He too gaped at the sight of Belle up in Owen's arms. "Fetch Princess and ride for Doctor Hargreaves. Tell him her ladyship has taken a tumble."

"Aye," the boy agreed, and he went running to saddle a horse.

Mr. Walters stepped to Unicorn's side and held up his arms. Belle slid into his grip, and he eased her down onto the stones. She shuddered as her legs protested. Walters looked stricken.

Owen landed beside her and put a hand on her arm. "I have her now. See to Unicorn, if you will." He didn't wait for a response before lifting Belle into his arms once more.

"You'll only scare them, you know," she said as he strode for the double doors to the castle. "I might be able to walk if I lean on your arm."

"I won't risk further damage," he said. "Catch the latch."

She reached down and opened the latch, and he pushed wide the door with his shoulder.

Mrs. Winters had been in the entry hall, watching as Davis came down the stairs with one of the trunks from their overnight guests. Her hands flew to her mouth.

"My word! Lady Belle! What's happened?"

"A minor injury," Belle assured her as Owen carried her past and into the withdrawing room. "Really, nothing to concern anyone. But you might let Mr. Quayle know that Mr. Canady's horse is missing."

Mrs. Winters must have done more than that, for Owen had just positioned Belle on one of the sofas when her mother came hurrying in.

"What's this about an injury?" she demanded, striding to their sides, blue skirts a blur.

"I'm just sore," Belle explained. "Gem's gone for Doctor Hargreaves. I daresay he won't find much to treat.

We needn't alert the rest of the household."

Her mother frowned as she dropped onto the chair nearest the sofa. "Your sisters, Tuny, Meredith, and Charlotte, at a minimum, will show up any moment. You're fortunate the Carroltons and Kendalls are busy collecting their children before departing, or we'd likely have to contend with them as well. But how were you injured? I thought Mrs. Winters said you'd gone riding."

"We did go riding, Your Grace," Owen said. He had been so pale when Belle had first opened her eyes. He'd stared down at her, as if he had lost his last hope. At least now some of the color was returning to his cheeks above his beard.

"I was thrown," Belle explained to her mother.

Her mother reared back. "Thrown? Since when do you allow one of our horses to throw you, my girl?"

"It was my fault," Belle said, even as Owen said, "It was my horse."

"I see," her mother said, and Belle thought she saw all too well. "I didn't realize your horse was so unruly, Mr. Canady. Perhaps we should speak to Mr. Quayle. I'm sure he could offer some suggestions."

For the first time Belle could recall, Owen's easy smile faltered. "I would be delighted for any advice, Your Grace, but Jasper ran off after throwing Lady Belle. Once I know she is well and safe, I must find him."

Her mother rose and enfolded him in a hug. Belle could see Owen blinking over her mother's shoulder, clearly shocked by the unexpected gesture.

"I knew you were a good man," she said as she disengaged. "It takes a lot for a horseman to walk away from his mount. You can leave Belle to me. Go find Jasper."

He hesitated, then dropped to one knee beside Belle. For an insane moment, she thought he meant to propose right then and there. Her pulse shot up like a firework on

Guy Fawkes Day.

"You're sure you're all right?" he murmured.

Now that she was reclining on the sofa, other aches from her shoulders and backside reminded her that she had collided with the ground. But she would not keep him here for such paltry pains, not when his horse could be in jeopardy.

"Fine," she told him. "Go."

Again, he hesitated. Then he took one hand and brought it to his lips. The kiss sent a tremor through her that had nothing to do with her injuries. Releasing her, he rose, nodded to her mother, and left.

"So he's THE ONE, is he?" her mother asked, looking after him.

"I think so," Belle said, another shiver going through her at the knowledge.

"He rides well," her mother said.

Belle laughed. A man's ability to manage his mount was high on her mother's list of required qualities in a husband. She had been a cavalry officer's widow, after all.

"I thought I heard him serenading you last night," her mother continued, returning to her seat. "Now, there's a romantic gesture." She wiggled her lips. "Perhaps it's time your father and I had a conversation with him."

"Mother," Belle started, but her sisters, Tuny, Aunt Meredith, and Fortune appeared just then, and Belle had to spend the next little while reassuring them all until Mrs. Winters hurried in with the physician. Then Belle had to answer questions and move this part of her body and that.

And through it all, her mind and heart followed the man desperately searching for his beloved horse.

Word must have spread about Belle's injury, and the reason behind it, for Owen found Leo, Fritz, and the three Imperial Guards waiting with saddled mounts in front of the stable.

"Sir Matthew wanted to come as well," the prince told Owen. "But he thought we'd make better time without him."

They might at that. The big baronet was none too steady in the saddle. Still, Owen could only be humbled that the Batavarians had offered their help.

Mr. Quayle had come up from the main stable. As the duke's Master of Horse, he seemed to feel compelled to take charge of the search. Owen couldn't mind. His thoughts continued to center on Belle.

"His Highness and Mr. Huber will take the western shore," the Master of Horse ordered. "Start nearest the canal and progress toward the north. Count Montalban and Mr. Roth will take the eastern shore, same progression. Mr. Canady, you indicated Jasper was heading north. Take Mr. Keller with you to the northern shore starting from the east and sweeping west. I'll take Walters and sweep the southern shore from west to east. If anyone finds Jasper, send a rider to alert the others."

It was a sensible plan. Owen thanked Mr. Quayle, then headed out, Mr. Keller of the Imperial Guard at his side, along with the prince's brother and Mr. Roth. Unicorn had been spared the trip, having just done yeoman's duty, and Owen found himself on a black-coated beauty named Meridien. The stallion had good confirmation and a punishing pace, but he was no match for Jasper. The thought made Owen's throat tighten.

No one seemed disposed to talk, so they rode hard and fast, keeping an eye out for Jasper along the way. The many times he'd ridden the island told Owen which lanes and paths to follow to reach the eastern corner, where the two parties split up, one going south, the other west.

"English gentlemen put a great deal of importance on their horses," Mr. Keller observed as he and Owen picked their way along the shore. The Thames rolled past, blue-grey and placid. Reeds bowed down along the shore as if to give the mighty river homage.

"Many do," Owen allowed, gaze sweeping the grassy fields inland. Even if Jasper had stopped to graze, his back should still be visible. Instead, golden grains waved with false cheer under a cloudless sky.

"I did not ride much in Batavaria," the guardsman admitted. "Or here, until recently. I like it." He patted the horse he had been given.

Owen managed a smile. "There is something about being able to survey your world and know you're sitting on the power to take you anywhere, fast."

"Indeed." The single word was smug.

They both focused on scanning their surroundings then. But though Owen watched and called on occasion, they caught no sight of Jasper before they reached the westernmost corner, where they met the prince's contingent.

"Nothing," Leo reported with a shake of his head. "Perhaps Mr. Quayle had better luck."

Owen could only hope the same, but the day seemed to be darkening as they rode back toward the stable. He craned his neck as they approached, and Meridien picked up the pace.

No pale grey stallion stood waiting for Owen's return. And neither the count nor Mr. Quayle had located any indication of the horse. Jasper had disappeared.

"But a lad from the village brought this for you," the Master of Horse said, handing Owen a sealed note. "Perhaps someone there has found him."

He did not sound optimistic. If a villager had discovered a Thoroughbred running loose, the family would likely have sent to the castle first, not for Owen specifically. The only villager he'd spoken with had been the barmaid, and she would not know to ask for him by name.

He stepped to one side and broke the seal.

You are careless. I have the horse, and I tire of waiting. Bring me news tonight, or I will dispose of him.

He crumpled the note in his fist. Mercutio thought he'd cut off all Owen's options. He could not know how wrong he was.

He raised his head to find the others watching him.

"Thank you all for your help," Owen said. "I believe I know where Jasper has gone. I must speak to His Grace. Immediately."

Mr. Quayle raised his craggy brows, but he sent his men to take charge of the horses.

The prince and his brother paced Owen as he strode for the castle doors. The need to explain to them, warn them, was strong, but he knew he owed Belle's father the truth first. Mercutio might be tired of waiting, but Owen was tired of hiding. These people asked nothing of him and offered their friendship and trust. It was time he returned those gifts.

"I have found the duke evenhanded," Leo mused, as if he thought Owen needed encouragement. "He prides himself on logic."

The count snorted. "Except when it comes to his daughters. Then he can be difficult to please."

That did not bode well for the coming conversation.

"Where is His Grace?" Owen asked the first servant he saw as he came into the entryway.

The olive-liveried footman nodded down the corridor. "In the library, sir, but he has a visitor. Shall I tell him you wish to speak to him?"

"Tell him it is urgent," Owen said. The footman hurried off.

"Do you wish company?" Leo asked, and Fritz nodded

as if willing to come along as well.

They were cautious of their future father-in-law, yet they offered to stand by Owen's side. Perhaps not once they knew the truth.

"No, thank you," he said. "But if things go as I suspect, I would appreciate the opportunity to speak with you both as well."

The prince inclined his head.

The footman hurried back. "His Grace will see you now. This way, sir."

Owen followed him down the corridor, feeling as if he walked toward the noose.

In the light of day, the library did resemble a cave, but even the vast space could not lessen the duke's presence. His Grace was standing behind the desk, hands clasped behind his back.

Another man stood in front of the desk, watching as Owen approached across the polished floor. Owen didn't recognize the face, but the russet hair and commanding stance spoke volumes. Had His Grace captured Mercutio's man? Hope and despair mingled.

Owen paused a few feet away and bowed to the duke. "Your Grace. Thank you for seeing me."

"I was about to call for you in any event, Mr. Canady," Belle's father said, green gaze glittering. "Mr. Tanner here, a member of the Imperial Guard, tells me you're working with our sworn enemy. I'd like to hear your side of the matter before I clap you in irons."

CHAPTER TWENTY

O WEN HELD HIMSELF still while his mind flipped through choices. He knew the words to deny, to deflect. He could likely spin a tale that would have both the duke and the guardsman swearing to his innocence.

But those were not the actions of the man he wanted to be, a man worthy of marrying Belle.

"I was blackmailed into spying on you, Your Grace," he said. "I can only commend Mr. Tanner for discovering it."

The fellow inclined his head in acknowledgement.

"Mr. Tanner has been very helpful," the duke agreed. "Prince Otto Leopold and I thought it best to have someone watching from the outside for trouble on the inside."

Tanner pressed his fist to his chest. "I live to serve." He looked to Owen. "And so, it seems, do you. The villagers say the man in the house you visit is a foreigner to your shores. I have reason to believe he has ties to Württemberg, but I have not been able to catch sight of him. Who is it?"

"His name," Owen said, "is Alonzo Mercutio."

Tanner stiffened.

So did the duke. Then Belle's father leaned closer, eyes narrowing. "You are certain of this?"

"I am," Owen promised. "He told me his name early on. He seemed to think it might impress me."

"Or strike fear in you," Tanner mused.

"Signor Mercutio is one of Württemberg's most successful agents," the duke explained. "We thought he had been sent home in disgrace."

"He has returned, with help," Owen said. "I thought Mr. Tanner to be his man here in the castle, the man who attempted to search your desk and shoved a note of warning under my door, but there must be another."

"Someone else from Württemberg?" the duke asked with a glance to Tanner.

"No," Owen answered for the guardsman. "I understand him to be recently hired from a neighboring town called Walton-on-Thames."

The duke's brows rose. "Indeed. That may be the very thing that allows us to identify him. I'll speak to Mrs. Winters. In the meantime, Mr. Canady, I must know. What does Mercutio hold over you?"

"The ownership of my horse," Owen said. When Tanner frowned, he hurried on. "That won't seem like much to you, Your Grace. You have a stable full of fine mounts. But Jasper is the sole source of my income. By winning races, he allows me to continue the pretense of being a gentleman."

The duke eyed him. "You were humbly born, then?"

"Oh, no," Owen said, bitterness creeping back into his voice again. "My mother was one of the Wentworths of Yorkshire, for all she married a dreaded Irishman."

Belle's father nodded. "I've heard of the family. I believe the senior member died some years ago now."

"That would have been my great-uncle," Owen agreed. "A distant cousin inherited his estate. He allowed me to keep Jasper, as no one else could handle him. There never was a bill of sale. Now, it seems, my perfidious cousin has sold him out from under me, and Mercutio holds the paper."

"And you would be willing to take the chance of losing your horse by turning against your blackmailer?"

the duke asked.

"This very moment," Owen vowed. "You, your family, and your friends have been nothing but kind to me, Your Grace. I regretted my agreement with Mercutio almost immediately. But I have not been able to find a way out of the bargain that safeguarded Jasper. I have recently realized that if I must sacrifice him to safeguard Belle, I will do so."

The duke's brows rose. "You claim yourself another in my daughter's train?"

"With all my heart," Owen told him.

He cocked his head as if he could not believe him. Who could blame him? He had to be questioning everything Owen had ever said.

"He has proven that truth," Tanner put in. "He allowed Lady Abelona to ride his horse, something I understand he has never allowed another to do."

"No one else ever could," Owen said. He wasn't sure why he was arguing with the fellow. But now that the truth was out, he wanted no more lies between him and Belle's family.

"And he stayed by her side when she was thrown instead of going after the horse," the Imperial Guardsman continued as if determined to paint Owen in a better light. "I saw his face. He thought only of her. That is not the mark of a rogue."

"Indeed," the duke acknowledged.

Hope blew like a fresh wind, until Owen thought he could feel the cool air on his face. "I would never do anything to harm your daughter, Your Grace. Please believe me. I will do anything to right the wrongs I have done."

"I will hold you to that, Mr. Canady," the duke said. He turned to the guardsman.

"Thank you for your report, Mr. Tanner. I will let His Highness know. As you leave, ask Davis to fetch Lady

Abelona. I believe Mr. Canady would like to confess to her as well."

Just as hope had come, it fled. Owen kept himself still as the guardsman bowed and took himself off.

"You have some trepidation about this conversation with Belle, Mr. Canady?" the duke asked in the silence that followed.

Owen managed a smile. "Some trepidation might be expected in confessing one's sins, Your Grace."

"So my children tell me." He suffered himself to sit at last and waved Owen into a chair in front of the desk.

"My children are very important to me," he continued. "I found it difficult enough to understand and meet their needs when they were little. Now?" He shook his head. "As they go off to their own households, I find I must trust others to help them should they need it. Marrying Prince Otto Leopold will make Larissa a princess without a country. Callie and Count Montalban are uncertain where they will settle. However, in both cases, I can see they are making fine matches with men who will love, honor, and protect them. I am struggling to see what you offer Belle."

All his fears, all his doubts rose up before him. Owen stood taller. "I offer a man who will always and ever put her needs before his own. Who will strive every day to be a husband worthy of her. Jasper's speed and my wits have earned my way until now. Whatever I have, whoever I will be, I pledge to your daughter."

He leaned back. "I suppose we will have to see what Belle says about the matter."

It would always have come down to that. He could only hope he had done enough to prove to her he was no longer the man he'd once been.

Every part of Belle tingled as she paused before the library door. She'd changed into a day dress with Anna's tutting help, then returned downstairs to see their guests off. She had just finished bidding farewell to Lord and Lady Carrolton and their family as well as Petunia's sister Ivy and her family when Davis had come to tell her that her father wanted her in the library with Owen. Had he asked her father permission to address himself to her? Was this her proposal?

Oh, how she hoped so!

She was ready to admit she was in love with Owen. He was everything she'd dreamed of. From the first, she had seen his qualities. How glad she was that Tuny had realized they would never suit!

She smoothed down her skirts with one hand, other hand gripping the cane Doctor Hargreaves had insisted on giving her. As she'd expected, she was merely bumped and bruised. She would be fine with a good night's sleep. At least her frilly muslin skirts did not impede her steps. She could very well walk in on the marriage mart and walk out betrothed. Taking the latch, she pushed open the door.

"You wanted to see me, Father?" she asked with a smile.

Her father and Owen stood at the sight of her. Her father's face was shuttered, as if she were a stranger he found in his library. Owen's shoulders were back, his chin up. Shouldn't they look happier? Some nervousness on Owen's part might be expected, but her father was so tense she might have thought he intended to order both of them from the castle.

Owen took a step forward, but her father waved her into the chair next to Owen's.

"Mr. Canady has something he must share with you, Belle."

So, was this to be a proposal after all? Why wasn't her father leaving? Shouldn't a declaration be made in private?

Using the cane, she maneuvered herself over to the chair and settled herself on it. Her father sat as well.

Owen remained standing. "What did the physician say?" he asked, face puckering as he looked at the cane.

"I'm fine," she assured him. "I don't really need this, but I will abide by Doctor Hargreaves' wishes, for now. Wasn't there something more important you wanted to ask me?"

He sat at last and leaned back in his seat. "Not ask you, Belle. Tell you. There is no easy way to say it, so allow me to speak with less than my usual eloquence. I furthered your acquaintance under false pretenses. I was blackmailed into spying on your father."

She could not have heard him correctly. Belle shook her head to clear it. "I don't understand."

"Continue," her father said, voice as cold as a blast of winter. "Tell her for whom and for what purpose."

"A man named Mercutio," Owen said. "To stop your father from supporting the Batavarian's cause of retaking their country."

Belle sucked in a breath at the name of the villain who had kidnapped Fritz, mistaking him for Leo, earlier in the Season. "That can't be right. Leo and Larissa captured Signor Mercutio, and Callie heard from Fritz that he had been deported weeks ago."

"I can assure you he is not only in England," Owen said, "but staying at Primrose Cottage in your village. He holds a bill of sale that says he owns Jasper, not me. Unless I do as he asks, he will take the horse. Indeed, I have received word that he holds Jasper even now and will destroy him if I don't bring him news of your father's plans."

She shook her head again. None of this made sense. He was THE ONE. She'd been so sure!

But she'd been sure he was meant for Tuny as well,

and she'd been so wrong. She'd been sure she could ride Jasper, and she'd been thrown for the first time in her life.

She suddenly wasn't sure of anything.

As if he saw the emotions crossing her face, Owen slid from his chair to kneel before her.

"I am so sorry if I hurt you, Belle. I promise you, I would have told you all under more congenial circumstances, but this demand from Mercutio forces my hand."

She stared at him, the truth nibbling away the last of her hope. "More congenial circumstances? What sort of circumstances could ever be congenial for betrayal?"

"I never betrayed you," Owen said, gaze imploring. "I've told Mercutio nothing. And what I feel for you is true."

"True!" She gripped the cane and surged to her feet. "You lied to me. You lied to us all. I don't know who you are. I can't even stand to look at you."

He rose, reaching out toward her. She recoiled and nearly lost her footing. He moved to steady her, but she held up a hand. If he touched her, if he tried again to explain himself, she would crumble. She turned and walked as quickly as her injuries would allow, away from him, away from the future she'd hoped they would share, and away from the love she'd thought she'd found.

CHAPTER TWENTY-ONE

OWEN SANK BACK onto the chair. Light had left the room. He'd lost her, and he could blame no one but himself. He'd lied so many times, thinking it the only way to succeed, given his background. Had it been an excuse? Was he simply that flawed, as his great-uncle had always claimed?

"You seem to have captured my daughter's heart," the duke said.

Owen raised his gaze to the duke's with difficulty. "I'm not sure how you came to that conclusion, Your Grace. I had hoped, but my actions seem to have ended anything we had begun."

"Time will tell," the duke said with maddening calm. "What do you intend to do about Mercutio?"

It was a wonder the man hadn't clapped him in irons as he'd originally threatened. Every good castle must have a dungeon. But no matter how Belle felt about him, he owed it to her and her family to make things right.

"With your permission, I'd like to capture him. I'll speak to the prince about it. But what of his servant?"

His jaw hardened. "I'll stop the servant, if you take on the master. That act will begin to atone for your original intentions. As to my daughter, you have a great deal of work ahead of you to mend that bridge. And if she refuses you, I won't argue on your behalf."

Oh, the scoundrel, the dastard! To put on perfection as if it were no more than a coat and parade around in it. The arrogance! How could she have so mistaken him?

She wanted to mount Unicorn and ride as far and as fast as she could, but somehow she didn't think it would be far enough to escape the pain inside her. As it was, she barely made it to the chamber story before needing to sit.

She managed to gain the padded bench along the portrait gallery. Surrounded by pictures of her ancestors, she let the tears fall. Oh, to have come so close! How could she have been so foolish as to give her heart without knowing she held his first? She'd feared his past had left a mark. This was much, much worse!

"Belle?" Petunia must have been coming down from the schoolroom, for she dropped beside Belle, face tight with concern. "Do you need help reaching your room?"

"Oh, Tuny, the world is bleak." She sank her head onto her friend's shoulder and sobbed.

Tuny patted her back and made conciliatory noises. After a few moments, Belle rallied and pulled away, sniffing.

"It's not just your injuries paining you," Tuny said, watching her. "What's happened?"

Belle swallowed. "It's Owen. He is not the man we thought him. He confessed to Father he came here to spy on us so he could report to the enemies of Batavaria."

"Why that sneaking…" Tuny snapped her teeth together as if she would have liked to take a bite out of Owen. "I'll speak to Matthew. He'll have something to say about this."

"Leo and Fritz too, I'm sure." Belle wiped away the last of her tears with her fingers. "I'm very sorry I ever suggested you and he might suit."

"And rather sorry you and he suited so well," Tuny commiserated.

Belle nodded. "That's the worst of it. I'd begun to hope, to dream…" She drew in a breath. "It doesn't matter. The man I cared for is a fiction."

"I know the feeling," Tuny said. "I had high hopes for Lord Ashforde once, but he proved himself to be someone else entirely."

Belle took her hands. "Then we are well off without them."

Tuny's brave smile faded quickly. "And utterly miserable."

Belle squeezed her hands in understanding, and they sat for a moment, feeling each other's pain.

Tuny roused herself first, removing her hands from Belle's and rising. "I should give him a piece of my mind."

"Lord Ashforde or Owen?" Belle asked, gazing up at her.

"Both," Tuny said. "Do you need help getting to your room?"

"No," Belle said. "I'll be fine."

"Then excuse me. I have some scoundrels to scold."

All his life, Owen had made promises. He'd vowed to his mother he'd be humble and obedient when he went to live with her relatives, and he'd chafed against their dictates. He'd told his great-uncle he'd serve him faithfully, and he'd immediately begun to plot how he might escape. It didn't matter that none of them had lived up to their promises to care for him, his mother through no fault of her own and his great-uncle from a lack of character. They'd done their duty, and he'd failed his.

Not this time. Belle had shown him a better way.

She relentlessly cared for those she loved, whether they appreciated or even knew of her deeds on their behalf. She welcomed everyone, regardless of their background. She believed in doing the right thing, no matter the cost. Even if she would not allow him in her life, he would honor what she valued. And so, he began with a talk with Prince Otto Leopold and his brother.

He found the two men with Lord Ashforde and Thal in the billiards room. Leo and Fritz were watching Belle's brother give Ashforde a sound drubbing, Thal's skills obviously surprising the baron. They readily stepped out into the corridor when Owen requested it.

"I must apologize to you," Owen told them. "I was blackmailed into joining this house party for the sole purpose of discovering the duke's plans to support your quest to recover your kingdom so that your enemies could stop you."

Count Montalban took a step forward, fists coming up, but his brother put out a hand to stop him.

"Who hired you?" the prince demanded.

"Alonzo Mercutio," he said. "I told you how we met in London. He's made his way back into the country and is looking for leverage against you."

Count Montalban's arms moved to cross his chest even as he widened his stance. "Where is he now?"

"In the village. I could lead you to him. But he has another man with him who has been spying as well. The duke is hoping to locate him, but if he cannot in time, Mercutio may be warned that we are coming, leaving him with sufficient time to lay a trap."

Leo inclined his head. "Thank you for telling us."

Count Montalban wasn't willing to be nearly so gracious about the matter, for he narrowed his eyes. "How do you know he's telling the truth, Leo? He admits to lying."

Owen held up his hands. "I have forsworn allegiance to the man."

"And the blackmail you spoke of?" the count challenged.

"I am resigned to the worst," Owen said, though the twist of his gut belied the words. "Mercutio has my horse. He intends to destroy Jasper if I do not comply with his wishes."

The prince cocked his head. "And what are his wishes?"

"That I bring him word of your plans, tonight."

The two brothers exchanged glances, and the count nodded.

"Tell him, then," the prince said. "I will give you the exact words to say. It may be that we can snare him in his own trap."

"You'll need to speak with the duke, then," Owen warned. "He's searching for the servant even now."

"There you are!"

All three of them turned as Petunia stormed down the corridor toward them. Head high, hands fisted in a way her brother would likely have approved, she moved with a purpose and a passion that set her blue skirts to flying. A winged fury would have looked less dangerous.

The prince and his brother took a step back. Owen held his ground.

She marched up to him and poked a finger into his chest. "You're a snake and a scoundrel, and I've half a mind to pummel you to the ground if Matty won't do it for me."

"You have every reason," Owen told her, holding himself still. "I can only say how sorry I am."

"Sorry you got caught," she sneered.

The prince seemed to feel compelled to defend him. "Mr. Canady is attempting to make amends."

"The more fool you for believing that," she spat out.

Their conversation must have been audible inside the billiards room, for Lord Ashforde stepped out into the corridor.

"Is something troubling you, Miss Bateman?" he asked.

She drew herself up. "Yes. The whole lot of you who think you're so much better than anyone else. What you want, what you need, must come before the needs and wants of others. In fact, you don't even consider what others might need before taking what you want. You make me sick!" She turned and stalked off down the corridor.

Lord Thalston glanced from Lord Ashforde's pale face to Owen. "What did you do?"

"Something I greatly regret," Owen said.

"Agreed," Lord Ashforde murmured, gaze following Petunia's figure.

"Perhaps that's another apology you need to make," Leo suggested.

Lord Ashforde nodded, but Owen was certain the prince meant him.

"Develop your script," Owen told the prince. "If you'll meet me in the library before dinner, we can make our plans. In the meantime, I will go speak with Miss Bateman."

The prince was agreeable, so Owen strode after Petunia. For a moment, he thought Lord Ashforde might join him, but the baron apparently decided his apology could wait until a more opportune time, for he returned to the billiards room with Thal.

Owen caught up with Belle's friend at the foot of the stairs to the chamber story. "Petunia, Miss Bateman, wait!"

She stopped, jaw working as if she were preparing to pepper him anew.

"I lied to you and to Belle about my reason for being here," he said. "But I did not lie about my feelings. I have greatly enjoyed our friendship."

"Friends don't lie to each other," she accused.

"Not about important things," he allowed.

"Not about anything," she countered.

"Then you are indeed fortunate in your friends," he

told her. "I learned young that it was best to hide my feelings, or they would be used against me."

She cocked her head. "That hard on you, were they?"

He could not appear any weaker than he already felt. "It was nothing that couldn't be handled with a ready address and a winning smile."

"And that's your answer to every problem," she surmised. "You built a wall of charm, and even you can't see over it to what's really inside."

The truth bit hard. "I see what's inside now," he told her. "The darkness makes me cringe. But there's a spark, a spark your friend Belle helped reignite. I won't let it go out. And so I must ask your forgiveness as well."

She nodded slowly. "Not just me but everyone you wronged."

"I've already spoken with the prince and the count," he assured her.

"That's not enough," she informed him. "Leo is marrying Larissa, and Fritz is marrying Callie. That makes them family. That means they care too."

Owen lowered his gaze, unable to meet the light in hers. "Until I came to know this family, I had not experienced such camaraderie. That's one of the reasons I knew I had to come forward."

"And the other reasons?" she pressed.

He glanced up. "The man who was blackmailing me has my horse," he explained. In for a penny, in for a pound. "And I'm in love with Belle."

She regarded him out of the corners of her eyes. "You're holding to that story."

"It's no fable," he promised. "She's captured my heart, and I never want to retrieve it."

"Save your flowery speeches. You're going to need them." She sighed. "She's terribly hurt, you know."

The words were a dagger. "I know. What can I do to make it up to her?"

"Helping Leo and Fritz is a start. That's why you were talking with them, wasn't it?"

She was too clever by half. "Yes. His Highness has a plan to capture the villain plaguing us all."

"Good," she said. "How can I help?"

Belle used the excuse of her injuries to remain in her room for dinner. All their overnight guests with the exception of Tuny and her family had left, so it wasn't as if she was needed to entertain. The truth of the matter was that she simply couldn't face Owen, not yet. Not until she rid herself of this desire to run to him, beg to know whether he actually cared about her. It didn't matter if he cared about her. He was not the man for her. She had to let him go.

She should have known her family would not be so willing to leave her be. Her mother and father came to see her right after dinner.

"Not feeling the thing?" her mother asked, tucking the covers closer as she had done when Belle was a child.

"Shall I have the physician back?" her father asked with a frown toward her legs, as if they had been the ones to betray her.

"I'm sure I'll feel much better by morning," she told them both.

They exchanged glances, then her mother smiled, rising from where she'd perched on the edge of the bed. "I imagine you will at that. Sleep well, dearest." She bent and pressed a kiss to Belle's forehead. Her father smiled his support.

Anna tiptoed out as well, but Belle's sisters filed in as soon as the others had retired.

"Tuny told us what happened," Callie said, dragging

one of the upholstered chairs closer to the bed, while Larissa came around the bed and snuggled next to Belle, careful to keep from bumping her in deference to her bruises.

"He's making things right," her oldest sister assured her, tucking a curl behind Belle's ear.

"I don't see how," Belle told her. "He spied on Leo and Fritz! He was going to tell their enemies everything!"

"But, because of him, Leo and Fritz have a chance to learn the identities of their true enemies," Larissa said.

Belle frowned. "What are you talking about?"

"Fritz and Leo met with Owen and Tuny before dinner," Callie supplied. "They have a plan, and Owen is a pivotal part."

Belle glanced between them. Both her sisters looked so earnest with their hair flowing down onto their nightgowns and their eyes warm.

"But he lied!" she protested. "How can you trust anything he says?"

"Because he claims to love you," Larissa said. "More than his horse, more than his life, apparently, because there's no little danger from what he's doing now."

Cold fingers wrapped around her heart. "You mean he's going out tonight?" No matter what he'd done, she could not wish harm on him.

"Any minute, I should think," Callie answered. "Owen will speak with Mercutio and give him a story about what Leo and Fritz are doing to convince King George to support them in reclaiming their father's throne. They expect Mercutio to send a messenger. One of the footmen we hired for the party is apparently his agent. Wills has been watching him this afternoon. As soon as he slips out of the castle, an Imperial Guard will follow and report back to us on where he goes, while another will keep Mercutio in sight."

It was a good plan, one she might have thought of

herself. She could see how Leo and Fritz would endorse it. But they were missing a critical part.

"What about Jasper?" Belle asked.

Larissa lay a hand on her arm. "Owen was willing to sacrifice him, if it meant undoing the wrongs he'd done."

"What!" Belle pulled away from her. "Unacceptable. Owen loves that horse. And surely Jasper must be considered in his own right. Besides, how can either of you talk of sacrificing an animal?"

Callie squirmed on the chair. "I didn't like that part of the plan."

Neither did she. She now knew the danger of interfering when those she loved needed to find their own way through a problem. It seemed Owen remained on her heart, and it sounded as if he was trying to find a way through the problems he'd caused. But she could not leave him to do it alone. She must put his needs first.

Belle threw back the covers. "I'm glad the plan troubled you, because I have a different one, and I could use your help."

CHAPTER TWENTY-TWO

IT WOULD HAVE been impossible for Owen to ride one of the duke's horses into town that night without Mercutio suspecting that Belle's father was on to him. Therefore, the plan was for him to walk down on foot, with Leo, Fritz, and the Imperial Guards on horses farther back, where they would not be noticed by Mercutio or his servant. Wills had reported that the servant, a fellow named Larsen, had asked for the evening off and repaired to the village but had gone first to the public house. Obviously, he saw no urgent need to return to his master, which suggested he knew nothing of their other plans.

Owen was taking no chances. Mr. Tanner had been alerted to follow anyone leaving Primrose Cottage, except for the Italian. The prince and his brother, with Huber and Keller, would be following Mercutio, should he take the bait as they all hoped. And Sir Matthew and Petunia were in position to keep everyone informed as to progress, one way or the other.

"And you're certain that's what you want me to tell Mercutio," Owen said as the grooms finished saddling the prince a horse.

Leo nodded. "The information gives us the best chance of following him or his servant to their master."

"Or masters," his brother said darkly before levering himself up into the saddle. "We have no idea who is ordering their movements now."

The stable doors had been closed for the night. Now one side cracked open. Everyone froze.

Belle slipped into the stable and shut the door behind her. Though a dark cloak swirled around her, Owen caught sight of the Cossack trousers and riding boots beneath. Finding herself the center of attention, she beamed all around.

"Good evening, gentlemen. I've come to offer my services."

Relief that she would speak to him vied with fear for her safety. "Lady Belle, you are all graciousness," Owen told her, "but we cannot impose on you."

The prince and his brother glanced his way, looks amused.

"You have yet to accustom yourself to dealing with a duke's daughter, I see," Leo guessed.

"Determined, stubborn, valiant," Count Montalban agreed. "If she wishes to come, resign yourself now."

Belle dimpled. "Why, thank you."

Owen could not give in so easily, not when her safety was concerned. As Walters went to fetch Unicorn, as if just as resigned, Owen crossed the straw-strewn floor to her side.

"Belle, I don't know how Mercutio will respond. If he suspects a trap, he could well mount an attack. I don't want you hurt."

"And I don't want Jasper hurt," she countered. "Callie says you're prepared to sacrifice him if need be."

The thought was still a bitter pill to swallow. But this mess was of his own making. He had to right the wrongs, for her sake if nothing else.

"I will do my best to rescue him, once I've spoken to Mercutio," Owen promised.

"Not good enough," she said, pert nose in the air. "Not when I can make sure of the matter." Her gaze met his, those great green eyes once more wide and imploring.

"Please, Owen, let me come with you. While you speak to Mercutio, I can find Jasper and ride him to safety."

Hope blossomed. He snipped the flower. "Jasper may be watched. And you know how he feels about anyone on his back except me. You could be truly hurt this time."

Her lower lip trembled. "But I love you, Owen, and I want to help."

Behind him, someone groaned. He knew the feeling. Everything in him demanded that he take her in his arms, pledge his undying devotion. But not here, not now.

"And because I love you, Belle," he murmured, "I cannot allow you to endanger yourself."

She took a step closer, face angled up to his, and he felt the pull all the more. He had to be satisfied with laying a hand against her cheek.

"Oh, Owen," she murmured. "Surely danger shared is danger lessened."

Or made so much worse. He glanced at the prince, who smiled. The count shrugged as if he would have agreed to the matter ages ago.

His heart would not bear seeing her harmed, but he knew he couldn't allow his fears to influence her actions. She was clever, she was determined. She could manage danger as well as the rest of them.

"Very well," Owen said, hand falling, and Belle squealed. The count's horse shied at the sound, but he quickly controlled the mount, even as she pressed her lips shut as if to prevent another peep from coming out. Her shining eyes still gave away her delight. Owen only wished he could be so pleased about the matter.

"Unicorn will not be needed," he told Walters, who stopped in the aisle between the stalls, brows up in surprise. "Lady Belle will be coming with me."

They left the stable ahead of Leo and the others, who would ride down shortly, after anyone watching followed Owen.

"Stay close," Owen said as they started for the village. "If this Larsen, Mercutio's man, is anywhere about, I want him to see one shadow, not two."

She clung to his side, arm anchored on his as if for support. Her cloak brushed his boots. There was pleasure in her presence, though he could have wished for a better reason to have her beside him.

"May I take it I'm forgiven?" he murmured, mindful of any listening ears.

"You may take it I am leaning in that direction," she murmured back. "I don't think people lie to me very often. I don't like it."

A better liar, and she might not realize the deception, but he decided not to point that out. "I won't lie to you again."

"And you will be careful," she urged.

"I promise," he said. Then they both fell silent as they slipped across the bridge into the village. Moving cautiously from cover to cover, he led her along the main street. The shops were shuttered for the night, and the only sound came faintly from the public house, punctuated by the occasional bark of a dog.

Owen drew her to a stop against the wall of the last shop and peered toward the drive to Primrose Cottage.

"This is the house I told you about," she whispered. "Father's owned it for ages. I always thought it a pretty place."

"Jasper will be in the stable at the back," he told her. "If you see anyone about, don't go in. Meet me at the bridge either way."

She nodded, then slipped her hand into his.

They clung to the hedges along the drive until the yard opened up before them. Once more, Owen paused, senses reaching out. No sound other than the breeze through the trees. Not even the scent of smoke from a fire in the hearth, but that was only to be expected on the balmy summer evening. A tiny sliver of light through the shutters on the front window said someone might be in attendance.

"The stable is that way," Belle whispered, pointing around the house. Then she reared up and pressed her lips against his a moment before murmuring, "See you shortly."

She disappeared around the side of the cottage.

Feeling as if the dark of the night clung to his soul, Owen approached the front door. Best to go humbly this time, as if he had been thoroughly cowed. He lifted his hand to the door.

It opened to his knock. "You do not remember your place," Mercutio complained, but he motioned Owen inside and shut the door behind him. "My servant returned from the castle fearing you would refuse even now."

So, the servant was somewhere in the house or on the grounds. He could only hope the fellow would steer clear of the stable and Belle.

"I had to wait until they were asleep," Owen said, trying for a wheedling tone.

Mercutio crossed both long arms over his narrow chest, not even bothering to admit Owen to the sitting room beyond. "Report what you have learned."

Owen had charmed and cozened his way into more races and more homes than he could count. He affected a pained look. "They don't spill their secrets easily, this duke and his friends."

Mercutio's arms fell. "So, you have nothing. A shame. He was a fine animal."

His stomach knotted. He would not allow the man to see he had scored. "I didn't say I have nothing. The prince and his brother have been gradually opening to my persuasion. You were right. They have plans."

His dark eyes lit, and he took a step closer. "Tell me."

Owen smiled. "When I have the bill of sale in my hand."

Mercutio scowled. "You will have the bill of sale when you finish your job."

"My job is finished," Owen assured him. "When I tell you what I learned, you can shake the dust of this village off your feet."

"Tell me first," he said.

Owen held out his hand. "Give me the bill of sale."

Mercutio puffed out a breath. He stalked away from Owen into the sitting room, where an alabaster box sat on the desk in one corner. Opening it, he retrieved some parchment, wrote something on it with a quill, and brought it back. But instead of handing it to Owen, he tucked it into the pocket of his coat.

"And so?" he demanded.

Owen knew that stance. He had pushed the fellow about as far as he could. He could only hope it was enough of a delay to allow Belle to rescue Jasper. If his horse would allow her to ride him!

"Prince Otto Leopold and Count Montalban will be meeting privately with His Royal Majesty, King George, on Monday next," Owen told him. "The king has indicated he may be willing to support their cause, if they send convincing proofs against their enemies in advance."

"And do they have such proofs?" Mercutio pressed.

"I have not seen them, but I understand a rider will leave the duke's household tonight, in about an hour, heading for Windsor with the documents."

Mercutio's mustache curled up with his lip. "Excellent. You are right. You are of no further use to me." He reached into the pocket of his coat. Instead of the bill of sale, he drew out a pistol.

"*Addio*, Signor Canady."

Owen leaped forward and shoved the pistol up. The Italian struggled, barking a string of what were no-doubt curses in his native tongue, but Owen brought the spy's arm down against his knee and wrenched the gun free. It was a miracle the half-cocked weapon hadn't gone off or the servant come running. Perhaps God was honoring his change of heart. He sent up a prayer of thanks.

Mercutio stumbled back and held up his hands. "You do not want to do this. I serve a powerful master."

Now, there was bait he could not refuse. "Who?"

Mercutio licked his lips. "I am not at liberty to say."

Owen raised the gun. "A shame. It seems you are of no more use to me either. *Addio*, Signor Mercutio."

"Wait!" There was desperation in the Italian's dark eyes. "He will be very angry should anything happen to me. I am his eyes, his ears."

"I care only for his name," Owen said, aiming the pistol at the miscreant's heart. He would never have pulled the trigger, but Mercutio could not know that.

Owen's look must have been convincing, for he spat out, "Von Grub."

He seemed to think Owen would tremble with fear at the name, but it meant nothing to him. He could only hope it would mean something to the prince.

Owen motioned with his free hand. "Give me the bill."

Mercutio pulled it from his pocket and held it out. Owen snatched it from his hand and glanced down long enough to be certain he held a signed bill of sale for Jasper. Satisfied, he backed for the door.

"Leave Surrey," he said. "Because I will be telling the duke everything."

He ducked out the door and ran.

Belle watched the stable, counting off the moments. The walls were thick enough that any noises from inside were muffled. But nothing moved, and no lantern flickered from the groom's quarters on the upper story. She crept to the door and rolled it open wide enough for a horse to exit.

A sharp snort greeted her.

The moonlight trickling into the space was just enough to show her the pale sides of the grey and the gleam of his eyes. He appeared to be the only occupant.

"There's a good boy, Jasper," she crooned, moving closer. "You remember me. We didn't get on well on our last ride, but I'm hoping you'll be willing to allow me up longer this time."

She kept up a steady stream of conversation as she felt along the walls for the bridle and her sidesaddle, banging her knee against the tack box in the process. Only rough wood met her fingers. Could she ride the horse with nothing but her hands and knees to guide him?

The idea would have been daunting with Unicorn. But with Jasper?

From a distance, someone shouted in a foreign language. Closer to hand, a horse whinnied, and a man's voice called for calm. Larsen must be near the rear of the house.

Oh, please, not coming this way!

As if he heard the sounds too, Jasper took a step closer to the door, coming up short.

His bridle had caught on the rope affixed to it. And now she could make out the shape of the sidesaddle on his back. How unkind to leave him like that all day!

And how fortunate. With a whisper of thanks to the One above, Belle hurried to untie the horse. He tugged immediately.

"Just a few moments more," she promised him, leading him over to the tack box. Her injuries protested as she climbed up. She would pay for tonight's work. But not with Jasper's life.

Clinging to the bridle, she managed to push herself up

into the saddle.

"Time to fly," she murmured. She pressed her heels against the horse's sides and urged him out of the stable.

In other circumstances, she might have stopped to determine the wisest way to go, but Jasper had a different idea. He bolted through the yard, up the drive, and out onto the street. Belle managed to turn him for the bridge. He raced toward it, then up and over it before she gained control.

"Easy, my lad," she told him, turning him in a circle. "We have to make sure Owen finds his way free as well."

Jasper shook his head as if he disagreed, but he suffered himself to be guided back across the bridge, hooves ringing on the stones. She managed to rein him in, and he stood, trembling, as Belle scanned the lane ahead. Where was Owen? Had Mercutio gained the upper hand? Should she be riding for her father or the village constable?

Owen loped out of the darkness to join her. Jasper began bobbing his head, whickering a welcome. Owen cupped his large face and leaned his forehead against the horse's nose. "Oh, how I've missed you."

"Is it done?" Belle asked as he leaned back.

He patted his coat pocket. "The message has been passed, and I have the bill of sale that proves Jasper is mine. I watched the cottage for a moment from the street. Larsen must have had a horse saddled at the rear, for he rode out immediately. There must be another for Mercutio. Now we wait to see if he follows our lead."

From beyond the village, light flared in the sky—a flaming arrow that arced up to plummet into the canal and wink out.

"And there's Petunia's signal," Owen said. "The Imperial Guards are on the tail of Mercutio's man, and the prince and Count Montalban will follow Mercutio. He won't escape this time. And I have a name for His Highness and your father."

Belle sagged, one hand on Jasper's warm neck. "Then we're all safe."

"Thanks to you," Owen said.

She straightened. There was something to be said for being on horseback. Generally, she was the shortest person in the room. Now, she could look down into Owen's eyes. Light from the streetlamps combined with moonlight to paint him in silver and gold.

"Thanks to all," she corrected him. "Larissa and Callie let me know what was happening. I gather Petunia shot the arrow to tell us the plan was working."

"She did," Owen said. "Sir Matthew is standing guard with her."

Belle patted the horse. "And even Jasper played his part by allowing me to ride him to safety. But I think he would be happier if you were to take the reins."

Owen laid his hand on the saddle and swung himself up behind it. Belle leaned into him, breath coming easier.

"I meant what I said, Belle," he murmured as he took the reins and guided Jasper up the bridge. "I love you. But I have little to offer except a horse faster than the wind and a heart that beats for you alone."

"That's enough for me," Belle told him. "I love you too, Owen."

His free hand closed over hers. "It won't be enough for your father."

Belle smiled. "Leave that to me."

CHAPTER TWENTY-THREE

OWEN SETTLED JASPER back into the duke's stable before returning to the castle.

"Keep an eye on him," he told Walters. "If there's any trouble, send for me."

"I won't let anyone take him, sir," Walters promised, eyeing the horse with no little awe.

Belle had thought it wiser if she slipped into the castle first. The door didn't so much as creak when Owen opened it. Wills, the grey-haired footman, was waiting.

"Her ladyship has retired for the night," he informed Owen, face solemn. Then he shot a quick glance down the corridor before leaning closer. "I was the only one who noticed she'd gone out. She told me you were successful. Just know that His Grace is waiting for a word from you in the library."

"Thank you," Owen said.

Wills nodded, then straightened to his former watchful position, eyes forward and head high.

The duke looked up from the desk as Owen entered. "Good to see you unharmed, Mr. Canady. My wife would be distressed if her house party ended in bloodshed."

After seeing what a convincing marauder Belle's mother had made in the tableau, Owen thought little daunted her. "Happy to be unscathed, Your Grace. Did you see Miss Bateman's signal?"

"Indeed. All seems to be going as planned. And your

horse?"

"Safe in your stable," Owen assured him, vowing not to explain the circumstances further.

The duke did not seem to expect an explanation. "Excellent. I'll send for you if there is any further word tonight."

He recognized dismissal. "Your Grace," he said with a bow. He backed from the library.

He reached his room with no one except the duke and Wills the wiser. He wasn't sure whether to be pleased or disappointed. He didn't want to jeopardize Belle's reputation, or his own any more than he already had, but he would have liked more of a celebration for Jasper's deliverance.

And Owen's engagement.

Oh, marriage hadn't been specifically discussed, but he and Belle had exchanged words of love, and she intended to soften her father toward him. Nothing less than a proposal was expected in the morning.

He went to sleep with a smile on his face, and he was still smiling when he woke.

He took particular care of his toilette. He lathered up his shaving soap and cleared his neck and cheeks. He trimmed his beard and combed his mustache, then chose his bottle green coat, green and gold shot waistcoat, and tan trousers with Moroccan boots. A dapper gentleman, in command of his faculties, looked back at him from the gilt-framed mirror. For once, his character felt nearly as shiny. He walked downstairs and into the breakfast room, ready to take on the world.

And every member of the duke's household and his guests.

He kept his smile in place as he met the gazes pointed in his direction. Belle's smile was so large it widened her pretty face. Her sister Larissa looked expectant, and Callie was leaning forward as if to catch every word. Leo and his brother must have reached the castle at some point last night, for they nodded a greeting from near the top of the table. Sir Matthew's eyes were narrowed; Lady Bateman's were wide. Lord Ashforde seemed puzzled by the entire affair, face creased in a frown. Petunia went so far as to offer Owen a grin. The duchess cocked her head as if measuring him for size, and the duke's lean cheek twitched.

"Good morning," Owen said, moving into the room.

A rumble of answers echoed around the table. Owen took his seat, and a footman brought him a plate of poached eggs and delicate slices of ham, with a fluffy roll waiting to be slathered with butter and jam.

"Sleep well?" Belle asked from across from him.

"Quite," he said, sharing her smile.

"Do get on with it," her mother said. "I don't think anyone will eat much until you do."

Owen's brows went up, and he looked to the prince.

"I explained our mission last night to those who were not privy to our plans," Leo offered. "And they know Signor Mercutio and his servant have been apprehended."

"They're locked in the cellar," Tuny volunteered with particular glee.

So, no dungeon in the castle after all. A shame.

"Signor Mercutio will not find British law so accommodating this time," the duke predicted. "I will see that both King William of Württemberg and King George are notified."

"You might notify them about another as well," Owen said, slicing off a bite of ham. "Mercutio told me he was under the direction of someone named Von Grub."

Breaths hissed out around the table.

"But I thought he was just the secretary to the Envoy from Württemberg," Petunia said, glancing around. "And he was sent packing too, wasn't he?"

"He was," the duke agreed. "After it was proven he'd

played a part in attempting to ruin Count Montalban, he was returned to his king in shackles. It seems he holds more power than we thought, that he could send Mercutio back to us and direct his movements."

"We will pursue the matter," Count Montalban promised with a look to his brother.

"Good," the duchess said. "Go on, Mr. Canady."

Owen blinked. "I'm not sure what else you'd like to know, Your Grace."

"The rest of the story?" she suggested.

Ah. She knew enough of the tale to realize he had nearly been its villain. She was giving him a chance to paint himself in a better light. Well, he'd come prepared to ask forgiveness, hadn't he? Best to get on with it.

Owen drew in a breath. "I was not as fortunate in my upbringing as to have a family or friends like yours. I have been able to make my way by racing my horse, Jasper, at various local meets around the country. His prowess and my dubious claims to the gentry through my mother have seen any number of doors opened to me, yours included."

The duke set down his glass. "You mistake the invitation, Mr. Canady. You are not here because of who you are or what you might have to offer but through the auspices of my daughter."

Belle held up her hand and pinched her thumb and forefinger together. "I had a little something to say about the guest list."

Her mother snorted.

"I realize I would not be the man I am today without your daughter's friendship, Your Grace," Owen said. "Until I met Lady Belle and the rest of your family and guests, I never knew what true friendship and family were. That's why I have to apologize for my actions."

He glanced around the table. "I came here because I was being blackmailed. Mercutio discovered that my cousin had given Jasper to me out of spite. I had nothing that proved I owned him. Mercutio convinced my cousin to write a bill of sale to him instead. In exchange for a similar bill from Mercutio to me, I promised to learn how the duke hoped to persuade King George to help the prince and his family retake their country. But your friendship, your kindness, made me realize I had aligned myself with the wrong people. I explained everything last night to the prince and Count Montalban and did what I could to help make things right."

"I am satisfied Mr. Canady is a true friend to Batavaria," Leo put in, and his brother, Larissa, and Callie all nodded.

"Always admired a fellow who could admit his mistakes and seek to right them," Sir Matthew put in. His wife squeezed his hand on the table.

"And were you able to gain your bill of sale?" the duke asked.

"I was," Owen replied. "There should be no question now that Jasper is mine."

"Well, then," the duchess said. "All's well that ends well. More ham, anyone?"

Conversation picked up around the table. Owen stared at them. That was it? No more recriminations? They were simply going to accept his word?

Warmth pulsed through him.

Until he glanced at the duke at the head of the table. Belle's father was still regarding him with jade-colored eyes slightly narrowed, as if he could see right through him.

There. It was over. Belle took a deep breath before adding apricot jam to her roll. If the others could accept Owen's apologies, her father would be less likely to hold a grudge.

She hoped.

She was one of the last to leave the table, taking Owen's arm and giving it a squeeze. "Well done."

"I'm glad your mother gave me the opportunity," he said, voice still tinged with surprise.

The Bateman family would be preparing to travel that day, so the guests had all dispersed to their rooms. Owen tugged Belle into the withdrawing room, as if to shelter her from the footmen and maids hurrying past.

"Are you certain you want to speak to your father?" His tone was as warm as always, but she heard the tension in it.

"Yes," she told him. "In fact, I may be able to catch him in the library before Uncle Julian and Aunt Meredith arrive this morning to wish everyone off. Give me a moment."

He bent and brushed his lips against her cheek. "Take all the time you need. I know how important his blessing is, to us both. Just know that I have some money put aside. I can't give you a castle, Belle, but we won't starve. And I will do everything I can to ensure you never regret accepting my suit."

Trembling with hope, Belle hurried for the library.

Her father had yet to take up residence, so she had a few moments to stroll among the tall stacks of books arrayed on the polished wood shelves. The scents of beeswax and fine leather hung in the air, along with a faint mustiness from some of the older tomes. How many times had she scurried through dim light, trying to find Callie and pull her back to the schoolroom before they were caught? How many times had she sat with her sisters as their father read to them? So many happy memories in this room.

And now, please, God, one more!

The sound of footsteps on the carpet told her she was

no longer alone. This time, those weren't the furtive steps of a stranger but the steady tread of the father who loved her. She came out from between the bookcases in time to see him taking his seat behind his desk. He must have heard her as well, for he glanced over one shoulder to meet her gaze.

"Ah, Belle. Looking for poems again?"

She smiled as she came to join him, remembering the times he had caught her as a child on just such an errand. "No. I came to talk to you."

He leaned back in his chair as she took the seat in front of the desk. "Oh? About what?"

That cool tone might fool others, but Belle was certain he knew why she was here. Another time, she would have wheedled, reminding him that he was a dear father who wanted good things for his children. Or perhaps she would flatter his wisdom, his perspicacity. But she'd wanted honesty from Owen. She ought to be willing to give it as well. No hiding behind flowery phrases and winsome smiles.

"I am in love with Owen," she said. "And he is in love with me. When he comes to ask your blessing, I hope you can see your way clear to giving it."

He cocked his head as if considering the matter from a different angle. "By his own admission, he has nothing to offer but a horse. Where do you intend to live? How will you pay your way?"

"Fair questions," Belle said. "He tells me he has some funds, but they might go farther if you were to offer that hunting box you have little use for, in Leicester. You've said you have trouble finding someone to manage it. Owen and I could do that, in exchange for the living."

"Your mother will not be pleased to have you so far away," he mused.

Not just her mother, she thought.

"I am open to suggestions," Belle said. "But I think you

can see that living in the castle might make it difficult for us to settle into our marriage. I'm sure you wouldn't have wanted to live with Mother's family, had they been alive."

One corner of her father's mouth turned up. "Point taken. I understand the lease on Primrose Cottage is suddenly available."

Belle smiled. "I'll see what Owen thinks."

Her father held up his hand. "Your Owen has been a charming guest and a cunning schemer. I'd feel better bestowing my blessing if I knew which man you were marrying. I'll speak to him, but I propose an understanding only, until he proves himself."

Belle sat taller. "But Larissa, Callie, Tuny, and I vowed we would all be married by harvest."

Her father's brows rose, then came thundering down. "Marriage, Abelona," he said, "is a lifelong commitment not to be taken cavalierly."

Belle drew in a breath. "And anything worth doing is worth doing well. I know, Father. By making that promise, we all agreed we would give it our best. No one wants to marry someone unsuitable, just to meet a schedule we set ourselves."

"Very well," he said with a nod. "I will do my best to be reasonable, but I cannot promise you will be wed to Owen Canady by harvest. It might be a little later."

Belle settled back in her seat. "I can be content with that, Father."

After all, it didn't matter when she married Owen, only that she married him. And having an understanding was every bit as good, in her mind, as being betrothed.

Her father was watching her. "You have changed. There's a calm I don't recall seeing before. Shall I credit this to Mr. Canady's influence?"

Belle stood. "You may credit it to my own good sense." She came around the desk and pressed a kiss to his cheek. "But I will own that Owen helps me consider how others might feel about my plans. Not everyone requires rescuing. And hearing of his unhappy upbringing has made me appreciate you and Mother all the more."

"Now that's the Belle I remember," he said with a shake of his head as she leaned back. But his cheek was turning red, and Belle knew he had taken that point as well.

She made her excuses and moved toward the door. The moment she opened it, Callie and Tuny scuttled back. Behind them, Owen spread his hands ruefully.

She shut the door before her father could catch sight of them. "Was that necessary?"

"I can't remember what I don't hear," Callie reminded her. "And I heard sufficiently that I can explain to Larissa."

"I didn't," Tuny said with a shrug. "But Callie can catch me up." She took Callie's arm and led her away.

Owen stepped into their spot.

"I didn't have my ear to the door," he told her. "And I would prefer to hear the news from you. How did he take our potential engagement?"

Belle linked arms with him. "You are to ask his permission. He is prepared to give it, with the stipulation that we wait a month or so before announcing our engagement. He'd like to be sure of you."

"And you?" he asked, searching her gaze. "Do you feel the need to be sure of me?"

"I am sure," Belle told him. "I intend to spend the rest of my life with you."

"Ah, Belle." He took her in his arms then. In his kiss, she knew herself loved, valued. A week, a month, a year was nothing to forever. And that's what she and Owen would have.

CHAPTER TWENTY-FOUR

MEREDITH AND JULIAN arrived to find things in an uproar.

"Part and parcel to life with the duchess," Julian murmured as footmen trotting out trunks and maids burdened by bandboxes sidestepped them in the entry hall.

"Jane runs an orderly household," Meredith informed him, holding Fortune close as the cat eyed trailing bits of lace and the open door to the courtyard.

"As orderly as three daughters and two sons can allow," Julian agreed.

Mrs. Winters came out of the withdrawing room to greet them. "Terribly sorry, my lord, my lady. Perhaps you would be willing to wait until Her Grace can see you?"

Meredith caught sight of Belle and her swain coming down the corridor. Those pink cheeks, those glowing smiles. Had something happened?

"We'd be delighted to wait," she said, raising her voice to carry. "I'm sure Lady Abelona and Mr. Canady will be sufficient company."

They exchanged glances. Then Belle put on one of her bright smiles. "Of course, Aunt. We'd be happy to join you."

The four of them entered the withdrawing room, and the housekeeper closed the door on the bustle.

As Belle and Owen took seats next to each other and

Julian settled himself on the sofa, Meredith bent and let Fortune free. The cat gave a delicate shiver as if shaking off the last of her touch, then fixed her copper-colored gaze on Owen.

He didn't stiffen, as some were want to do, at the scrutiny. Indeed, he smiled a welcome as her pet prowled closer. Fortune sniffed at his boots, nose twitching as if she found the leather offensive.

Belle clasped her hands together tightly in her lap.

Fortune raised her head and began twining around his legs. The deep rumble of a purr was audible.

"It seems you've made more than one conquest, Mr. Canady," Meredith said, smiling. "She may allow you to pet her, if you'd like."

As if cognizant of the honor, he reached down gingerly and ran his hand along the grey fur. "Thank you, Fortune."

She arched her back against the touch then went on to give her attentions to Belle. Belle scooped her up and cuddled her close. "Yes, thank you, Fortune. I had thought I'd lost your esteem as well. I'm glad to know we both earned it." She glanced up to meet Meredith's gaze. "Owen and I are engaged."

"Or will be shortly," Owen put in.

That called for congratulations and kisses, and Meredith soon learned they were not the first to hear the news. By the time the last guests departed, Callie had shared the story, and everyone knew that Belle and Owen would be marrying in the next month or so.

"Which leaves Petunia," Meredith said as she and Julian headed for Rose Hill in their carriage later that morning.

"There's always Lord Ashforde," her husband said from his spot beside her. "I still think he has some interest. And with his growing influence at Court, she could do worse."

"I am not as interested in worse as better," Meredith informed him, hand running down Fortune's fur as the cat lay between her and the window. "Petunia deserves a gentleman who will hold her in high esteem, not worry about how she will affect his esteem. I fear Lord Ashforde may fall in the latter camp."

"Agreed," Julian said. "I only wish I'd had more of an opportunity to speak with him. He'll shortly be advising the king about the Batavaria question, and I'm not sure where he stands."

"I'll leave that matter to Leo and Fritz," she said. "If only we knew someone suitable for Petunia."

Fortune pulled out from under her touch and glanced back at her, a gleam in her eyes.

"Have an idea on that matter, do you?" Julian asked fondly.

Fortune turned her gaze out the window, as if she couldn't wait to return to London.

THANK YOU FOR choosing Belle and Owen's story. Belle is such a force to be reckoned with. I'm glad I could find her a man who appreciated her spirit. If you missed the earlier books in the series, look for *Never Pursue a Prince* (Larissa and Leo) and *Never Court a Count* (Callie and Fritz).

Want to make sure you don't miss a new release or sale? Sign up for my newsletter at *www.reginascott.com* so you'll be the first to know. I offer my subscribers exclusive, free short stories and behind-the-scenes glimpses. Don't miss out.

Keep reading for a sneak peek at the final story in the Wedding Vow series, *Never Love a Lord*. Tuny may hold the key to winning Batavaria back from their enemies, if she can convince Lord Ashforde to see her side of things, in logic and in love.

SNEAK PEEK

BOOK
FOUR
THE WEDDING VOW

REGINA SCOTT

CHAPTER ONE

Chelsea Palace, England
Late August, 1825

PETUNIA BATEMAN MIGHT have been a commoner, but she was far from common.

Tuny took some pride in the fact as she followed her brother and sister-in-law through the crowds thronging the ornate reception room. How many other young ladies of her acquaintance were invited to a soiree at the palace being leased by the King of Batavaria and his sons outside London? Well, her dear friends Larissa and Callie were here, but they were betrothed to the crown prince and his brother, so they had a reason. Like their sister, Belle, they were daughters of a duke, so they might have been invited regardless. In a space full of titled lords and ladies in fine clothes, Tuny was probably the least notable.

But she did her best not to goggle.

It wasn't as if His Majesty was in attendance. The king was being very careful to distance himself from the Batavarian question, as the papers called Prince Otto Leopold's quest. The prince and his brother wanted King George to support their cause to see their ancestral lands restored. King George wanted little part of it.

Neither did the stunningly handsome fellow approaching on their left. Panic threatened, and Tuny tugged at her sister-in-law's arm.

"Bit warm in here," she said when Charlotte looked at her askance, green eyes wide and russet brows up in question. "I think I'll wander closer to the window."

"I'll come with you," Charlotte offered with a smile. She in turn tugged on the burly arm of Tuny's brother, and Matthew promptly shouldered his way to where two tall windows overlooked the grounds.

"Still avoiding Lord Ashforde, I see," Charlotte murmured, strategically placing her back to the gilded wall and smiling at the passing company.

"And will until I have a husband standing next to me," Tuny whispered.

"You might find it easier to attract a husband if you smile more often," Charlotte shot back.

Tuny smiled, but she wouldn't have been surprised if it looked more like a grimace.

Three Seasons, *three Seasons*! And she'd yet to attract a suitor she felt comfortable accepting. Belle had elicited a vow from her sisters and Tuny that they would all be married by harvest. Tuny had lived her entire life in cities, so she had little knowledge of when farmers harvested their crops. But she had a feeling the time was drawing near. And not a suitor in sight.

"That Ashforde fellow seems determined," Matty said with a tip of his chiseled chin toward the tall, ascetic gentleman who was once again strolling in their direction. "Should I speak with him, Tuny?"

"No!" The word came out so forcefully the elderly matron promenading past stuck her nose in the air and plied her ostrich plume fan so quickly Tuny felt the breeze.

"That is," she said, tempering her tone, "there's no need for you to speak with him, Matty. He means nothing to me."

Something inside her informed her the statement was a lie. She forced down the thought.

"May I have your attention, please?"

The words rang out over all the other conversations, and heads turned toward the dais at the top of the room. In an old-fashioned powdered wig and green velvet coat with gold buttons the size of saucers, Mr. Lawrence, Lord Chamberlain for the Batavarian Court, stood tall and proud. His sharp gaze alone demanded that conversation cease. Quiet settled on the room.

"Thank you," he said. "His Royal Highness, Prince Otto Leopold, has an announcement."

"It can't be his betrothal," Tuny whispered to Charlotte. "They announced that ages ago."

Charlotte patted her hand, gaze on the Lord Chamberlain.

Whose eyes were now trained on Tuny, as if he'd heard her murmur. She pasted on another smile.

Leo, as he was known to friends and family, rose from the throne and looked out on his guests. "On behalf of my father, King Frederick Augustus of Batavaria, I would like to thank you for your kind support these last weeks we have been in your beautiful country. Your welcome, your offers of friendship, have touched our hearts. I would be remiss if I did not recognize those who have provided not only friendship, but material support. Their Graces, the Duke and Duchess of Wey, have been particularly helpful."

Across the room, Larissa's father inclined his head in acknowledgement, while her dark-haired mother beamed.

"Sir Matthew Bateman and Lady Bateman have also given of their time most generously."

Now all gazes turned their way, and Matty tipped up his chin in a nod, smile hovering. Tuny couldn't help her grin.

"But tonight, I want to thank someone who went above and beyond to support our cause. She provided wise council to my brother and myself in matters of personal importance, and, when danger reared its head, she was among the first to step forward to help us combat it, at no small risk to her person and her reputation."

Was he talking about Larissa? Tuny craned her neck to catch sight of her friend, but Larissa didn't appear particularly excited or honored. In fact, she was frowning as if she wasn't sure of the identity of this paragon either.

"Miss Petunia Bateman, step forward."

Tuny's head jerked back to face Leo. His look was solemn, and he held out his hand, palm up, as if expecting her to walk up and put her fingers in his. Around her, she could see gazes turning, as the glittery company recognized her presence, perhaps for the first time.

"Go on," Charlotte whispered, giving her a nudge with her elbow.

Heart pounding in her ears, Tuny started forward. The crowd parted before her, leaving her a clear path to the dais. Every gaze was on her. She tried not to meet any of them. If she did, she might stumble to a halt. As it was, she barely managed to stop just short of taking Leo's hand.

It dropped to his side. Mr. Lawrence scurried forward to offer him a gold coronet surmounted by pearls.

"For services to the House of Archambault," Leo intoned, taking the coronet and raising it over his head, "I hereby award you the status of a baroness of Batavaria and the title Lady Moselle." He settled the coronet on Tuny's hair. "You have all my gratitude, your ladyship."

She must be dreaming. Her brother had been given the title of baronet when he'd saved the life of the then Prince Regent. Her oldest sister had earned the title of marchioness by marrying a widowed marquess. She'd done nothing of such importance.

Yet the weight of the gold felt so real on her forehead. And was that... applause?

She turned, careful not to put her back to Leo. She

knew that wasn't done, at least. All around the room, gloved hands clapped, and titled faces smiled.

"Huzzah!" Matty shouted.

From the back of the room, the Imperial Guards on duty shouted back, "Huzzah!" and clapped their fists to their chests in salute.

Tuny couldn't even find a smile at the moment. Any moment, she was going to wake up and discover herself tucked into her childhood room in Matty's house, just off Covent Garden. Girls whose fathers owned mills, much less worked in one as her father had, didn't become baronesses in their own right.

Leo linked his arm with hers. That too felt real. She clung to him, afraid she might fall over from shock!

"Will you join me for a moment of private conversation about your duties, Lady Moselle?" he asked solicitously.

She must have nodded, for the coronet slipped on her hair as if even the gold and pearls knew that they didn't really belong to her. She reached up a hand to right the coronet nonetheless. Leo began strolling toward the tall doors that led out onto the gallery, nodding to that acquaintance and that friend. She felt the weight of their stares, heavier than the crown he'd set upon her head. Mr. Keller, one of the Imperial Guards, held open one of the doors for her. Though she knew he was the shiest of the guards, his face broke into a grin before he carefully schooled it.

This must be real. She was a baroness. She had a title. The door closed behind them with a funereal thud she felt to her bones.

She rounded on Leo, pulling away from him. "You've gone mad. There's no other explanation. Shall I call for a physician?"

Leo chuckled. Like his twin brother, Count Montalban, he had curly blond hair just brushing the collar of his scarlet tunic and sharp blue eyes. Diamond eyes, Larissa called them.

"You earned that title," he assured her, voice hinting of a complicated number of accents from his time abroad. "I will not forget how you ventured out that night to make sure we could track our enemies to the source."

Earlier this month, she and the prince had attended a house party at the duke's estate. While there, enemies of Batavaria had attempted to stop the prince and his brother from cementing a place in King George's regard. Everyone had pitched in to help stop the villains. Tuny's part, to wait and watch with Matty, then to shoot a flaming arrow into the sky to warn the others their enemy was on the move, had seemed small to her, but it had been exciting sneaking around in the dark, knowing she was part of making history.

"It was nothing," she told him. "No more than a lark."

Leo shook his head as if he disagreed. "Even before that, you gave me and Fritz sound advice."

"I gave you a piece of my mind, more like," Tuny reminded him. "And I ought to again. Me, a baroness? No one will believe that."

Leo drew himself up. "I am the representative for the King of Batavaria in England. I have his authority to grant honors and favors. I know of no one more deserving."

The door from the reception opened, and Larissa and another of the Imperial Guards came out. Tuny recognized Mr. Huber, whom she had also met at the house party. He inclined his head in greeting, brunette hair catching the light from the chandelier overhead.

"Tuny's elevation is the talk of the room, just as you'd hoped," Larissa told Leo as she joined him, Mr. Huber staying at a discreet distance. "Have you told her yet?"

Something hitched inside her. She should have known being elevated couldn't be this easy.

"Told me what?" Tuny asked, glancing from her friend to Leo.

"As a member of my court, you may be called upon you from time to time to continue your support," Leo said.

Oh, was that all? She already provided support to the Society for the Prevention of Cruelty to Animals by arranging benefits and mailing pamphlets. "Anything for a friend," Tuny said.

"You might not say that when you hear him out," Larissa warned with a look to Leo.

Leo squared his shoulders as if about to march into battle. "You are aware that King George has appointed a group of respected lords to advise him on whether to support our cause?"

Tuny nodded. "Lord Wellmanton, the Foreign Secretary Lord Canning, and others. It was in *The Times*."

"We are aware that Lord Wellmanton and Lord Canning are against the idea," Leo told her. "Some of the others are more supportive. Still, they remain fairly evenly divided. The final decision may well depend on the advice of one lord."

"Lord Ashforde," Larissa said, as if determined that Tuny understand.

Her stomach sank. "Lord Ashforde?"

Leo nodded. "Given that you are known and respected by his lordship, we were hoping you could convince him to see things our way."

Once more panic approached, this time so swift and hard that Tuny took a step back.

"What you mean is that you want me to turn him up sweet!" she cried. "You really are mad!"

Lord Ashforde meandered about the reception hall, greeting this acquaintance and chatting with that. All the while he kept the doors through which Petunia Bateman had exited in view. Ever since returning from the house party given by the Duke of Wey, he had looked for opportunities to engage her in conversation. Perhaps, if he could manage a private word, he could apologize for the tension that now held them apart.

Especially since that tension had been all his fault.

"Lady Moselle," Mrs. Richmond moaned as he passed. "As if that family needed another reason to gloat."

"Indeed," Ash said, pausing beside the white-haired matron who herself was once removed from a banking family. "Intelligent, devoted to one another, contributors to the church and their community. They are to be envied."

Mrs. Richmond drew herself up and stomped off, obviously looking for someone who would agree with her dismal assessment of the Bateman family's progress into Society.

She wasn't likely to find many, especially here. The prince and his brother were obviously admirers. Most of the Englishmen and women in the room would know the story.

Ash had been newly home from university when the Beast of Birmingham, a legendary pugilist, had saved the life of the Prince Regent and been made Sir Matthew Bateman. His marriage to Charlotte Worthington, sister to Viscount Worthington, had been reported in the gossip rags Ash's father had left lying about. But the marriage of Sir Matthew's oldest sister, Ivy, to the Marquess of Kendall had quickly eclipsed that news.

Since then, thanks to the auspices of Lord and Lady Belfort, the Batemans had become friends with the Duke and Duchess of Wey and their family and were well known to the Earl and Countess of Carrolton and Sir Harry and Lady Orwell. The family was fortunate indeed in its acquaintances.

And Petunia Bateman, now Lady Moselle, was no exception, even if she was exceptional.

That thought was not reflected in the cool smile he directed at the next group of people who sought conversation. For three years, he had been trying to convince himself, without success, that there must be another lady on the *ton* her equal. He could name her attractions. With her sleek dark-blond hair and wide, warm brown eyes, she had a pleasing face. She was nearly tall enough to look him in the eye, and she wasn't afraid to do so. She had a quip for every occasion, a handy trait when having to converse with strangers ready to censor her for her family antecedents. She was unrelentingly loyal to those she called friends.

But the emotions she raised in him were nothing short of dangerous to his plans. And so, he had told himself to look elsewhere for a bride. A decided shame that no other lady had yet to rise to her stature.

She hurried through the doors now, face white and steps unsteady. He was moving closer before he could stop himself.

"Miss Bateman, Lady Moselle, are you all right?" he asked, hand cupping her elbow.

She yanked back out of reach. "Fine. Perfect. Never better." Her smile was a ghastly parody of its usual warmth. "Enjoying the evening, my lord?"

Until this moment, immensely. There was something right and good about her being given her due. He could only applaud the prince for his decision to elevate her.

"A fine soiree," he assured her, careful to keep his voice level. "Allow me to offer you my congratulations on your elevation."

"My demotion, more like," she said with a glance back the way she had come.

Ash stiffened. "If His Royal Highness has in any way discomforted you, I would be happy to take him to task."

Where had that come from? There came that urge again, to gather her close with one arm and brandish a sword at her foes with the other. He wasn't some barbarian! He was an English lord, one who prided himself on his composure, his logic.

She rallied. "No need, my lord. I can take care of myself. Excuse me. I should find my family."

She hurried away, head down and coronet slipping.

That had been the longest conversation they'd had since the evening three years ago, when he'd told her he would not be making an offer for her hand. It had been the worst decision of his life, one he'd paid for with sleepless nights and endless days. This Season, he'd told himself to look closer, reconsider his decision. Perhaps it might be possible to rebuild the friendship they had once had. Such a friendship might lead to marriage. It was all very logical.

But something wasn't right with the new Lady Moselle. Even the night he had rejected her, she'd shown more spirit, more fire. The prince had said something to her that had caused her to pull even farther away from him.

He owed it to himself, and her, to discover the truth.

Learn more at
www.reginascott.com/neverlovealord.html

OTHER BOOKS BY REGINA SCOTT

Fortune's Brides Series
Never Doubt a Duke
Never Borrow a Baronet
Never Envy an Earl
Never Vie for a Viscount
Never Kneel to a Knight
Never Marry a Marquess
Always Kiss at Christmas
Never Pursue a Prince
Never Court a Count

Grace-by-the-Sea Series
The Matchmaker's Rogue
The Heiress's Convenient Husband
The Artist's Healer
The Governess's Earl
The Lady's Second-Chance Suitor
The Siren's Captain

Frontier Matches
The Perfect Mail-Order Bride
Her Frontier Sweethearts

Uncommon Courtships Series
The Unflappable Miss Fairchild
The Incomparable Miss Compton
The Irredeemable Miss Renfield
The Unwilling Miss Watkin
An Uncommon Christmas

Lady Emily Capers
Secrets and Sensibilities
Art and Artifice
Ballrooms and Blackmail
Eloquence and Espionage
Love and Larceny

Marvelous Munroes Series
My True Love Gave to Me
The Rogue Next Door
The Marquis' Kiss
A Match for Mother

Spy Matchmaker Series
The Husband Mission
The June Bride Conspiracy
The Heiress Objective

And other stories for Revell, Mirror Press, Moonshell Books, and Love Inspired Historical.

ABOUT THE AUTHOR

REGINA SCOTT STARTED writing novels in the third grade. Thankfully for literature as we know it, she didn't sell her first novel until she learned a bit more about writing. Since her first book was published in 1998, her stories have traveled the globe, with translations in many languages including Dutch, German, Italian, and Portuguese. *Never Romance a Rogue* marks her sixtieth work of warm, witty romance.

Alas, she cannot have a cat of her own, as her husband is allergic to them. Fortune the cat belongs to her critique partner and dear friend Kristy J. Manhattan, who supports pet rescue groups and spoils her four-footed family members. If Fortune resembles any cat you know, credit Kristy.

Regina Scott and her husband of 30 years reside in the Puget Sound area of Washington State. She has dressed as a Regency dandy, driven four-in-hand, learned to fence, and sailed on a tall ship, all in the name of research, of course. Learn more about her at her website at *www. reginascott.com.*